DRAGON SLIPPERS

DRAGON SLIPPERS

Jessica Day George

BLOOMSBURY
CHILDREN'S
BOOKS

3 7547 00029 6472

Published by Bloomsbury U.S.A. Children's Books
175 Fifth Avenue, New York, NY 10010

Library of Congress Cataloging-in-Publication Data
George, Jessica Day.
Dragon slippers / by Jessica Day George. — 1st U.S. ed.
p.   cm.
Summary: Orphaned after a fever epidemic, Creel befriends a dragon
and unknowingly inherits an object that can either save or destroy her kingdom.
ISBN-13: 978-1-59990-057-5 • ISBN-10: 1-59990-057-2
[1. Dragons—Fiction. 2. Orphans—Fiction.] I. Title.
PZ7.G293317Dra 2007   [Fic]—dc22   2006021142

First U.S. Edition 2007
Typeset by Westchester Book Composition
Printed in the U.S.A. by Quebecor World Fairfield
4 6 8 10 9 7 5

For Mikey, who has put up with an awful lot over the past nine years, but who never gave up on me or let me give up on myself.

And for the dragons.

DRAGON SLIPPERS

The Brown Dragon of Carlieff

It was my aunt who decided to give me to the dragon. Not that she was evil, or didn't care for me. It's just that we were very poor, and she was, as we said in those parts, dumber than two turnips in a rain barrel.

My father had been a terrible farmer, and too proud to admit it, so he had struggled on year after year despite countless failed harvests. It had only been my mother's skill with embroidery that kept us from starvation. She had sewn fancywork for all of the merchants' wives and once for the lady of the manor. But now Mother and Father were dead of a fever, leaving me and my brother, Hagen, to the mercy of my father's sister and her husband, who weren't exactly wealthy themselves.

After the sale of our farm brought only enough money to pay off the mortgage, my aunt proposed the idea that I might marry into money and so pull the rest of the family out of poverty. But while I was pleasant enough to look at, with blue eyes and a small nose, my straw-yellow hair was also straw-straight and I was sadly freckled. To be blunt, I was no beauty, and as I could not spin straw into gold or cry diamond tears, there was no reason for a wealthy suitor to overlook the fact that I had no dowry whatsoever.

"It will have to be the dragon," my silly aunt declared as we all sat around the hearth, holding what my uncle called a council of war. "Surely a brave adventuring knight will save her from its clutches," she continued, "and then we shall all be taken away to live in his castle." She was also very fond of reading romantic tales.

"All of us?" My uncle looked up from where he sat by the fire and whittled a rattle for my newest cousin. "Throwing yourself and myself and our youngsters into the mix as well?" He winked at me behind her back. He had a sly sense of humor after years of dealing with my aunt.

"It's the least he could do," she said stiffly.

Which really made no sense at all. Why should any-one be rewarded for defeating a dragon by being saddled with a dowryless, freckled wife and well over a dozen daft and impoverished in-laws?

No matter how I pleaded and my uncle argued logic, my aunt would not be swayed. That my uncle fi-nally agreed to the plan made me realize just how badly off they were. Their farm, like my father's had been, was on the brink of ruin. Hagen was fourteen and could help in the fields, so there was no need to get rid of him, but I was just another mouth to feed, blood kin or not.

Rolling my eyes, I went into the hills above our town and stood outside the great smoke-stained entrance to the cave where everyone agreed that the dragon of Carlieff lived. My aunt came with me, to make sure that I didn't try to skive off, and brought her two oldest boys and Hagen as well. She promised them each a penny candy if they would pitch rocks at the cave mouth to awaken the dragon once she was safely back on the trail to town.

Hagen just shook his head and grinned at me. "Not to worry, Creel," he assured me. "All us lads dare each other to come up and yell at the dragon. He's never been seen, not since Grandad's time. Dead as a doornail, I bet. Just wait here until dark and then come on home. Uncle says mebbe you can get work at the manor."

I smiled and nodded, suddenly choking back tears. My scanty possessions were in a satchel slung over my shoulder, including any yarn or embroidery floss I had managed to save from Mother's supplies before my aunt sold them. I didn't want to upset him, but this would likely be the last time I saw Hagen for a long, long time.

My uncle had mentioned working at the manor to me as well. He told me to go to the caves to humor my aunt, and when I got back he would take me to see the manor housekeeper about a job. But I had seen the doubt in his eyes and knew that it was a slim hope. I had my own plans, once Hagen and the other boys had gone back to town. And they didn't involve scrubbing floors.

My aunt started down the trail, shrilly directing the boys to start throwing rocks and admonishing me not to forget whose idea it had been to bring me to the dragon. I promised her cheerfully that I would not, snickered with Hagen, and even threw a few rocks myself.

Either the dragon had risen from the dead, however, or it had been away visiting friends since our Grandad's time. It appeared soon after we began our bombardment. The first thing we heard was a great rumbling and scraping, audible even over the sound of our shouts. Then a plume of smoke came out of the cave, followed by the beast itself. My two cousins took off, screaming like anything, while Hagen and I stood there numbly, staring at the dragon.

It was brown and scaly and looked impossibly old, with a great rack of shining golden horns on its massive head. My throat was so dry that the sides stuck painfully together, and a cold river of sweat started down my back beneath my worn gown.

Hagen touched my elbow. "Run," he whispered. He sounded as terrified as I felt, and I was grateful that he had stayed with me. "Run."

"You run," I said. I didn't think my legs would work. "I'll be right behind you."

I felt the stirring of air as my brother wheeled about, needing no more urging, and took off down the trail like a young deer. My legs failed to carry me after. I was mesmerized by the ancient beast's great golden eyes.

"What do you want?" Its voice rumbled and grated and hurt the bones behind my ears.

"I am a virgin, pure and true," I recited as my aunt had coached, not knowing what else to say. My voice came out in a wheeze, and my legs were now trembling so hard I feared that they would rattle me right off my feet.

"And what am I supposed to do with you?" The dragon snorted, and a ball of fire shot out and burnt the grass to ash not two paces from me.

"N-nothing. I am sure that a noble knight will come to save me from your clutches." I blushed to say something so ridiculous, but I didn't know how else to answer. I wasn't actually in his clutches, and the Lord of Carlieff's son was the only noble knight for miles around, and was known more for his skill at dancing than his fighting prowess.

"Are you a princess?"

"No."

"Then what are you?"

"I'm the daughter of a farmer," I said, lifting my chin. "My name is Creelisel Carlbrun."

"Oh, by the First Fires," the dragon moaned. "I have no desire to deal with this." He shook his rack of horns. "I am old and tired and bored with all the foolishness that humans cause."

"Oh," I said, feeling as foolish as they come. It had not occurred to me, or to my family, that even the dragon might not want me. Its words also made me wonder: Who *would* come after the daughter of a poor farmer? Would some knight or lord really be moved enough by my plight to risk his life for a nobody like me?

"I'm sorry," I told the dragon sheepishly. "I can leave." I had a vague idea of where I would go: I thought to carry on my mother's dream of opening her own dress shop in one of the larger cities. And anything would be better than being eaten by a disgruntled and elderly dragon.

"I don't think so," the dragon rumbled. "Get into the cave, go on!" It waved one claw toward the entrance. "I'd like to find out exactly how much trouble you're going to cause before I decide how to dispose of you."

"I'd really rather save you the worry," I said desperately.

"Go," the dragon said again, pointing into the dark cave. "Hurry."

I had to admit, scared though I was, I was also quite curious about what a dragon's lair would be like. Would I be permitted to see the great mound of gold on which he slept? Was the floor carpeted with the bones of fallen knights? Steeling myself, I cautiously preceded the dragon into his cave.

It was quite a disappointment. Really, there was nothing out of the ordinary about the dragon's lair at all. It was almost exactly like the caves to the east where my girl cousins met their swains to canoodle. Nothing more than a large, damp room with some imposing but not particularly inspiring rock formations. I breathed a faint sigh of regret, inhaling the odor of stone and cold and just a hint of sulfur. Perhaps I would not be treated to a sight of his hoard after all.

I was no longer as worried about being eaten as I had been. This dragon did not seem that inclined toward munching on human flesh. I was more worried that he would send me away empty-handed, without either a champion or a generous dowry. I didn't want the champion, but the dowry-money would come in handy. It seemed that I had heard stories of noble creatures such as dragons taking pity on dowryless girls and gifting them with ancient treasures. Hadn't I? Perhaps it wasn't dragons. But surely, to avoid having to fight some overzealous knight, this one might make an exception. . . .

"Don't step in the pool." The dragon's rough voice intruded on my reverie.

I halted in time to avoid putting my foot in a perfectly circular pool in front of me. I looked down and couldn't see the bottom. And, to my alarm, I couldn't see my reflection either. Just the dragon looking back up at me.

But it wasn't *my* dragon, I realized with a start. It was a blue-gray dragon with only two horns on its head, and it was looking up at me from the pool with an expression of what I guessed to be surprise.

"By the First Fires, Theoradus, what is that you've got there?" The voice of the blue-gray dragon rippled the waters of the pool just slightly, but his image didn't waver. It was an unsettling sight. "It looks like a human female."

"It *is* a human female," the brown dragon said with disgust. "It appeared at the entrance of my cave, demanding that I fight some knight over it. And I never wanted it to begin with."

"Half a moment," I protested, tearing my gaze away from the alarming vision in the enchanted pool. "I never demanded any such thing! I've been offering to leave quietly, and you wouldn't let me!"

"Its clan sent it here," the brown said woefully, "and now it thinks that a knight will come to save it, even though it is not nobly born."

"Coo-ee," the blue-gray breathed. "It's been years since I've had to fight a knight." It licked its chops with a long forked tongue. "I don't know what you're complaining about. She looks tasty enough, and you'll get to eat her champion, too." A rattling laugh stirred the water. "It's almost enough to make me fly over to your territory to share the feast."

My knees were knocking together so hard that I was sure the dragons could hear them, and my teeth had begun to chatter. The brown dragon rather reminded me of the local tailor, who was much plagued by his wife and eight children and liked to pretend that he couldn't stand the lot of them. Secretly, though, he doted on the entire brood. But this great beast wasn't the local tailor; he was an animal, a monster, really.

And it seemed that he did eat humans.

Or at least he was acquainted with dragons that did.

I hated my aunt suddenly, with a ferocity that startled me and kept me from hearing the brown dragon's next words.

"Beg pardon?" I shook my head to clear my thoughts. It was certainly the wrong time for me to be daydreaming, but there was something so surreal about my situation that I could hardly focus on the here and now.

"We were not speaking to you," Theoradus said in his dry voice.

"If you must use the pool, you must." The blue-gray dragon sighed. "But promise me that you will summon me right back, Theoradus. I am *dying* to know how this is going to turn out."

"Very well," Theoradus agreed in a much put-upon tone. "Now go."

He put one claw into the pool and stirred it, breaking up the image of the other dragon, which had something that nearly approached a grin on its face. Theoradus withdrew his claw and then blew a gust of hot, sulfurous breath across the surface of the pool.

The surface boiled and then the bubbles were replaced by an image I recognized as the gates to the lord's manor. Standing before them were my aunt, Hagen, and the entire host of my cousins. There was a large crowd of townsfolk as well, and I groaned in despair. Even if the dragon did let me go, there would be no living this down. I was going to have to leave Carlieff for certain. Theoradus dipped a claw into the water briefly and the sound of my aunt's piercing voice filled the cave.

"Swooped down out of the sky, like some great demon from the Holy Writings," she squawked, waving her arms for emphasis, while my female cousins all sobbed into their aprons and nodded in carefully coached agreement. "Simply carried her off! And a finer, prettier, more accomplished girl there never was!"

It took me a moment to realize that she was talking about me, and I felt a surge of liking for my aunt. Then I recognized her listener as the lord's son, and groaned again. She didn't truly think that I was pretty or accomplished, I told myself. She was only trying to stir him up so that he would ride out to save her poor dragon-abducted niece.

The townsfolk were muttering and weeping in appreciation of the story. The women clutched their children closer and the men scanned the skies for more dragon activity.

"You must do something," a woman screeched. "Our lord must protect us!"

"This is going to be irritating, at the least," Theoradus rumbled.

"And at the most?" There was a quaver in my voice that I couldn't hide.

"Painful." He bared all his teeth in a jagged grin. "But not for me, of course."

"What if he should slay you?" I didn't want to offend the beast, but I was a touch skeptical about his blithe attitude. The lord's son was very brave, even if he wasn't very muscular.

"You don't get to be six hundred and seventy years old by being slow or weak," the dragon informed me.

"Oh." I shivered. In the pool, the lord's son was striking his chest with a large fist and proclaiming that he would rescue the fair maid or be killed in the endeavor. "Oh, dear," I said.

A Fine Pair of Shoes

While I sat glumly on a stone outcropping with my pitiful bundle of belongings beside me, the brown dragon dispersed the image of my aunt and her audience and summoned his blue-gray friend again. I was trying to think of some alternative, some way that I could get out of this mess and go home. . . . No, not home. I didn't have a home anymore, and I was old enough to make my own way in the world, one way or another.

First, however, I needed to get out of this cave.

"The Lord of Carlieff's son is coming," Theoradus told his friend in a dry growl, "to rescue the fair maiden."

"*Is* she fair?" His friend squinted up out of the water at me. "I never can tell with these humans." He shook his head. "Is he decked out in shining armor and already madly in love with the poor maiden?"

"Yes," Theoradus admitted, an expression of distinct embarrassment crossing his face.

The other dragon roared with what I realized was laughter. "I might come and watch. Earnest young knights are my favorite sport. I love the looks on their faces when they realize that they're being slow-cooked in their own armor."

An idea was forming in my brain, though I had to take a moment to quell the horrifying image of the lord's son being slow-cooked in his own armor. This outer chamber of the dragon's lair was very plain, but there was a wide opening beyond the pool that surely led to more caves.

I hopped down from my cold seat. "If I may suggest something," I began.

"No," the brown dragon said curtly.

"If you would please listen to me, I could save you the inconvenience of having to fight the lord's son," I wheedled.

"No one asked you," Theoradus retorted.

"But I don't want to stay here and have you fight him," I said, taking a bold step toward the beast. "And you don't want to fight him, either."

"What is it trying to say?" The blue-gray dragon peered curiously up at me. There was a look of amusement on its muzzle.

"I will happily leave here, and take the lord's son with me," I said in a rush. "That way, you won't have to worry about me, or fighting the lord's son or any other knight. And all I ask in return is a small trinket from your large and no doubt magnificent hoard."

A single jewel-encrusted goblet from the dragon's hoard would pay my way to a city . . . perhaps even to the King's Seat itself. . . . And surely the dragon would not miss a single item from what I was sure was a prodigious treasure trove, considering his age.

"You want something from my hoard?" The brown dragon looked stunned.

My heart sank. Perhaps in dragon society this was a horrible faux pas. I prayed fervently that it wasn't the sort of mistake that was remedied by roasting the offender.

The other dragon guffawed, stirring the water of the pool from underneath. "What in the name of the Seven Volcanoes do you want a pair of shoes for?"

"I beg your pardon?" I stared from one dragon to the other. "Shoes? A pair of—No . . . I wanted . . . a goblet or some such."

"A goblet?" The brown dragon looked mystified. "I don't collect dinnerware."

The other snorted, rippling the surface of the pool. "She's heard the stories," he explained. "She thinks we all lounge about on piles of gold."

"You don't?" My voice was a squeak.

"Of course not," Theoradus said. "Well, I'm sure there are some who do. It takes all kinds. I myself fancy shoes." His golden eyes half-closed. "There's just something so fascinating about the way they're made, and the way the styles change over the years. . . ."

The blue-gray dragon in the pool was laughing quietly,

a sound that made my eyes water. "Go on then! Let her take a pair of shoes if she likes, and be off!"

I looked down at my rough sandals. I thought again about going back. I thought about my aunt and the bed I shared with my cousins, who pinched me when they wanted more blankets.

"One pair of shoes," I bargained with the brown dragon of Carlieff, feeling my heart hammering in my chest at my boldness. "And I'll never trouble you again."

There was a long, terrible silence.

"Oh, why not?" He sighed. "Come this way."

He led me past the pool where the image of the other dragon still laughed, and through the entrance to the inner chamber of his lair. Here, too, I was disappointed as this proved to be just another large cavern, but with a huge oval depression in the floor to one side that I suspected might be the dragon's bed. Beyond the bed was yet another rough opening and this one was curtained by a large and somewhat moldy tapestry.

The dragon pulled the tapestry aside with a gesture that was almost reverent, and motioned with his foreclaw for me to precede him into the inner cave. I took a deep breath, still secretly hoping for a pile of gold, and stepped forward.

Shoes. Shoes as far as the eye could see. This third cavern was the largest yet, and every square foot of it was covered in wooden racks holding shoes. Women's shoes, men's shoes, children's shoes. There were boots and dancing slippers and sandals. Shoes made of cloth

and leather and wood. There were fanciful pointed slippers with bells on the upturned toes and men's work
boots with thick soles.

I marveled at fur-lined boots embroidered with red
silk and clusters of small shells. The dragon watched carefully as I caressed a pair of high-heeled dancing slippers
so encrusted with emeralds that I doubted the wearer
would be able to walk in them, let alone dance. I could
not imagine what sort of person would wear such shoes,
and I stopped to imagine briefly where the woman had
lived, and when.

"Make your choice," the dragon said as I reached out
a hand to a tiny pair that were apparently carved of crystal. The dragon's voice sounded nervous, and I wondered if he was afraid that my rough peasant's hands
would damage the delicate footwear.

I withdrew my hand and moved on, searching for
shoes that looked to be my size. Something sensible, I
thought, boots perhaps, or at the least, sturdy brogues.

Nevertheless I paused before a delicate pair of green
satin slippers embroidered with gold. My mother would
have loved them, I thought with a pang. I remembered
how she had sighed over some of the fancy embroidery
that she had done for the wealthy women of the town. It
had always saddened me that she was forced to wear
such plain gowns, when all the while she was toiling over
beautiful and intricate garments for women who did not
even look her in the eyes when they paid her.

"No, Creel," I told myself firmly, moving on. "You
have to be sensible."

Sensible. I was not going back to Carlieff Town. I had to make my own way in the world, and if I was going to take a pair of shoes, they would need to reflect that.

I began looking at sturdy shoes with thick soles. They should fit well and be comfortable, or there was no point in having them at all. Fortunately, in the six hundred or so years that the brown dragon had been collecting shoes, he had amassed quite an array in all shapes and sizes, and I soon had a large selection to try on.

He still seemed tense about me touching his hoard, but I was careful to treat each pair gently, no matter how plain or fancy. I set them down on the far side of the room and crouched down to see which ones fit.

The embroidered slippers made me think of my vague plan, and as I tried on pair after pair of shoes, I worked it over. My mother had taught me to embroider, and to knot and weave sashes and lace. She herself had been an assistant dressmaker in the King's Seat, before a visit to some cousins had resulted in her meeting and marrying my father. She had never let me do anything for an actual customer, explaining that they had paid her to do the work and she had an obligation to do it. She had trained me using scraps of fabric and tag ends of thread, and I could admit without any false modesty that I was good. Very good, in fact. After I surpassed even my mother's skill, she had often lamented that my talent would be wasted in Carlieff, with no money to send me to a larger city where I might find a place at a fancy shop.

I had thought that with a piece of the brown dragon's hoard I could pay my way to a city and buy the materials

I would need for a sampler set to show potential employers. If I was as accomplished as Mother had said, then I hoped to earn enough to one day open my own shop. But without silver to buy what I needed, I would have to try another way. Perhaps if I went to the King's Seat, where I was totally unknown, and claimed that bandits had robbed me of nearly everything during the journey, the scanty bits of cloth and yarn I had with me would be enough to find me a job.

I had been so caught up in my plans that it took me a moment to realize that I had gone through all the shoes I had originally selected and none of them fit. I heaved a sigh and put them all back, then began searching for more. Perhaps some sturdy boots meant for a boy, or a better pair of sandals would have to do.

There was a sound from the outer cavern, and the dragon left off his anxious scrutiny of me. I gathered from the rumbling that his friend was impatient to hear what was happening.

At the far end of the last row of shelves I found a strange pair of shoes. Well, not really all that strange—they were sitting beside two somethings made of black and white feathers, which could not possibly fit human feet—but they caught my attention nonetheless. They were a rich azure blue, and made from very soft, thick leather. They had no laces, but slipped over the foot to reach a little way up the front and back of the ankle. The heels were low, the soles were made of some stiffer dark gold leather, and the interiors were lined with white silk.

They were much too fancy for my needs, but I couldn't tear my eyes from them all the same. They looked to be just my size, and terribly comfortable. Besides, I reasoned, they were obviously new and of good quality. And if I wanted to pass myself off as a master artisan I would need to dress better.

And that meant wearing nice shoes.

I picked them up and went back to the center of the room, where I had been gathering another group of shoes to try on. I left the blue slippers for last, but I already knew in my gut that they would be the only pair that fit.

I was right.

None of the boots or sandals, the brogues or even the crude moccasins I thought came from the southlands fit my feet. They were too big or too small, the toe pinched or the heel did. They were too stiff, or too floppy, for proper walking.

And then I slipped into the blue pair.

They fit as though they had been made for my feet. They were so light that I felt as if I were barefoot, yet the soles were thick enough that I could not feel the uneven stone floor beneath them. They were supple as I walked and didn't slide or chafe my feet. I had a sudden urge to cut the skirt of my gown off at the knee so that everyone could admire my beautiful new shoes.

"By the Seven Volcanoes!" The brown dragon had returned, and steam was rising from his nostrils as he surveyed my footwear. "What are you doing?"

I was taken aback by his reaction. "You said I could

have any pair of shoes that I wanted," I said stubbornly. I had never owned anything as nice as these shoes, and longing for them made me bold. "And these are the only ones that fit me. I want these."

"Any shoes but those!"

I frowned up at him. "No, it was to be any shoes I liked. You never said that there were some pairs I could not have!"

"What's going on?" The voice of the blue-gray came wafting into the shoe cave. "Which shoes did she pick?"

"She picked the—" Theoradus began, roaring back over his winged shoulder to the cave entrance. "She picked the—" Then he looked back at me and snapped his fanged muzzle shut.

"You said any pair of shoes," I reminded him. "Or I will stay here, and let my aunt rouse the entire town to come after you." I folded my arms and put my chin in the air. "You gave your word just as I gave mine."

"You don't know what you're doing," the brown dragon said, its eyes narrowed to slits.

"They're only shoes," I pointed out. "They are very nice," I hastened to add. "And they are certainly the finest slippers I have ever worn. They fit me perfectly."

Theoradus studied me carefully for some minutes, while the sound of the blue-gray's voice grew ever more petulant. The brown monster stared at the shoes, still visible because I was holding up my skirt so that I could admire them, too. He looked into my face, and smoke continued to billow from his nostrils, making my eyes water.

"Just a pair of shoes, you say?" His voice was rougher than normal. "I did indeed give my word. And you will hold me to it?"

Mute and confused, all I could do was nod.

He heaved an enormous sigh, even more bone-rattling than the ones he had emitted when I'd first arrived, and then he turned away.)

"Then—I may keep them?" I called after him.

"I gave my word," came the heavy reply. "You wish to have those shoes, and I cannot refuse you." There was the scraping of his claws on stone as he walked back through the sleeping chamber. "She has selected a pair of shoes," I heard him tell the blue-gray dragon.

"Oh, come now!" The other dragon was obviously still highly amused by the situation. "Did she winkle out your favorite pair? You look as though your fire has gone out!"

"Come forward, girl," Theoradus snapped. "And show Amacarin which shoes you have chosen."

Still holding my skirts at my knees, I walked over to the edge of the pool and held first one foot and then the other over the water. The blue-gray dragon reflected there hissed and drew back in shock. His eyes flicked from my feet to Theoradus and back several times before he could speak.

"*Those shoes?*" He was gasping for air. "Out of all the foolish human footgear you have collected over the years, she selected *those*? Why do you even have them?"

The great brown dragon bristled, literally, at having his hoard referred to as "foolish," but he did not otherwise reply. I looked from one beast to the other. "What is so remarkable about these shoes?"

Amacarin, as the blue-gray was apparently named, hissed again. "Those shoes—"

"Those shoes were made by a master craftsman, many years ago," Theoradus interrupted. "And no dragon parts lightly with something he treasures."

"Especially something like—" Amacarin began.

"*Any* choice would have been difficult for me to see on your feet," Theoradus broke in.

"Er," I said. "Well, I'm . . . sorry . . . to have upset you." I looked from one dragon to the other, but neither spoke for a long time.

Then Theoradus turned to me. "You have your shoes, girl, now go. And remember to keep your part of the bargain."

"Yes . . . sir," I squeaked, my attention being drawn from my new shoes to the fact that I was standing just a pace away from a large and upset dragon.

I let go of my skirts and hustled back to the shoe room to fetch my things, slipping my old sandals into the bundle just in case. I had toyed with the idea of leaving them behind, a little addition to the dragon of Carlieff's collection, but decided they were far too crude and shabby. Besides, I might want to wear them for a while, to spare my new shoes.

"Thank you, sir," I said sincerely as I made my way out of the caves. "You have been most kind and understanding about this whole, er, business."

"I have kept my part of the bargain," Theoradus said. "Now you must keep yours."

"Yes, indeed," I replied, and hurried down the path toward Carlieff Town.

Shards of Glass, Colored Brightly

Iwas halfway down the path to the town when I ran into the lord's son on his fine chestnut stallion. He was making good time for all that he was fully rigged out in armor and bristling with boar-hunting spears and a very long sword. I say that I ran into him because I had to hurry forward and get right in front of his horse in order to catch his attention. It must have been the narrow eye slits in the bucket-shaped helmet he wore.

"What are you doing roaming about these hills, girl?" He removed the helmet and glared down at me. "Don't you know that there's a fearsome dragon rampaging about and stealing away maidens?"

I curtsied neatly, as my mother had taught me. "Pardon me, young lord," I said politely. "But there has been some mistake. I am Creelisel Carlbrun."

He looked distracted, staring past me toward the hills where Theoradus's cave lay. "What are you babbling on about?"

"I am Creelisel Carlbrun," I repeated, louder. "*Creel?* The girl who was taken by the dragon?" I prompted when he still failed to recognize me.

"What?" A flash of disappointment crossed his face, along with one of relief. "You have fought your way free?" Then he drew himself up and began to speechify: "Do not fear that the noisome beast shall try to recapture you, fair maid! I shall defeat it once and for all!"

"Please don't!" I raised both hands in alarm when he made as if to ride on by. I was a little irritated that he appeared more eager to fight the dragon now that he knew its supposed prey had gotten free on her own.

"What are you saying, girl? That I am craven?" He glared at me, his face flushed.

"Of course not, young lord," I assured him hastily. "I merely wanted to save you the trouble of traveling all the way to the dragon's cave, only to find it dead."

"What?" He lowered his spear, dismayed.

"The dragon is dead, young lord," I told him in a firm voice. "It was very, very old, and the effort of carrying me off quite undid it. By the time we arrived back at its cave, it was reeling with exhaustion. It collapsed and did not rise. It is quite dead, and carrion birds are already gathering." I hoped that the rather thickheaded lordling would fail to note that there was not a bird in the sky.

"Well," the young lord said, taken aback. "Well." He squinted down at me and adjusted one of his spears. "I would deliver you safely into the bosom of your family once more," he intoned, "but as my horse is heavily laden with the accoutrements of war. . . ." He trailed off, raising his eyebrows to see if I caught his meaning.

I did.

"I shouldn't think of overburdening your fine steed, young lord," I agreed, feeling much more cheerful now. It had been easier than I'd thought to keep my part of the bargain. "If you would do me one favor?"

"Anything for a fair maiden!" He thumped his steel-clad chest with one gauntleted fist. He, too, was looking quite chipper. And why not? He wouldn't have to fight a dragon or marry a plain, low-born girl with freckles.

"Please inform my family that I am well, and have decided to go to the King's Seat to find work," I said, speaking carefully to make sure that he understood me.

"I shall be pleased to do so," he said.

I made another curtsy.

He wheeled his horse around, riding off without a second look at me. I waited until the dust had died down and then continued on the path until it forked. To the right it led back to Carlieff Town. To the left it joined the main road and wound its way south through any number of villages and towns until it ended where all roads in our land ended: the King's Seat, the greatest city in all of Feravel.

Surely in the King's Seat there would be a place for a freckled girl who wore blue slippers that had been given to her by a dragon.

I turned to the left and began to walk, my bundle securely tied to my back and my arms swinging free. I whistled as I went, and broke into a little song as I stepped onto the King's Road. This had been quite an exciting day for a farm lass. I had faced a dragon, bargained with him, and walked away free. I had deterred the young lord who had set out on his mighty steed to save me. I had a fine new pair of shoes and was on my way to the King's Seat to find work. It was the stuff of fairy tales.

Of course, in fairy tales, the young heroine did not get too hot and feel sweat running down the back of her neck and into her bodice. Nor did she get hungry, and wonder what her family was eating for their midday repast. I did have some bread and cheese in my bundle, so I stopped to eat a little. As I sorted out the small packet of food, a knotted skein of finespun scarlet yarn tumbled out and I barely managed to catch it before it touched the dusty road.

As I ate a small portion of the bread and cheese and drank a few warm sips from my leather water bottle, I contemplated the red threads. Most of my bundle was yarn or embroidery floss that I had spun myself, along with a packet of needles and my belt loom. I had a long, boring walk ahead of me, very little food and water, and no money. I would need something to trade for food and lodging when I reached the next town.

I repacked my food and water and tied my bundle back on, keeping out the red yarn, a skein of blue, and the belt loom. I threaded the ends of the yarn through the loom, tied them to my belt, and began to walk again.

It was called a belt loom because it was only wide enough to weave a belt or sash and because you tied it to your belt to create tension. I had made so many of these woven sashes (every woman and girl in Carlieff Town had at least a dozen for worship-days and feast-days, myself and my impoverished cousins included) that I could probably make one in my sleep. Or while I walked.

And walk I did, my eyes on the lengthening sash in front of me, and every so often, on the toes of my blue slippers, which peeped out from my skirts as I strode. The sun was hot, especially for spring, but the road was well maintained and my new slippers very comfortable.

All the same, by the time the sun had started to sink into the western hills, I was exhausted. I lifted my eyes from the sash, which had grown long enough that I had to tuck several loops of it back through my belt to keep it from dragging on the ground, and began to search ahead for some lodging.

By the time I found a farm that would take me in, I was ready to drop. The piece of dried venison and crust of brown bread they gave me tasted like a feast, and the pile of hay that I slept in was as soft as new-spun wool. In the morning, I didn't even mind when the farmer roused me at dawn and told me to be off. That is, until I started to walk again. My legs were sore, my mouth was dry, and I kept finding bits of hay in my hair and clothing. The only bit of comfort I had was that my new slippers hadn't raised any blisters—in fact, my feet didn't hurt at all—and they had yet to show any wear.

"No wonder Theoradus didn't want to part with them," I said aloud as I began another sash. "They really are the work of a master!"

Whistling through dry lips, I walked on.

For three weeks I had been walking, endlessly walking, and I had managed to weave four sashes so far. I traded the sashes where I could, and when I had none to trade I gathered eggs or darned socks or mucked out stalls. If I was lucky, I was given stale bread and dry cheese and the occasional boiled egg and sent off to the hayloft to sleep. In the morning I was roused at dawn, given a rusk and a drink of water, and sent on my way.

While a carter or two did take pity on me and give me a ride every few days, it seemed that most of them, like the householders, were wary of a young lass traveling by herself. They believed my story of being an orphan; I had no doubt of that. But they also suspected that I was a runaway apprentice or a maidservant who had stolen her mistress's necklace.

Two days' walk from the King's Seat I ran into real trouble. Infinitely worse trouble than having to walk all day or sleep in a drafty hayloft while pigs snored loudly from the barn floor beneath me. The King's Road curved west here, actually heading away from the King's Seat, so that it skirted the edges of the Rath Forest before it doubled back to reach the gates of the city. Very few people braved the more direct route through the forest, which was rumored to be full of wolves, imps who guided travelers to their doom just for fun, and even dragons. It was said that tinkers and bandits lived in the fringes as well, but the King's Road was well trafficked, and I had not concerned myself with them until that day.

A group of young men, hardly older than I, came out of the trees as I walked along the edge of the forest. There were eight of them, and they were filthy, with straggly beards, which I took to be a personal choice rather than an indication of desperation. They wore a motley assortment of clothes that were in dire need of laundering, but nonetheless seemed to be of good quality, which made me swallow hard. The easiest explanation that came to my mind was that they had taken these clothes from a wide variety of travelers—some of them women, I realized, as I got a closer look at the brocade vest sported by one lanky bandit.

"Good evening, gentle maiden," a tall youth said, stepping forward. He would have been handsome if he had been more careful about washing. And had his teeth not been stained and worn down from the pipe he clenched in the corner of his mouth even as he leered at me.

"Good evening," I replied, giving them a faint nod. I continued to walk along, working hard not to alter my pace. I was sure that, like dogs, they could sense my fear, so I did my best to show no outward signs of it.

"Won't you stop a while with us? It is growing dark, and a pretty young maiden should not be traveling this dangerous road alone." The leader moved to keep pace

with me, stepping over the low curb of the King's Road
and joining me on the smooth pavement. The others
stayed on the grassy verge, but trailed only a pace or two
behind.

The bitter truth was that he was right. It *was* growing dark, and while my prettiness was debatable, an un-
escorted maiden should not be anywhere near this road
alone. My legs shook, but I kept walking. I thought about
inventing a large and loving family waiting for me at our
cottage just around the bend of the road, but feared that
my voice would tremble if I opened my mouth again. Besides, they knew the region far better than I, and would
see through my lie in an instant if there was no cottage
around the bend. Truth be known, I had already begun to
worry about the fact that I had seen neither fellow trav-
eler nor human habitation for some hours. I was in trouble, and I knew it as well as the vagabond youths dogging
my steps did.

My family had never been very devout, but my
mother had taught us how to pray to the Triune Gods and
when to beseech them individually for favors. I wanted to
pray now, but took a moment to think first. Should I address my plea to the mighty, stern-faced Regunin, ruler
of the heavens, and beg him to smite my harassers? Or
should I pray to his gentle brother, thrice-dead Caxon,
lord of animals and plants, and ask that a bear or wolf
come out of the forest and eat the bandits? Jylla, their
merry, golden-haired sister, was the patron of women and
I normally prayed to her. But her nature was on the lusty,

pleasure-seeking side, and I was not sure that she would see my situation as perilous.

"O Gods," I prayed silently, deciding to throw the matter open to all three and hope for the best. "Please help me. I am young and foolish, but innocent, and have done no harm to man nor beast on this journey. Please deliver me from these bandits. Please."

I sped up just slightly, trying to seem casual about it, and forced a tiny smile to my lips. The leader was saucily continuing in praise of my beauty, and jesting that I had blinded him to all other girls. I did not make eye contact, but thought that my tight smile might at least somewhat mollify him.

"Please, please," I begged in my head. "Please let someone come along and save me. Please let there be a camp of friendly tinkers just through those trees . . . a shepherd on his way to market with a flock coming 'round the bend . . . a farmhouse just over that rise. Please, Regunin, Caxon, Jylla, *anyone*."

"Come now, pretty maiden, don't walk so fast," the chief bandit said in a cajoling voice. "It's getting cold out. You should join us at our fire."

"No, I thank you," I said, and began to walk even faster, doing my best not to break into a trot.

"Yes, *I* thank *you*," he sneered back, and lunged at me.

I couldn't help it: I screamed. Then I grabbed my skirts, hiked them as high as I could, and literally ran for my life. As I ran I yelled and screamed for help, even though I knew deep down that no help would come.

It did not take them long to catch me. One of the youths trailing behind leaped forward and tackled me, wrapping thick arms around my legs and bearing me to the ground. The leader stepped forward, almost leisurely, and removed my small pack from my back, tossing it aside. He clucked his tongue at me as I screamed and struggled, clawing at my attackers.

"That's not at all friendly," he chided.

"You mangy dogs!" I spat back. "Let me go!" I was crying out of anger and fear, and continued to writhe and scratch. "Someone help me!"

The leader opened his mouth, displaying the brown stumps of his teeth, and started to speak. Probably to mock my pleas and tell me that there was no one to help me. But whatever he meant to say was lost in a shout as a huge flat object fell out of the sky and struck the bandit's head before shattering into a million pieces on the road.

A shard of something bright blue bounced up from the ground and then ricocheted off my forehead with a small prick, coming to rest right before me. It was a piece of thick blue glass, with a small segment of lead attached to one side.

There were more brightly colored pieces all around, strewn like flowers over the body of the fallen bandit. There was also a heavy wooden frame and more dark gray pieces of lead. It took me a moment to recognize the remains of what must have been an enormous stained glass window.

The other bandits were looking from their leader up to the sky, trying fearfully to reason how a window had crashed down on him from nowhere. They had let go of me, and I staggered to my feet and stumbled through the broken glass, grabbing my bundle as I went.

"Stop!" One of the more clearheaded youths seized my wrists. "What's happening? Are you a witch?"

"Let me go!" I tried to twist free, but fear had given him extra strength, and I couldn't even make him shift his grip.

A roar filled the air. The bandit released me, and I clapped my hands to my ears and squeezed my eyes shut in agony. When the noise stopped I opened my eyes a crack, then took my hands from my ears. The bandits, including the one who had accused me of witchery, were fleeing with yelps of fright down the highway, slipping on the scattered shards of glass as they went.

I began to run, myself, but in the opposite direction, my skin crawling and my arms and legs trembling more than they had when I first encountered the brown dragon of Carlieff. What in the names of the Triunity had attacked us? Was this the miracle I had prayed for? I hadn't truly believed that Regunin would smite my attackers . . . but what else could it have been?

My question was answered a heartbeat later, when a large pair of golden claws swooped down into my line of vision, wrapped themselves around me like a cage, and carried me off into the air. I looked down at the King's Road becoming narrow in the distance below me, and up at the body of the massive beast that had captured me, and fainted dead away.

I woke briefly and found myself still being carried at a great height by what could only be a dragon, and felt the blackness rising again in my mind. My last coherent thought was that I was glad my brother, Hagen, wasn't here. He would laugh until his sides split to see me swooning like some lord's delicate daughter.

And then I was blissfully unconscious.

The Gold Dragon of Rath Forest

When I finally woke up I was lying on a mound of fern fronds, and the brown stone walls around me were craggy and strange. It took a while to remember what had happened.

Bandits.

Broken glass.

Dragon.

Oh, dear.

My aunt's hysterical lies had come true: I had been abducted by a dragon and taken away to its lair. But now the question arose of who was going to carry the tale to the nearest village and rouse the local hero to rescue me. I had serious doubts that my terrified harassers would think to do so.

There was a smooth shiver of scales on stone, and the smell of brimstone intensified. I squeezed my eyes shut, pretending to still be asleep, and listened as the dragon breathed like a bellows only a few paces from where I lay.

"You are awake, human child, I saw you looking about," the dragon said. Its voice rumbled deeply as Theoradus's had, but there was a softer, more mellifluous tone to it.

"Yes, noble dragon," I said, opening my eyes and then scrambling to my feet to face my abductor.

This dragon was even larger than the massive dragon of Carlieff. His scales were a rich, mellow gold, and the horns cresting his head gleamed sapphire-blue, matching his eyes. With his wings folded neatly along his back, he was studying me with those huge blue eyes.

"I thank you for saving me from those vagabonds," I added, remembering my manners.

"I had little choice," the dragon said, in a voice that sounded stiff, as though somehow offended or upset about the situation. "It was a strange thing . . ." He trailed off. "I saved you," he continued, "but my window was smashed beyond repair."

"Er, yes, I noticed that," I replied, then hazarded a guess. "Do you collect, um, windows?" It would be an odd thing indeed, if this cave-dwelling creature hoarded chapel windows. But no more odd, I thought, than Theoradus hoarding shoes he could never wear.

"Yes, I *do* collect windows," the dragon said testily. "And that one was particularly fine." Then his gaze sharpened on me. I took a step back, feeling the rough stone wall behind me and wondering wildly where the entrance was. "Do you not assume that I hoard gold?"

I lifted my chin. "You are not the first dragon I have conversed with," I said in lofty tones, hoping to impress

this one with my experience. Perhaps if he thought I was
a friend of Theoradus's he wouldn't eat me. "I am well
aware that dragons napping on piles of gold are the stuff
of old grannies' tales. Why, just the other day I was admiring the shoe collection of Theoradus of Carlieff, and
he gave me this pair as a gift." I raised my skirts to show
off my blue slippers.

A gout of flame issued from the gold dragon's snout
as it gave a loud roar. I only just managed to leap out of
the way as my bed of ferns and moss was torched by
blue-white dragonfire.

"By the Seven Volcanoes," the gold dragon swore.
"Where did you come by those slippers?" Its head
dropped down so that its long muzzle lay on the ground
and it could gaze at my feet from a distance of less than
a pace. I twitched nervously but tried not to move otherwise, still feeling the heat of its fire on my face.

"I got them from Theoradus, the brown dragon of
Carlieff," I repeated, my voice hardly more than a whisper and all my false bravado gone.

"He simply *gave* them to you? There must have been
a reason. Tell me, girl, what caused him to do such a
thing?" He lifted his head a little to look at my face.

"Well, my . . . my aunt started it all," I said, deciding that it would be better to tell the truth. After all, this
was a very *large* dragon. "She made me go up to his lair
so that she could tell the lord's son I had been abducted.
They wanted him to rescue me, y'see, so that he would
have to marry me even though I don't have a dowry."

The gold dragon raised its head all the way off the ground and stared at me in astonishment. "Go on," he urged in a strangely gentle voice.

I stumbled my way through the entire strange story of talking with Theoradus and his friend Amacarin, of making the bargain, and trying on hundreds of pairs of shoes.

"They both acted shocked that I had chosen these," I reported. "But Theoradus did not go back on his part of the bargain: he let me keep them even though he clearly didn't want to."

"Of course he did," the dragon said with a sulfurous snort. "Continue."

On I went, through meeting the Carlieff lord's son on the path and starting out for the King's Seat. I told him about the less-than-kindly farmers I had met and my ambition to find work. By the time I was finished, my throat was hoarse and my nose was running. I pulled out a handkerchief embroidered with delicate spears of gladiolus flowers and blew my nose.

"I see." The gold dragon's voice was hardly more than a murmur, or what passed for a murmur coming from a creature so huge. "Those slippers. . . . This is a most intriguing situation."

"Why?" I asked. What was so fascinating about a pair of women's shoes? One would think that these enormous, fire-breathing monsters would have something more to do with their time than bicker and snort and stare at my slippers!

The gold paused again. "You truly have no idea what makes those shoes any different?"

"If I had," I answered, letting my confusion and frustration show through, "I wouldn't keep asking every dragon I've ever met about them." I folded my arms, taking the same stance my mother had always used when she was in a huff with one of us.

"How many dragons have you met?" The dragon sounded almost amused.

"Three so far, and that's more than most humans can claim," I retorted.

"True," he said. He sounded melancholy. "Things were different once, you know."

"Were they?" I edged along the wall, trying to look for a way out as stealthily as I could. I hoped that he was not going to reminisce about the olden days, when dragons carried off young girls all the time, or so the town storyteller had led me to believe.

"Yes, four hundred years ago it was not unusual for a human and a dragon to be friends."

That stopped me. Friends? None of the stories I had heard ever mentioned dragons being friends with a human. They were always eating them or kidnapping them or burning them to ash.

"I-I didn't know that," I stammered finally. "But what has that got to do with my slippers?"

"You were given those slippers because Theoradus, whatever else he might be, is a creature of honor," the gold dragon said with a snap of his jaws. "He promised you any shoes you wanted."

I had a very strong feeling that there was much more going on here than he was telling me. But I was not foolish enough to pester a dragon, no matter how badly I wanted my questions answered.

The dragon drew his head back and looked off into the dimness at the far end of the cave, which was not large. He hummed a little to himself and it made my back teeth vibrate in a not altogether unpleasant way. I dared to ask a question, carefully avoiding the topic of footwear.

"So, did you have many human friends?" I was hoping that he would say "Yes," which would indicate that he didn't always eat the humans he encountered.

"I had one," he replied shortly.

"Oh," I said, cursing myself. He probably *had* eaten them.

"Since you have shared your story, allow me to share mine," he said finally, with a sigh that blew my skirts against my legs. "I am called Shardas, and I have lived in this hill within this forest for some seven hundred years."

"Pardon me?" I interrupted as politely as I could. "May I ask two questions?"

"Of course." He nodded genially.

"First: May I sit down?"

"Oh, certainly! Forgive my lack of manners. It has been some centuries since I have hosted a human."

I seated myself gingerly on an outcropping of rock, which proved to be surprisingly comfortable. Although my feet were not sore despite all the walking I had done in the past week, they felt sort of itchy, and it was bothering me. I wiggled my toes, but the itching did not subside.

"And your second question?" Shardas prompted.

"Oh, yes. If you're over seven hundred years old, and Theoradus said that he was six hundred and something, what does that make you?"

"What does that make me what?"

"Are you an old dragon, or a young one? You seem very . . . spry. But the oldest human I've ever heard of was Gammer Tate, and he was only eighty-four when he died."

"Ah. Let us say that we are comfortably in our middle years, Theoradus and I, though I am a full century older."

"Goodness."

"Yes. The oldest dragon I have ever heard of was Minchin One-Eyed, and she lived to near three thousand years." His scales rippled in a strange motion that I recognized as a shudder. "But if I have to linger on in that state—toothless, blind in my only remaining eye, and with my scales coming off in patches—I want to be harpooned through the ear instead."

"Er," was the only response I could think of. Though, remembering what Gammer Tate had looked like at the end of his life, I had to agree. The harpoon seemed a bit excessive, however.

"Where was I?" A long forked tongue ran out of Shardas's muzzle as he thought.

"Sorry. You've lived in this forest for seven hundred years," I recited.

"Ah. Thank you." He shook his head. "And in that

time, we dragons have all but completely withdrawn from human interaction, though you seem to be the exception to the rule."

"Well, I hadn't believed that there really was a dragon living in the Carlieff hills until I met Theoradus three weeks ago," I admitted. I pursed my lips and thought. "Speaking of Gammer Tate, he always used to tell the story of how he had once seen two green dragons flying together above the trees when he was cutting wood. And my mother was from a town just outside the King's Seat. There was supposedly a red dragon living near there; it used to fly over the town every autumn." I nodded my head. "Everyone talks about dragons, but I've never heard of anyone else ever seeing one face-to-face, let alone talking with it. Him."

"Precisely. The stories of maidens being carried off by dragons and rescued by knights have persisted, but for the most part they were never true.

"We used to be sought out by the truly gifted alchemists, for shed scales or drops of blood to use in their medicines and experiments, but no more." He heaved a sigh. "My friend was an alchemist. We became acquainted during my third century. He very nearly found a cure for the tumor-sickness that afflicts you humans."

"What became of him?" My grandmother had died of the tumor-sickness, and it had been a terrible thing to see.

"He died of old age on the brink of his breakthrough," Shardas said sadly. "And I had not enough knowledge of his experiment to finish it."

"If you used to be friends with an alchemist, and most of the stories about maidens being carried off really are just stories, then why do you continue to avoid humans?" I cocked my head to the side. "What happened?"

"King Milun the First came to the throne," Shardas said heavily.

"And that was a bad thing?" The teacher of the local school I had attended until the age of twelve had always raved about Milun the Protector, as he was known. In her learned opinion, he was the greatest king Feravel had ever had. "He saved our land from being overrun by the Roulaini."

Shardas blew through his nostrils a few times, looking at some point over my shoulder. "Let us merely say that while he was a great king for the humans, he was a disaster for the dragons."

"I didn't know that he ruled over the dragons, too," I remarked, bemused. "Although, I do remember that some of the dragons fought with him to repel the Roulaini invaders."

"He *didn't* rule over the dragons," Shardas said in a haughty voice. "And lest I forget myself and let loose a stream of flame that would almost surely singe the hair from your head, I shall not elaborate on what Milun the First did to the dragons. Suffice it to say, after he came to the throne, my people found it prudent to withdraw from human society."

"I see," I said, although I didn't really. And while Shardas seemed to be kind, I didn't know how many questions I dared ask before he would grow tired of me, or (worse) burn me to ash or eat me.

"I need to go into my inner chamber and bespeak another dragon," Shardas said. "You may follow, if you like."

Lacking anything better to do, I trailed behind his spiked tail. It would be senseless to run, I realized, since I had no idea where I was or how to get back on the King's Road.

Then I stepped into the inner, much larger chamber and all thought of escape left me. My mouth hanging open like the northern bumpkin I was, I gazed around at the most gorgeous sight I had ever seen, tears coming to my eyes at the beauty of it all.

Glass. Everywhere I looked there was glass. I had had no idea that there were so many colors in the world, let alone that glass could be made in such hues. The cave was filled with stained glass windows of every size, and depicting every beast and god and legendary hero imaginable. They hung from the ceiling on fine silver chains, and somehow, despite the fact that we were deep in a hill in the middle of Rath Forest, light shone through them.

"How did you do this?" I asked the question reverently, humbly. My fingers itched to find silk and floss and embroider the colors and patterns I was seeing, but I knew that I would never be able to capture the light that gleamed through them. Squares of sapphire blue, emerald green, and ruby red made a patchwork quilt on Shardas's folded wings and gleaming scales.

"There is a small opening at the top of the cave," he said in a pleased voice. "And I use mirrors to reflect the light through the windows."

"Beautiful," I said, but the word felt inadequate.

"Jerontin, my alchemist friend, helped me position the mirrors," Shardas told me. "Would you like to see his laboratory?"

I sensed that I was being offered a rare opportunity and nodded my head in a respectful manner. It occurred to me, as Shardas led the way to the curtained doorway into another cavern, that I had never seen an alchemist's laboratory. I found myself very curious.

It did not disappoint. There were clear glass jars of strange liquids and wooden utensils whose usage I could only guess at. There was a set of brass scales ranging in size from small enough to measure a pinch of salt to large enough to weigh a horse. Heavy pottery crocks stoppered with cork lined a wall, each one labeled with a piece of yellowed vellum that had been glued to the side.

"Yarrow, tansy, juniper, powdered dragon scale, dog hair, tiger teeth, monkey bile," I read in fascination. "Everything in here is so clean," I said, after looking around some more.

"I have tried to keep it as he left it," Shardas said in a sad voice. "Jerontin was very particular about keeping things clean."

"It's very—" But then I couldn't think of anything to say. How could I tell a dragon that I thought it sweet he was keeping up his friend's laboratory centuries after his death?

"Shardas? Are you there?" A rumbling dragon voice came from the main cavern, saving me from having to think of what else to say. "Shardas?"

"I am here, Feniul," Shardas called over his shoulder. He turned and walked through the opening at the far end of the cave.

Once again I followed his long tail through the curtained doorway and back into the glory of his glass collection.

"By the First Fires, what is that?" The voice that had summoned us came from a still pool on the floor only a pace away, and I jumped.

"It's a human," Shardas said in his dry way. "You've seen a human before, haven't you, Feniul?"

"Of course I know it's a human, but what are you *doing* with it?" The other dragon, which I could now see was a bright green, made a disgusted face as best it could. "You're not going to eat it, are you?"

I started again, and looked anxiously at Shardas.

"No," Shardas said, rolling his eyes. "I'm not going to eat it. And it's a she, actually."

"You haven't taken to collecting them, too, have you?" The green dragon sounded as if there were nothing more appalling than collecting humans.

"I still prefer glass," came Shardas's mild reply. "I was just about to bespeak you, Feniul. But what was it you wanted?"

"Er. Well. The sight of that human female has quite driven it out of my head," Feniul said prissily. "It was something about this summer's migration of . . . Stop that, Azarte!" The dragon's head bobbed out of view.

Shardas looked at me and said in a low voice, "He collects dogs."

"I beg your pardon?" I stared down into the pool, but all I could make out was a massive green shoulder and part of a wing. "*Dog* dogs? Live dogs?"

"What other kind of dog is there?" Feniul's face had reappeared. "Azarte is altogether too fond of treats," he said in the tone of a harried mother whose favorite child has gotten into the jam again.

"Er, yes, that must be a great trial to you," Shardas replied. "That's why I *don't* collect living things," he murmured to me, and I stifled a giggle.

"What was that?"

"Nothing, Feniul. What did you want to ask about the migration?"

"I didn't know dragons migrated," I put in, fascinated.

"Little human, what you don't know about dragons would fill my cave," Feniul said nastily. "*We* don't migrate. *Your* species does."

"Humans don't migrate," I argued, more puzzled than offended.

"Then explain why flocks of them clog the roads and paths to your king's city every summer," Feniul huffed at me, rippling the water of the pool.

"He's speaking of the Great Fair and the Merchants' Ball," Shardas explained. "We try to keep out of the way of the humans traveling in the forest in general, but at that time of year there are so many that we must plan our hunting even more carefully."

"What would happen if some humans *did* see you?" I looked from one dragon to the other. "A farmer traveling to the fair with his prize pig is hardly in a position to slay a dragon, by accident or on purpose."

"So *you* say," Feniul muttered darkly.

"Since the unpleasantness with Milun the First, it is not our habit to allow humans to see us if at all possible," Shardas told me in his patient way. "It is better like this. For both our kinds."

"You let me see you," I pointed out. "You rescued me from those bandits."

"You did what?" Feniul shook his emerald head with a rattle of scales and horns. "I will never understand you, Shardas. Never."

"Nor I, you," Shardas responded, giving a significant look to the brown puppy that could be seen squirming between Feniul's forelegs. "And yet we remain friends."

"I suppose," Feniul said in his prissy manner. "Shall we simply keep to the same schedule as last year, then?" He was giving me the eye, as though he didn't trust me, which he probably didn't. But then, I could hardly blame him.

"Yes. If you would be so good as to inform the others?" Shardas folded his legs and gazed down into the pool more intently. He, too, was watching the puppy, his long, forked tongue protruding from the corner of his fanged mouth in what I took to be a sly grin.

"I would be happy to—" Feniul turned his face away sharply, looking at something neither Shardas nor I could see. "Azarte! No! Bad dog! *Bad dog!*"

We both stared into the enchanted pool in fascination. Feniul had turned mostly away from us, so that all we could see of him were part of his massive hindquarters and his long tail. The fat brown puppy, released from his master's grip, was happily scrambling among the spiny ridges along Feniul's tail. Other dogs could now be seen tumbling around the rush-strewn floor of Feniul's cave or napping on piles of blankets. Large bones that I hoped were from sheep or cattle were scattered around or in the process of being chewed by various dogs.

"Do a lot of dragons collect live animals?" I whispered to Shardas.

"Not really, but Feniul's always been a bit odd." Shardas sighed. "He's a cousin—a very distant cousin, mind you—but I still have a clan obligation to him," he told me in a mutter.

I recoiled from the pool as a long narrow head suddenly came into view. A lolling red tongue framed by sharp yellow teeth made a startling contrast to the sleek black-and-white fur and backswept ears.

It looked like a hairy dragon.

"Yipe!" I squealed, much to my embarrassment. "What is that? Are baby dragons furry?"

"Of course not." Shardas snorted. "That's Azarte, I believe."

The dog grinned at us and then backed away from the pool, giving me a better view. As dogs went, he was larger than most. In fact, I was willing to bet there were few ponies that could match up to this leggy animal. He was long and narrow, mostly white with a couple of large black patches on his head and back, and he had a long, bushy tail. The woolly fur on his chest was matted with something red and sticky and he was drooling red as well. At first I thought it was blood, and almost averted my eyes in disgust, but then I noticed a definite pinkish hue that was not found in nature.

"Bad dog," Feniul reasserted, coming back into the frame of the enchanted pool. "He's broken into a bag of mallow sweets and eaten them all," the green dragon said with frustration. "No matter where I hide my sweets, he finds them within a day. He's going to make himself sick!" The enormous beast sounded near to tears.

Azarte, apparently sated, laid his long body down alongside his enormous master and heaved a great sigh. In a matter of seconds he was sound asleep and snoring.

"Yes, well, that's too bad, Feniul," Shardas said when it became clear that the other dragon was going to be clucking and fussing over his dog for some time. "But I had better go and figure out what to do with this human maid now."

"What? Oh, yes! Why was it you picked up that human?" Feniul's attention was pulled away from his dogs with an effort.

"For reasons that I will explain to you at a later date," Shardas said. "Perhaps." And he stirred the pool with one long claw, breaking up the image of his (distant) cousin.

Shardas heaved a sigh not unlike Azarte's and turned to me. My knees started shaking again. No matter how many hours I spent conversing pleasantly with dragons, they were still *dragons*: mighty, ferocious damsel-eaters, if the legends were to be believed, although, according to Shardas, at least, they weren't.

I bit my lip as I looked up at Shardas. He blew smoke out of his nostrils and looked down at me.

"You want to go to the King's Seat," he stated finally.

"Yes, sir," I said in a small voice.

"I'm not going to hurt you," he told me gently. "I'm trying to figure out what the best and safest way will be for you to take. What are your plans, again?"

"I want to find work embroidering," I said. I pulled the gladiolus-decorated handkerchief from my pocket and held it up.

He lowered his head and studied it with one sapphire eye, then the other. He reared back after a moment's scrutiny and nodded at me.

"I am not a collector of fine embroidery," he admitted, "but it looks well made to me."

"Thank you. My mother was very skilled, and she taught me."

"What do you think you will need in order to find work of this kind?" For a dragon he had a very practical mind.

"Better samples of my work than this dirty handkerchief," I said after thinking for a moment. "I had some embroidered scarves and woven sashes, but I've had to trade them all in return for food or lodging. I need to have different types of embroidery to display, to prove that I know the various techniques. I don't have the cloth to make a dress or anything, so I suppose my own gown will have to do, to show my skill with plain work." I sighed at this: my gown was an uninspiring brown color and not new.

"I see." Shardas nodded thoughtfully. "What do you require in order to make more embroidery?"

"Just some time." I shrugged. "I have some linen and a lot of yarn and embroidery floss in my pack." Then I looked up at him in dismay. "My pack!"

"Your pack is right over there," he reassured me, pointing with a long claw.

"Oh, thank you!"

"You are welcome. Take all the time you need. I shall not charge you for bed and board, as your people say. And when you are ready, I shall take you to the King's Seat myself." He nodded his great head.

"A thousand thank-yous," I said, tears pricking my eyes. Then a thought struck me. "But why are you being so kind to me?" I tried to keep suspicion out of my voice and simply sound humble. Was he trying to catch me off guard, or fatten me up for better eating?

"Perhaps to prove to you that we dragons are not all as bad as the bards would make us out to be," he said with an airy wave of one foreleg. "Or perhaps because I miss my alchemist friend." He strolled over to one of the larger windows and gazed intently at the scene it depicted: a young woman in a green gown playing the harp while a dragon wheeled overhead. "Or perhaps because something about you reminds me of a fair drag-oness I knew long, long ago," he finished in more somber tones.

"Oh. Thank you."

I went over to my pack and began to lay out my em-broidery floss and needles. I was starting to feel hungry, but ignored it. When my stomach growled loudly, how-ever, Shardas laughed and went into another chamber. He came back with an immense wheel of cheese and a basket of apples. Putting aside my silks, I let the dragon show me how to impale the fruit and chunks of hard cheese onto a stick. I held the stick away from me, and he used the barest trickle of flame to toast our food. We feasted until I thought I would burst. Then Shardas settled himself down in the middle of the room to contemplate his win-dows, and I began my sampling set.

A few hours later, we heard Feniul call from the pool, insisting that Shardas give Azarte a talking-to. Shardas and I rolled our eyes in unison, and then he began to sing to drown out the sound of barking dogs.

In a great deep voice the gold dragon sang "The Bal-lad of Jylla and the Fair Youth of Trin," a song my father had often sung in the evening. Tears pricking my eyes, I bent over my sewing. The piece I was working on was meant to be a curling vine, but in my mind it was the sinuous curve of a dragon's tail.

A Cave Like Home

I slept that night on a fresh pile of leaves and branches in the main chamber of Shardas's lair. The next morning, I awoke stiff and groggy, with hair like a bottlebrush and my gown sadly creased.

"You look awful," Shardas said.

"Thank you," I muttered.

There was a roast pig and a bowl of strawberries the size of a washtub sitting on the floor in the middle of the chamber. Still half asleep, I ate berries and pork and tried to get my bearings. Shardas attempted to make conversation, but when I replied only with grunts, he gave up.

After breakfast, during which he ate most of the pork and all but a handful of the strawberries (stems and all), he took me down the passageway and into another cave.

"This will refresh you, I hope," he said.

The floor of the chamber sloped away from the entrance to a pool of turquoise-blue water that steamed in the dim light. Shardas's bulk would fill the pool with only just enough room to turn around, but it was still bigger than the pond I had learned to swim in at home.

"The water is quite hot for humans, though I enjoy it," Shardas said. "If you do not get too close to the middle, I think you will find it comfortable enough."

"Is it a natural hot spring?"

"Oh, yes, there are many such in this land."

"Not around Carlieff Town."

"You didn't spend enough time in caves, then. That is why we dragons came to Feravel in the beginning: so many deep caves, with air vents and hidden pools." He gave a great sigh, rippling the water. "Even Milun the First couldn't get rid of us entirely." And with that he left me to bathe.

I ran back down the passage and fetched my pack. There was a little nub of soap tied up in a spare handkerchief and a clean set of underthings in the bottom of my pack. Keeping to the edges of the pool as suggested, I scrubbed myself clean. My straight hair was horribly tangled, and I broke two teeth off my comb working through it. Then I took the rest of the soap and scrubbed the dirt and sweat out of my gown and laid it over a rocky outcropping to dry.

Having nothing else to wear, I crept back down the passageway with a shawl draped over my underthings. I sat and sewed with the shawl around me until the heat of the pool had dried my gown enough to make it wearable again.

After a lunch of peaches and mutton, Shardas asked if I would like to have a proper sleeping chamber, and I gave a heartfelt nod. He took me down the passage that led to Jerontin's old workroom. On the far side of the laboratory was a curtained opening too small to admit Shardas. Shifting the curtain aside, I found a small sleeping chamber, thick with dust.

"I have not been able to clean it," Shardas said, his great voice heavy with regret. "I tried reaching in with a cloth to dust from time to time, but it was too awkward."

"I see."

Stepping inside the room, I walked around slowly. There was a bed of heavy carved wood, and a red-lacquered chest. The bedcoverings looked to be not only dusty but also disintegrating from age, and the rug that covered the rough stone floor was more holes than cloth. Shelves had been carved into the wall, and on them were books with spines faded from age and use.

"More of Jerontin's alchemical books," Shardas explained.

"I will clean them off and put them in the laboratory," I said.

"Thank you."

Shardas provided me with some of the cloths he used to shine his windows, and I set to work. I carried out the rotten bedding and rugs, and Shardas gathered them up and took them away. When he came back a few hours later, he had a collection of blankets held carefully in his claws.

"I'll find you a new rug tomorrow perhaps," he told me.

"Where did you get these?" I held up the blankets: they smelled freshly laundered and two of them were still damp.

Shardas scraped at the stone wall beside his head with the tip of a blue horn. "Oh, I found them." He looked like a little boy who had stolen a pie.

"Where did you find them?"

"Hanging."

"Hanging?"

"Hanging on clotheslines near some farms," he confessed in a rush.

"Shardas!" I was shocked. "You stole these?"

"I only took one from each clothesline," he argued.

There were four blankets. That meant there were four farmer's wives wondering just what had happened to the blankets they had washed and left to dry in the spring sunshine.

"But you stole them!" Then a thought struck me. "The food that we've been eating—the fruit and the meat . . . you stole them, didn't you?" I thought of my father, working so hard to make our farm a success. Imagining a dragon swooping down and denuding our fields made me feel sick.

"No, no, it's not like that," Shardas assured me. He reached through the doorway into the little bedchamber as though thinking to pat my head or back with his claws, and then withdrew without touching me, still looking guilty.

"Then what *is* it like?" I was torn. I really liked Shardas, and I was deeply flattered that a dragon would want to please me this way. But, having been raised on an impoverished farm, the idea of stealing was more than I could bear.

"I only go to very prosperous farms: lots of buildings in good repair, farmhands bustling around. Then I take very, very little. A single blanket, which I haven't done since Jerontin died. A clawful of peaches. The pig was wild: I caught it here in the forest, and the sheep was a stray."

That soothed me to a certain extent. "Oh. Well, I suppose the food is all right then. But maybe you should take some of these blankets back."

"I'm afraid I wouldn't know which farm I had gotten which blanket from," he admitted. "And it does get cold in these caves at night, for humans."

He was certainly right about that. Last night, after pulling my shawl around me and then putting on my winter stockings, I had still shivered. No wonder I had woken up so out of sorts. Aside from waking up in the lair of a dragon, I mean.

At last I accepted the blankets, though I politely refused a rug for the floor. Most of my days would be spent in the window room, I argued, where it was warm and there was better light to sew by. After that I stopped asking where Shardas got our food, and he never told me. But soon I learned to trust and respect him, and I was comforted by the fact that his gentle soul would not allow him to ruin a family's livelihood.

And so, as stitch after stitch found its place on the

handkerchiefs and swatches I embroidered, our days fell into a routine. Shardas with his windows and I with my embroidery sat together companionably for hours while light fell through the jewel-like glass panes and made patterns on the floor of the cave.

Though I missed Hagen, and sometimes found myself choking back tears as I thought of my parents, I didn't miss life on our farm. It was delightful to sit and embroider all day without having to worry about wasting candles, or getting my chores done. There was no scrawny cow to milk, no chickens to peck at me as I tried to gather their eggs. My aunt's shrill voice was nowhere to be heard, and the depressing sight of wilting potato vines did not greet me when I went outside to relieve myself. After only two weeks, I had to admit it: I had never been so happy.

The King's Seat

When a month had passed in pleasant harmony with Shardas, however, I felt that I should leave. I had woven four sashes and had a respectable sampling of my work exhibited on a number of handkerchiefs and linen squares. Since I had more thread than cloth, I had even decorated the hem, neckline, and sleeves of my own gown with stylized floral patterns I copied from Shardas's windows. I kept nervously asking him if he thought it would be enough of a reference for a future employer, and he replied quite honestly every time that he had no idea. I soon stopped asking.

"Are you certain you want to do this?" Now Shardas was the one asking repetitive questions as we prepared for the short journey to the King's Seat.

"I have to," was my automatic reply as I packed my things and made ready to leave.

I would be arriving at the King's Seat in grand style aboard the back of a mighty golden-scaled dragon. Not

that anyone would know: Shardas would leave me outside the city gates just before dawn to avoid being seen.
When the guards opened the gates for the day, they
would find me waiting there, pretending to have walked
in from the country.

Packing my things made me sad. I would miss Shardas
and it had been wonderful to have a room all to myself. I
had reveled in the freedom of rising late, lingering in the
steaming bathing pool, and eating as much as I liked.
Making my sampling set had been a thrill as well, because
for once I was doing things I liked, not the patterns that
my mother assigned me, copied from the dull, squarish
designs the ladies of Carlieff favored.

I liked to think that Shardas appreciated my company
as well. We would talk for long hours as I embroidered.
Sometimes he would sing strange dragon songs or human
ballads and hymns. I would return the favor by reciting
the epic poems popular in Carlieff. He had once asked me
to join him in a duet, and with a blush I confessed that I
had no singing voice to speak of. He complimented the
sewing I was working on, and chose another song.

And then there were the times when we both sat
silent, watching the light shift through the gorgeous panes
of Shardas's windows and thinking our own thoughts.
We also liked eating peaches and watching the moons rise
from atop the hill that housed his lair.

If I hadn't been so scared at the prospect of flying—
and worse, falling—I think I would have been embar-
rassingly weepy as we climbed to the top of the hill. We
had decided to take off four hours before dawn from the

top of the wooded hill that housed Shardas's lair. The hill never looked as big from the outside as it felt on the inside, and I mused aloud about how long it would take to excavate a hill, burrowing deep enough to provide such large chambers within.

"An hour, perhaps two," Shardas said in an offhand way as he scanned the skies. He was looking for the tell-tale smoke of tinker and bandit fires, in order to plot a course that would take us over the less-traveled areas of the forest.

"What?" I said.

"You don't think I spent months digging it out with my claws, do you?" He turned his attention to me with amusement. "And your eyes aren't playing tricks: it really *is* bigger on the inside than on the outside." Humming to himself in a satisfied way, he picked up my bundle and hunched a shoulder so that I could clamber up.

"Oof! Sorry!" Scrambling up the side of a dragon was not as easy as I had thought. For one thing, Shardas's gleaming scales were very slick, and some of the edges were sharp. For another, my gown and slippers had not been made for dragon riding. By the time I settled myself between two of his neck ridges, my cheeks were hot, my hair was coming unbraided, and my gown was uncomfortably twisted around. I settled it as best I could.

"Are you all right?" Shardas asked. "My alchemist friend was much more graceful at mounting."

"Well, la for him," I replied testily. I clutched the neck ridge in front of me and gritted my teeth. "Whenever you're ready."

Almost before I had finished speaking, Shardas leaped into the air. His enormous wings unfolded with a snap like wet silk being shaken out and we soared upward. My stomach rose into my throat and I squeezed my eyes shut. I invoked all three gods, and promised that I would enter a hermitage for life if they would just let me live through this.

I'd thought it would be easy to ride a dragon, but found that I had to concentrate on holding tight to the spiny ridge in front of me, clamping the sides of Shardas's neck with my legs, and not being sick all over the both of us. He carried my bundle for me so I wouldn't have to worry about losing it mid-flight. I thanked the Triunity that no one would be able to see me with my skirts hiked up and my teeth chattering from fright.

Wind rushed past my face as my stomach settled back where it belonged. Surprisingly, there was little movement and no sound other than the wind. I cracked open one eye. Then the other.

Shardas's wingspan was so great that he glided through the air as smoothly as an eagle. I had imagined a more unwieldy, frantic motion, but I should have realized that after centuries of practice, the gold dragon would be an expert flier.

I stared upward in amazement. The stars didn't appear to be moving at all. Yet when I looked down, the moon-silvered forest was rushing past at a dizzying rate. It was disconcerting, but not unpleasant.

We soared higher so suddenly that my sweaty hands slipped off the ridge in front of me. Fortunately, Shardas's neck was wide enough that I didn't fall. Instead, I threw my arms wide and closed my eyes again, pretending that *I* was the dragon, and that it was I alone who flew over the forest. I opened my eyes and let out an exhilarated whoop of joy.

A vibration shook my legs: Shardas was laughing at me. I whooped again, my arms still flung wide, and he swooped left and then right in a leisurely fashion, glided down to rattle the tops of the trees with his claws, and then flew higher until I felt that I could reach up with either hand and grab hold of a moon.

And then it was over, and we were standing on the wide, paved highway a half mile or so from the gates of the mighty King's Seat. Even in the wee hours before dawn there were so many lanterns and candles alight in the city that I could no longer see the stars, and the moons seemed sickly and dim.

I had known that the King's Seat was the largest city in Feravel, but I had not been prepared for what that truly meant. The construction of stone and wood before me was vaster than I ever could have imagined, and in the darkness I could hardly see all of it. My legs quaked from nervousness and the aftereffects of keeping my seat on Shardas's back.

"I had better go, the guards might see me," Shardas said, but his reluctance was clear in his voice. "Please be careful."

"I will." I hefted my bundle into my arms, scuffing the road awkwardly with one blue slipper. "And you be careful with the migration and everything," I said.

"We'll be fine, despite Feniul's annual histrionics," Shardas assured me, and we both chuckled. Feniul had bespoken Shardas through the enchanted pool nearly every day that I had been in the gold dragon's lair. Between his frustration with his dogs (I managed to count roughly twenty, but Azarte seemed to be the most trouble) and his fears that this year something would go horribly wrong with the migration, he was grating on Shardas's nerves and mine.

"You may call on me if you need help," Shardas said. "Please promise me that you will."

"Thank you, I shall certainly do so," I said with polite puzzlement. "But how?" I wondered if he would give me some sort of enchanted water pot or something, and worried that it might attract too much attention.

"Simply call out my name, and I will hear you and come," Shardas said. His large muzzle opened as though he were about to say something else, but then closed again with a snap of his jaws. "I will hear you."

And with that he leaped into the air and glided away, leaving me blinking dust from my eyes and waving sadly. I shouldered my burden and trudged up the road to the gate, then sat on the neatly tended grass beside the road to wait for dawn and the opening of the gates.

Just before dawn a cart carrying wicker cages of geese came along the highway. I slipped into the city in its wake, letting the honking and flapping and flying feathers distract the guards. Anyone might enter the King's Seat, but the guards took down the number of people in the party, their business, and ultimate destination. Not wanting to admit that I had no idea where I was going, I stood near an exhausted young gooseherd and let them put me down as one of that group. The driver of the cart looked at me curiously, but I just shrugged. It wasn't my fault if the guards were lax.

It was then that things got complicated. I didn't know how to find work as a seamstress or fancyworker. The tired gooseherd only knew where the poultry market was, and the cart driver shrugged and spat when I asked if he could give me a ride to the cloth-workers' district.

"Never seen it, never cared to," he grunted, and slapped the reins for his mule team to walk on.

The broad central street of the King's Seat stretched away before me. If I kept walking along it, I would eventually come to the Jyllite Square, where the two palaces were, or so I had been taught in school. But the walk from the gates to the Jyllite Square would take several hours, as I had also been taught. I started up the street anyway, hoping that the cloth-workers' district branched off the main thoroughfare.

The King's Seat sloped gently uphill toward the palaces, but after an hour of walking it felt more like a mountain. I had passed a number of inns, but didn't have any money to buy food or drink or a bed. I passed cattle markets and horse auctions and the glassblowers' district. But no seamstresses. No weavers or dyers or cloth workers of any kind.

At the next inn I passed, the innkeeper's wife was

industriously sweeping the front steps, and I stopped to ask the way to the cloth markets.

"Just in from the country, are you?" She paused and leaned her beefy forearms on the broom.

"Yes, good mistress, I'm looking for a place as a fancyworker." I held out my sleeves to show off the decorations I had sewn there.

"Well, then, be off with you and your country fancywork," she sneered, and swept a cloud of dust straight at me.

I ran, trying to keep away from the worst of it, my cheeks burning with embarrassment and my eyes smarting with tears at the sound of her raucous laughter. What was I, little Creel of Carlieff Town, doing in the King's Seat? Did I really think that my crude provincial skills were wanted here in the city?

I kept on going because I had nowhere else to go, but I didn't ask for directions again. After three hours, when I hadn't seen anything that looked like the cloth-workers' district, and yet still was nowhere near the palaces, I turned down one of the side streets, my fingers crossed that it would lead where I wanted to go.

I passed through a market that sold all sorts of exotic fruits and vegetables, and even more exotic animals for fine ladies to keep as pets. There were fantastically plumed birds and brown bears no higher than my knee, and little black monkeys, with wild manes of white hair, that could fit in a pocket.

When I stopped to gape at these last creatures, the

trader displaying them smiled at me kindly. He had a very brown face with very white teeth, and wore a strange, conical blue hat. I dared to ask him if he knew the way I wanted to go, but he merely smiled and shook his head.

"Please?" My voice wavered a little from tiredness and frustration.

"Gaal matto," the man replied, shaking his head again.

Across the way, the man selling bright-feathered birds called out, "He don't speak the language, maidy."

I turned around, hope rising in my breast, to address the friendly-sounding bird seller. "Sir? Do you know the way to the cloth-workers' district?"

"Aye, that I do. But come here so I don't have to shout, you're a fair way off."

But as I took an eager step toward him, I tripped over what had to be the world's smallest dog.

The Princess's Pippin

Watch where you are going, you horrible cow!" The voice snapped at me over the sound of a small dog yipping with pain.

"Oh, I'm so sorry!" I looked at the young woman standing behind me and then down at the little animal I had stepped on.

The girl had a cascade of brown curls falling from a coronet of stiffened silk and ribbons, and her brown eyes were narrowed in anger. The dog was white, and barely larger than a bedroom slipper. Its long hair was tied up with a lavender bow on top of its head, revealing two round black eyes and a small brown nose. In contrast to its mistress, the dog wagged a long plumed tail at me in greeting, apparently already recovered from being trod upon.

"Pippin! Pippin darling! Come here," the owner shrilled, holding out her manicured hands to the dog. "Let Mummy see if the nasty big peasant hurt my darling!"

But Pippin didn't want to be comforted. She wanted to smell my shoes. That done, she trotted over to the monkey seller and stood on her hind legs to get a better look at the little black-and-white creatures.

"Pippin!" The girl's voice was sharp now. "Come here to Mummy right now!"

Pippin seemed to sigh and slowly wandered back over to her mistress, giving a casual stretch rather like a cat before condescending to being picked up. Her "mummy" fussed over her for several seconds, looking for any sign of injury, while I stood red-faced and stammering over and over again how sorry I was.

"You're very lucky, country cow, that you didn't break one of my Pippin's little paws." The other girl sniffed at me. "She cost more than your family's entire farm, I'm sure."

"I am so very sorry," I said for the thousandth time, bristling at being called a country cow. "I truly didn't see her."

"Well, how could you? In that great dragging old-fashioned gown and with those huge boats for feet," the girl sneered.

As I got a better look at what she was wearing my heart sank. She was right: my gown *was* old-fashioned, or at the least, dreadfully countrified. While I wore a single long gown with a fitted bodice and flaring skirt all of a piece, she was elegantly dressed in layers of skirts that had been pinned up in the front to reveal each successive garment. Her bodice had the look of a tightly fitted jacket over a foamy white shift.

There was embroidery along the neckline and in long panels down her skirts, though. I gave it a quick scan and saw that it was nothing I couldn't do.

"How dare you stare at me in that way!" The rich girl stomped one pink-slippered foot. "Who is your mistress? I will have you fired at once! First you try to kill my precious Pippin, then you ogle me with your horrible country eyes!"

"I'm sorry," I mumbled, looking down at my dragging country skirts. What more did she want from me?

"Do you know who I am?" she demanded.

"No," I muttered.

"No? No what?"

"What?" I looked up at her and blinked again. Did she want me to call her "mistress"? We were the same age, as near as I could guess.

She looked over one shoulder and screeched something in a strange tongue. Four hulking brutes in scarlet tunics with heavy swords belted at their hips stepped forward. I hadn't even noticed them before, since all my attention had been focused on the dog and its excitable mistress.

She pointed her finger at me and babbled some more in that foreign language, and one of the brutes pulled a length of cord from a large belt pouch while the other made as if to grab my arm. I dodged out of his reach and for a wild moment I considered knocking over a cage of monkeys to create a diversion.

"Hey!" I yelled. "What's going on?"

"You need to be taught a lesson," the girl said.

"I say, what's all this?"

A tall and fairly good-looking young man in a rich green velvet doublet and leather riding breeches stepped forward. He frowned at me and then at the girl. "What's the to-do, Amalia?"

"This great peasant tried to kill my poor Pippin," the girl said in a voice that suddenly sounded on the verge of tears. She pulled out a dainty handkerchief and sniffed into it. As it wafted past the dog's face, "poor Pippin" tried to bite it. "I thought she had crushed my sweet doggie! And then she said rude things to me!"

"I did not!" I was astonished at this turn of events. She had gone from being shrill and demanding to weepy and victimized in a matter of seconds. And I *liked* dogs, even small fussy ones, and felt quite bad about stepping on Pippin.

"I say!" The wealthy young man turned gray eyes on me, looking stern. "What is the meaning of this? Is it true that you accosted Princess Amalia and attempted to kill her dog?"

I didn't even know how to answer. "P-Princess Amalia?" I stammered finally. "She's a princess?" I shook my head to clear it, and remembered some Carlieff Town gossip about the crown prince being engaged to marry a foreign princess. Oh, dear.

"Yes, she's a princess." The young man drew himself up stiffly and stared at me. "The Princess Amalia of Roulain." Then he looked at my clothes. "Ah, just in from the country?" He relaxed a little.

I blushed. Was it so obvious that I was a total bump-kin? But not so backward that I didn't realize who this wealthy young man was. If the shrill girl was Princess Amalia, than this richly dressed youth must be the Crown Prince Milun.

"Yes, your Highness," I murmured politely, making a small curtsy as my mother had taught me. "Forgive me. This is my first day in the King's Seat, and I did not recognize the princess. I didn't mean to step on her dog, truly I didn't."

"There!" The prince gave me a patronizing smile. "Very prettily said. You see, Amalia?" He turned to his betrothed. "She didn't mean any harm." He waved his hands at the brutes guarding the princess. "Pippin looks quite all right, as well."

It seemed a bit much to me that the princess needed four enormous men to guard her on a simple shopping trip, but I didn't remark on it. Who was I to know the ways of royalty? Particularly foreign royalty.

The little dog was watching all this with bright black eyes, and didn't seem to even remember having been stepped on. She looked very much like she would prefer being on the ground, investigating the black-and-white monkeys, to being squeezed by her royal mistress.

"Well, I think she did it on purpose," the princess said, refusing to be mollified. "If you ever come near me again, I'll set my guards on you!" She shook her fist at me.

"I'm sorry, your Highness," I forced myself to say. What I really wanted to do was slap the silly wench, royal or no, but I was sure I would be spending the rest of my life in a dungeon if I did.

The princess whirled around and stormed off, her guards and the crown prince in tow, and I breathed a sigh of relief. After I had calmed myself, I turned to ask the bird seller the way to the cloth district.

"Please go away," he said uneasily, refusing to meet my eyes.

"What? But you said—"

"I don't want no trouble, maidy," the man said, and made a shooing gesture at me, still not meeting my gaze.

"But can't someone please just point me toward the cloth-workers' district?" I looked around at the other exotic pet sellers, who busied themselves with cleaning cages or untangling leashes. The brown man with the black-and-white monkeys smiled back, though, and gabbled something I couldn't understand. "Please?" I tugged at my clothes and raised my eyebrows at the monkey seller, trying to mime what I wanted.

"Dorfath," he said merrily, and pointed down the street in the direction I had come from. "Dorfath!"

"Thank you!" And I marched off in that direction, hoping he knew what he was talking about.

The Curfew Bells Toll

By the time the sun began to set, I had to admit that either the monkey seller *hadn't* known what I wanted, or he was playing a cruel joke on me. I had plodded up and down the streets and found no sign of a dress shop or even a glove maker. In fact, for the last hour I hadn't seen any shops at all. Instead I had been wandering among large houses with brightly painted shutters and window boxes full of flowers. No one I passed would give me directions. The people on foot looked to be servants hurrying about their errands, and the rest were fine ladies and gentlemen riding horses or closed up in carriages.

As the streets darkened, lamplighters came along with their long torches and lit the polished lanterns that hung from posts in front of every house. I tried asking one of them for directions, but they were all foreigners, and only brandished their torches at me and shouted, "Fire hot, maidy! Fire hot!" so that I would stay clear.

"Here now, what are you doing out and about?"

I wheeled around to see a guardsman in a green leather jerkin glaring at me. I clapped my hands in relief.

"Oh, please, sir," I said, so tired that I was swaying where I stood. "Could you direct me to the cloth-workers' district? I just came from the country today, and I'm looking for work."

"It's nearly curfew, girl," the guardsman said in a rough voice. "It's not time to be lookin' for work. Get on home with you!"

"I haven't got a home, sir," I began.

"Vagrant, are you?" He frowned at me.

"Er, no. I've only just arrived in the King's Seat," I repeated. "I'm looking for work, but haven't found the cloth-workers' district—"

"So you don't have work or a home?" He chewed his lip. "I'll have to take you in for violating the curfew," he warned me. He glanced up at the sky, where the sun had set and the smaller moon was just rising.

"Please, I don't understand," I pleaded. "I've only just arrived; what is this about a curfew?"

"What town are you from?" The guard's eyebrows were approaching his receding hairline. "The curfew, girl, the curfew!"

I looked at him with a blank expression. None of the traders who stopped in Carlieff Town had ever said anything about there being a curfew in the King's Seat.

"The curfew 'til the crown prince's wedding!"

"What?" I still didn't follow.

"Can I help?"

The guard and I both turned to look at the young man who had come up while we'd been trying to understand one another. He looked to be about my age, some sixteen years or so, but was far better dressed than I in a tunic of fine gray wool and black leather breeches. He had brown eyes and brown hair with streaks of gold in it.

"Your Highness!" The guardsman tapped his fist to his chest in salute.

"Another one?" The question burst out of me in a squeak before I could stop it, and I stared at the young man in horror.

The prince and the guardsman looked at me with amusement and shock, respectively. I covered my mouth with both hands, wishing I could take those two words and shove them right back into my mouth.

"Another one?" The prince looked momentarily confused, and then he burst out laughing. "Don't tell me you're the maid who faced off with Amalia this afternoon? The one she claims tried to assassinate her lapdog?"

My face turned red and I put my hands on my cheeks. "Oh, no, has the entire city heard that story?" I silently cursed the princess and my clumsy feet. "I wasn't trying to kill her dog! I swear!"

"Oh, this is too wonderful," the prince said. "Did you hear that, Tobin?" He looked over his shoulder at someone.

Out of the shadows came a large man neither I nor the guardsman (judging by his flinch of surprise) had seen. He was huge, taller than any man I had ever met, his shaved head rising even above the prince's, and the prince was quite tall. Blue tattoos ran up both bare arms and over his scalp, and there were fat gold rings in his ears. He opened his mouth and laughed soundlessly, looking at me with kind blue eyes.

"This is the person who attacked the Roulaini princess?" The guard gaped at me. "I shall take her into custody at once!" He reached toward me.

I skipped out of the way. "I didn't attack her! She was only . . ." I couldn't say that she was being mean, or foolish; she was a princess, after all. "It was a misunderstanding."

"Yes, yes," the prince said, waving his hand. "My brother was quite satisfied that no harm was meant."

Suddenly, bells began chiming all across the city, making me jump. Both the prince and the guardsman looked up at the sky, checking the position of the moons, I guessed. The tattooed man, Tobin, continued to simply stand and watch.

"It's curfew, your Highness," the guard said, a trifle unnecessarily, in my opinion.

"Indeed it is," the prince said lightly. "So I had best escort this young lady to her lodgings. Carry on there, guardsman." And with that, the prince took my elbow and steered me away.

I was too numb to protest. I had not thought it possible to be more tired or frightened or lonely than I had been as I had made my weary way along the King's Road from Carlieff. But I was wrong: right this moment I was so exhausted and terrified and homesick that it was all I could do to stay on my feet. "I don't have any lodgings," I mumbled.

"Yes, I heard. And you're trying to find work in the cloth-workers' district?"

I could only nod and blush; he had heard me pleading with the guard. I was embarrassed, though I wasn't entirely sure why.

"I'll take you there, or near there. I know someone who has an inn just a few streets over."

"Why is there a curfew?" It was the only one of the many questions buzzing around in my head that I could think to ask just now.

He looked at me, seeming surprised. "You haven't heard? You must be from far away, then."

I didn't say anything, so he went on.

"It's because of Amalia and Miles getting married. A lot of people don't like the idea of him marrying a foreigner, especially one from Roulain." A shrug. "Old prejudices run deep. There have been protests, and even attacks. Mostly little things: mud thrown at her carriage, threats of harm from people who couldn't possibly do anything to a heavily guarded princess." He shrugged again. "But as a precaution my father has ordered that everyone stay in after dark, at least until after the wedding."

"Oh." I felt I owed him some sort of explanation, since he was helping me, after all. "I'm from Carlieff Town, all the way in the north. We had barely even heard that the crown prince was betrothed."

"I'm hardly surprised, it's been rather sudden." The

prince flashed his bodyguard a grim look, which Tobin returned with an eloquent expression, making me realize that he wasn't taking part in the conversation because he was a mute. Despite his handicap, it was clear that he shared his prince's distaste for the speed of this controversial marriage.

"So," I began, thinking to change the subject, "who exactly are you taking me to? Not that I'm not grateful to you, your Highness, for all your help," I added hastily.

"Tobin's older sister runs an inn just outside the cloth-workers' district," the prince explained patiently. "Ulfrid was my nanny when I was a child, and will be happy to help you."

"Oh, thank you." I looked back at Tobin, who was shadowing us with one hand on the hilt of his sword. "And thank you, Tobin," I told the bodyguard.

He raised his eyebrows and nodded curtly.

I slowed my steps, though, as we passed beneath a brightly burning lamp. "But, your Highness, if I may ask: *Why* are you helping me?"

He stopped and raised his eyebrows. "Why shouldn't I help you?"

"Because . . . well, I'm nobody. I'm a farm girl from Carlieff. You're a prince: Why do you care if I get locked up for vagrancy?"

The prince looked at me thoughtfully. "Had a hard day, eh?"

I looked down at the blue toes of my slippers, peeping out from under my hem. "You have no idea," I said softly, thinking of the endless walking, the dust, the raucous laughter of the woman who had shaken her broom at me. And that was before I had stepped on the princess's dog.

"Well, that's why. Because it is my duty to make up for the harsh treatment you have received thus far," he said, striking a noble pose.

Now I raised my eyebrows.

He grinned. "Actually, I like to walk around at night. I think the curfew is stupid. And the city jail is no place for a young girl." He stuffed his hands in his pockets. "Also, Ulfrid makes some very fine sausage rolls." He took a few steps forward. "Shall we?"

I was so tired. I nodded.

Tobin's sister was not a mute, but neither was she much of a talker. She opened the door after her brother gave it a few loud knocks and ushered us inside without saying a word. She had seated us by the remains of the common room fire, stirred the ashes to life again, and brought sausage rolls and tea before I heard her say a thing.

"Do that, did you?" Ulfrid was pointing at the cuffs of my gown. She had a heavy accent. But then, from the looks of her brother's tattoos and earrings, and the strange way her long white-blond braids were wrapped around her head, I had figured that they weren't from Feravel. "Your work?" she asked.

"Er, yes, it is." I straightened my skirt to display more of the hem, now rather dusty, that I had also embroidered. "And these." I pulled open my bundle and showed her the woven sashes and embroidered ker-chiefs. She grunted and nodded.

"Think you can help her find some work?" The prince smiled cheerfully at her. "I would hate to have her carted off by the guards for breaking curfew again." He winked at me cheekily and I pulled a face, forgetting for the moment that he was a prince, and treating him as I would my brother, Hagen. Then I remembered my place and looked away, cheeks hot.

"There are places," the woman said, nodding her head. "I will take her tomorrow." Her tone was neither encouraging nor discouraging, merely neutral.

"Excellent!" The prince put down his mug with a bang, then looked sheepish when his former nanny frowned at him. "Well, Tobin and I need to get back to the palace, or Father will be sending out the army to find us."

I wondered what it would be like to call a man "Father" when everyone else called him "Your Majesty." And to know that if you went missing, he would and could send an army to look for you.

"Yes, Luka, it is late," his nanny said in a voice that was almost fond. "You need more sleep."

I heard his given name with a start. I hadn't even known the name of a prince of my own land! Carlieff Town really was far out in the country. I knew that King Caxel and Queen Temia had had two sons and a daughter, and that the queen and the young princess had died during an outbreak of blue fever ten years ago. But beyond that I knew only that the crown prince was named Milun and would one day be Milun the Fourth. And here I was, being rescued from breaking the curfew and given food and lodging by a kind prince whose name I had never bothered to learn! I shook my head, trying to clear it of all this strangeness.

"Is something wrong?" Luka got to his feet and stretched, smiling down at me.

"Not at all, your Highness." I hopped to my feet as well, and curtsied. "I still don't know why you're doing this for me, but I want you to know that I am truly, truly grateful."

Now Luka blushed. "It was my pleasure, maidy. Ul-frid would have my hide if she found out that I had seen a fair maiden in need of aid and failed to render it." He shot a playful look at his former nanny. "Or even an ugly maiden," he added.

Ulfrid, with long, skilled fingers, twirled a bar cloth into a rope with one quick snap and then whipped the prince's shoulder with it.

"Ouch!" He rubbed his upper arm. "That hurt!"

"Begone with you, begone with you both," she said, threatening her mute brother with the towel as well. "The girl needs rest, and so do I."

Prince Luka and his bodyguard fled, laughing, while I sank back onto a stool, exhausted. When she had barred the door behind them, Ulfrid returned and surveyed me with bright blue eyes like her brother's.

"You can have a room at the top of the house, on the left." And she turned away to gather up the teapot and cups.

I trudged upstairs and collapsed onto the bed. Just

before I fell asleep I thought to wriggle out of my gown and lay it across the room's one chair, to prevent it from being too crumpled in the morning. Then I laid myself down again and was instantly deeply asleep.

Scarlet Ribbons

The next morning I was too nervous to eat breakfast, even though all I'd had the day before was a couple of peaches I'd brought with me from Shardas's cave and a sausage roll. Instead I washed as thoroughly as possible in the basin in my room, combed and recombed my yellow hair and braided it neatly. Ulfrid loaned me a clothes brush, which I used to make my gown as presentable as I could. It was countrified, and not new, but it had been laundered just two days ago in Shardas's bathing pool, and the embroidery showed off my neat stitches.

By mid-morning I was as ready as I thought I would ever be, and Ulfrid agreed in her laconic way. She gave curt orders to the staff, took off her apron, straightened her own gown, and off we went.

Two streets over we encountered a booth selling some badly dyed wool. A girl peddling ribbons from a tray was strolling up and down in front of the booth, as were a number of women with shopping baskets on their arms or overburdened servants trailing behind. It wasn't far from Ulfrid's inn, but from where I had met the prince last night it was a confusing walk through a tangle of side streets. For the tenth time, I sent up a prayer of thanksgiving to the Triunity for sending Prince Luka to take me under his wing.

Ulfrid marched past the booth and the ribbon seller, and even past the first few shops. I didn't know what she had in mind for me, but her stride was so long and purposeful, it was all I could do to keep up.

"But what about that one?" I finally gasped, touching her elbow as she marched past yet another shop displaying a rack of finely woven sashes in the window.

"Common," grunted Ulfrid, and strode on.

At last, nearly a mile from the inn, she stopped. We were standing in front of a tall and very imposing dress shop. It had a large bay window, but there was nothing displayed in it, unless you counted the beautifully made curtains drawn across the gleaming panes of glass.

The women going in and out were testimony enough to the type of shop this was: they had bodyguards walking before and footmen scurrying after. Maids carried small dogs on cushions, and young boys in livery held sun-canopies over their mistresses' heads the moment they stepped into the open air.

My jaw dropped. Was Ulfrid mad? Did her foreign upbringing differ so much from mine that she actually thought a shop like this would hire a nobody from the country? It would be much easier to convince a smaller shop that I was a master, but a place like this? Impossible! I slumped in despair. Ulfrid threw her shoulders back and glared at me until I straightened. Then she took my bundle of handkerchiefs and sashes from my arms and stepped into the shop without looking back to make sure that I followed.

Startled, I followed.

The room was furnished with cushioned chairs and little tables laid with snowy cloths. Pretty maids in embroidered aprons rushed to and fro, supplying the customers with refreshments, while other girls in pink dresses with scarlet sashes hurried about with armloads of silks and satins. Ulfrid walked through the maze of delicate chairs and gossiping customers without looking right or left. My face flamed as all conversation stopped and the finely dressed ladies and their daughters paused to stare at us. Nevertheless, I put my chin up and strolled behind Ulfrid as though I did this every day.

At the back of the shop there was a long counter of highly polished wood. Beyond it was a pair of doors that must have led into the backroom and the kitchens. Maids went into one with empty trays and came back laden with delicate cakes and pots of steaming tea or chilled bottles of wine, and the pink-gowned shopgirls went through the other to reemerge weighed down by bolts of cloth or large wooden spools of thread.

Presiding over it all from a position behind the

counter was a stout woman in deep blue silk with a wide pink sash. When we reached the counter I saw that, like the princess the day before and most of the women in the shop today, she wore layers of skirts that had been kilted up to display the fine embroidery along the hem of each garment. With a critical eye I inspected the work, and had to admit that it was quite fine. I also thought that the style and technique bore a strong resemblance to that decorating Princess Amalia's gown, and wondered with trepidation if she had her dresses made here.

"Ah, dear Mistress Ulfrid, what have you brought me?" The proprietress had bright black eyes and fat little hands that she clapped in delight at seeing Ulfrid. "More samples of that foreign embroidery?"

Without saying a word, Ulfrid laid my bundle on the counter and spread out its contents. She lined up the sashes and smoothed out the handkerchiefs and the two squares of linen I had used as samplers. The customers waiting at the counter leaned in closer to have a look.

The proprietress eyed my stitches beadily. She fingered the sashes, and lifted the two samplers up to study the stitches more carefully.

"It's amateur work," she declared with a sniff, casting down the handkerchief she had inspected last. "Crude cloth, crude threads, old-fashioned techniques. But the pattern is certainly unusual, and she has a good eye for color and form."

I bristled at this dismissal of my work. "I have embroidered for the Lady of Carlieff Town," I said in a

tight voice. "My stitches were skilled enough for *her*."
That was not entirely true: my mother had had me copy
exactly the work she had done for the lady, but had not
let me work on the actual gown. Still, how would this
woman ever find out the truth?

"Of course they were," the stout woman fired back.
"She's the Lady of *Carlieff Town*. Things are different in
the King's Seat!" She raked me up and down with her
fierce eyes. "And mind your tongue, girl."

"It was for the patterns that I brought her," Ulfrid
said placidly, as though my outburst had never happened.
"I've never seen this style of embroidery before. And this
knotwork is exceptional." She lifted one of the sashes
and showed the proprietress.

"Where did you copy these patterns from? Who was
your mistress?" The proprietress's voice lashed at me.

"My mother taught me to embroider and weave," I
said, only just managing to keep the snap out of my
own voice. I wasn't only irritated with her, I was irritated with myself for thinking that it would be easy to
find work with my poor samples. "I had no other mistress," I confessed, not very humbly. "But the patterns
are my own."

"I see." The woman looked me over again, and then
looked back at my work. Her brows were drawn together as though to say she didn't quite believe me. "I'll
take her on," she told Ulfrid after long consideration.
"If she can keep a civil tongue in her head."

I opened my mouth to make some biting retort, but

then realized that I had just been offered work. "Thank you," I said meekly.

Neither of the older women looked at me.

"She has only a small bundle of things, other than this," Ulfrid announced. "I will send the potboy with them this afternoon."

"Very well. Would you care for some wine? Cakes?" The proprietress made a gesture at the door to the kitchens. "I wouldn't mind sitting down for a bit in my private parlor."

"Thank you, Derda, but I must go back to my inn." Ulfrid grimaced. "That new serving wench spends far too much time making eyes at the soldiers and not enough time scouring mugs."

And with that, Ulfrid turned and stalked out, once more ignoring the sneering looks of the patrons. I called a feeble thanks after her, but she didn't acknowledge it in any way I could detect.

"Come along, girl," Derda said, gathering up my samples and sashes with a quick movement. "You cannot work in the shop until you've made yourself a proper shopgown."

"I will begin work on it immediately," I told her. I didn't much care for the way she and Ulfrid had ignored me and talked so condescendingly about my skills, but she *was* my employer, and it wouldn't do to get myself fired before I'd even earned any pay.

Derda snorted. "There you go again, talking when you're not wanted to talk. You'll work in the backroom until closing time, your old gown is good enough for that. Then there's the cleaning. And *then* you'll start sewing yourself a pink gown, like Marta's here." She pointed at a pretty girl with strawberry blonde hair who was whirling by with a bolt of lavender satin. Marta gave me a saucy wink, and I felt a bitter surge of jealousy for her perfect curls and neat city-style gown.

"How much will my wages be?" I dared to ask as I was stepping through the door into the large backroom where the bolts of cloth and spools of thread and ribbon were kept.

Derda gave me a calculating look. "You'll be paid a silver every two weeks. But it will cost you two silvers for the cloth to make your shopgown. And another silver for the proper underthings and a sash."

My jaw dropped as I quickly did the figures in my head. I would have to work here for six weeks until I was finally paid? And, though two silvers would have been a respectable sum in Carlieff Town, I'd heard hawkers calling out prices for things in the street and knew that, in the King's Seat, that sum a month would buy precious little.

"Additionally, you will room and board in the dormitory at the top of the shop," Derda went on. "I charge only a copper a week for that, and expect my girls to keep the shop and their living quarters tidy. There will be no gentlemen callers of any kind."

I could only stare at her. How did her girls make any money at all? It was ten coppers to a silver, and she charged them four coppers a month to live above the shop.

"Stop gawking that way, country girl," Derda said gruffly. "If you don't like my terms you're welcome to try to find work elsewhere. I think you'll find that I'm more than kind to my girls, at least compared to some.

"Now I've customers to attend to. Larkin will show you what to do." And she pushed back through the doors and into the front room of the shop.

The backroom was at least two stories high and the walls were lined with shelves. There were more ranks of shelves to each side of a long table running down the middle, scarred by sewing shears. Here and there a footstool or ladder allowed access to the highest shelves.

"Um, Larkin?" I looked around, but couldn't see anyone else. I put my bundle on the edge of the table. I raised my voice: "Larkin?"

What appeared to be a moving pile of cloth came lurching toward me, and I took a step backward. A good half-dozen bolts of fabric tumbled onto the table, revealing a rather plain girl with brown hair in two braids and wide gray eyes.

"I'm Larkin," she said, limping around the table to take my hand in her own. "Are you new? Welcome."

"Yes, I'm Creel," I replied. "I'm supposed to help you back here until I can get my shopgown made."

"Of course," she said simply. "You're so pretty; I assumed that she would have you work in the front."

"Oh, I'm not pretty," I protested. "You have much better skin; I'm covered in freckles."

"No one wants to be waited on by a cripple," Larkin said in her mild voice.

I realized with a pang that her limp was not from a recent injury. As she moved away from me to sort through the bolts on the table, her skirts swept around her legs, revealing an ankle that was twisted in a way that made her lurch from side to side. I fought the urge to tell her I was sorry; after all, it wasn't my fault, and an apology would only sound hollow, so instead I put my bundle on a half-empty shelf and wordlessly began helping her lay out the bolts.

Larkin quietly showed me how measuring marks had been burned into the edge of the table on both sides, and told me how much was wanted from each bolt. I took up a pair of heavy shears from the basket dangling from a hook on the wall to cut lengths of cherry-red silk. I hesitated at first, though. I had never seen such fine silk, and it was almost frightening to think about cutting it. What if I cut it the wrong length? What if my hands, calloused from farm work, snagged the fabric?

"Do you need help?" Larkin looked at me with a crease between her brows.

"Oh, no. Sorry." Taking a deep breath, I began to cut. The rip-rip sound of the shears biting into the silk was exciting as well as scary, and when I was done I held up the length with a triumphant expression. Perfect!

"Larkin, have you got the cherry and the powder blue done yet?" Marta, the pretty strawberry blonde came bustling through the swinging door. "Oh, hello!"

She waved a hand at me. "I'm Marta, are you the new girl?"

"Yes, I'm Creel," I told her, wary. Pretty girls like her always made me nervous, and Derda's attention made me suspect that this one was a favorite of hers.

"I guess you'll be stuck back here with Larkin until you can make your pink gown," she burbled. There was a looking glass hanging from one of the shelves, and she turned to it to rearrange her curls. "I couldn't make mine fast enough."

I frowned at her back, thinking that it was extremely rude of her to talk this way, and right in front of Larkin, too! "Well, I am very good with a needle," I said.

"You would have to be." Marta laughed. "Derda only hires the best. Not that she lets any of us do anything interesting. I don't know why she bothers to inspect our handiwork so closely. I've done nothing but hem underskirts since I got here last summer." She yawned. "Larkin, are you finished or not?"

I folded the cherry-red silk loosely, all but throwing it at Marta. "Here! I did the cherry."

"Oh, thank you," Marta said, sounding confused at my unfriendly tone. She refolded the fabric into a neater square. Larkin handed her an equally tidy parcel of powder blue.

"I'm just glad we talked Lady Catta out of having these two silks on the same gown," Marta said, wrinkling her nose. "When she first came in, she wanted layers of these sewn together . . . ugh. But now she just wants two skirts to wear separately." And she bustled back out again.

I looked at Larkin, wanting to say something kind, something reassuring, but I couldn't think of anything. Instead, I just helped her put away the bolts we had finished with, and cut more lengths from the others. Marta continued to flash in and out collecting swatches and bolts and cut lengths, and so did another girl named Alle, who seemed nice, if rather light-minded.

I had been cutting away with Larkin in companionable silence for about an hour when a horribly familiar voice came knifing through the door as Marta swung it open. Two spots of angry color were burning on her pale cheeks.

"I want scarlet ribbons for this gown!" the voice from the shop shrieked.

"Gah!" Marta shuddered. "I don't care if she *is* a princess—gah!"

"What seems to be the problem?" Larkin put down her shears and looked up at Marta in her mild way. "The Princess Amalia is one of our best patronesses," she chided the other girl. "You are fortunate to be waiting upon royalty."

"Again: I don't care," Marta fired back. "She's a horror!"

I was frozen for a moment, but then shook myself. "Is it really her?" I couldn't keep the dismay from my voice. "The Roulaini princess?"

"Yes, why?" Marta looked at me with curiosity.

"Oh, nothing," I mumbled.

"All right, suit yourself!" And Marta bounced over to the shelves where the spools of ribbon were kept. "I don't see it anywhere! I could have sworn we had some, but Alle thought we didn't, and she made the mistake of telling the princess that!"

"What is it exactly?" Larkin struggled to her feet.

"Scarlet ribbons, from the sound of the shrieking," I said under my breath.

Marta snickered. "But not just *any* scarlet ribbons. Not for the Princess of Roulain! *Wide* scarlet ribbons— two fingers wide to be exact. And of the finest southern silk, if you please."

I let out a low whistle. "Every handspan would be worth our monthly wages," I said.

"*Twice* our monthly wages," Larkin corrected me, going back to her task.

"We *are* the finest dress shop in the King's Seat," Marta shot back. "Which is why Derda charges her customers such outrageous prices." She shuffled through more spools of ribbon. "Well, I can't see it anywhere!" She sighed. "I guess I'll have to go back out and face Princess Shrill-malia."

"Marta, do you think it wise to disparage both our employer and our future queen?" Larkin's downcast eyes never left the lilac velvet she was cutting.

"Gah! Our future queen! I feel sick!" was the other's reply as she swept out.

"That girl is going to end up in trouble one day," Larkin murmured.

The shrieking continued from the front of the shop, where Princess Amalia was letting Derda and Marta know, in no uncertain terms, what she thought of the lack of scarlet ribbons. A cry of distress followed by the sound of breaking crockery told me that the princess had either knocked a serving tray from the hands of one of the maids, or had thrown it.

It was all I could do not to make some comment about spoiled rich girls. But the demure look on Larkin's face kept stopping the words before I could speak them. We finished the bolts we had been cutting, and Larkin made a laborious move to gather them up and put them back on the shelves.

"No, no! Let me do it," I protested, taking them from her. "I need to learn where they go," I went on, to spare her pride. "I can see that they are arranged by color, but does the fabric matter?"

"The heavier fabrics go on the higher shelves, the lighter on the lower," Larkin instructed. "In the cooler months, we rotate them." She was watching me, hovering on the verge of standing up to help.

"It's all right, I can do it," I assured her.

And I could. My mother had kept her silks and yarns arranged in the same way, and I knew just how to find the shelves of blue and green and yellow, pink and gray. I was using a stepladder to shelve the last bolt, but something seemed to be blocking it.

"There's something stuck back here," I called over my shoulder to Larkin.

"I'll take care of it." She lurched to her feet and limped toward me, faster than I would have thought she could. "I'm used to it. Let me."

"No, it's all right, I've got it." Stretching my arm as far as I could, I reached back and snagged what felt like one of the large ribbon spools. It was caught for a moment, then came free so suddenly that I fell back off the stepladder and only just managed to catch myself before I tumbled right onto my rear. "Hey!" I held up my prize with a grin. "Scarlet ribbons!"

This had to be what Marta had been looking for. Holding the spool high in triumph, I started for the swinging door.

"What are you doing?" Larkin caught my arm, her face crinkled with concern.

"I'm going to take this out and make her Highness stop screaming," I said, bewildered at her reaction.

"But you haven't a proper shopgown," Larkin protested.

"Don't be silly," I said. "What if the princess leaves without anyone knowing that we had the ribbons she wanted?" I grinned at her, ignoring my own internal anxiety at having to face Amalia again. "I'm sure I will be forgiven for appearing in my country gown when they see what I've got." And with that, I pushed through the doors into the shop proper.

As I'd thought, the rest of the customers had left,

with the exception of a stately matron wearing a hat so covered in feathers that it looked as though a large bird had settled on her head. She was standing to one side of the princess, looking resigned, while Derda and the rest of her staff fluttered around the princess and her entourage, offering her sweets and bolts of silk.

"I found it," I called, striding forward and waving the spool of ribbon. "It had been misplaced."

Marta rushed forward to take the ribbon from me, whispering a string of breathless thank-yous. She offered it to the princess with the expression of a vestal virgin giving sacrifice to a vengeful god. The princess snatched the spool from her hands, and Marta backed off quickly, almost treading on me in her haste to get out of slapping distance of Feravel's future queen. One of the first things I had noticed on entering the room was that Alle and several of the serving maids had red cheeks and moist eyes, as though they had been struck.

Derda gave me a beady look and a sharp nod and then gestured with one hand for me to return to the backroom. Only too grateful, I nodded in answer and started to creep away in as unobtrusive a manner as possible.

"You there, girl who finds things," the stately matron barked, halting me in my tracks. "Come here."

"Madam?" I looked to Derda, who nodded her permission, though she did not appear pleased.

"Yes, yes, come here and let me see your gown," the

woman said with impatience, though her expression was not unkind.

"Forgive me, Madam," I apologized. "I have only just come to work for Mistress Derda, and have not yet made myself a presentable gown. This is the poor farm garb I arrived in." I had to grit my teeth to say such a thing, since my dress had not been all that mean back home, but I was hoping for a quick escape.

"Let me have a closer look at that embroidery," the stately woman said, her tone softening. She snapped her fingers and her maid pulled a pair of green-tinted spectacles from a purse. The woman held them a few inches from her eyes and squinted at my hem. "I have never seen the like."

"Er, no, Madam, it is my own design," I told her, and I held up my skirt a little so that she could see it better.

"You!"

My head jerked around and I found myself meeting the princess's angry gaze. Princess Amalia let her little lapdog, Pippin, down and the creature began happily eating the crumbled cakes that adorned the floor. The princess advanced on me.

"You're that awful, clumsy country cow who assaulted me yesterday," the princess said, pointing a sharp-looking finger. "What are *you* doing *here*?"

"Some very remarkable embroidery, I hope," the older woman said, handing her spectacles back to her maid. "I heard about what happened in the marketplace yesterday, Amalia, and I'm sure it was an accident, so please stop fussing about it.

"Derda." The stately woman turned her gaze from the princess, who was gasping like a hooked fish at this injustice, and addressed my employer. "You must have her do something for me. I've never seen the like. It's breathtaking."

"Well," Derda said, coming to my side. "We shall see. I'm afraid the girl is new, and some of this work is not really fit for such as yourself, your Grace."

Not caring if Derda was my employer, or the woman facing me a duchess, I opened my mouth to protest, when Princess Amalia said something that made me wish I had taken Larkin's warning to heart and not left the backroom.

"Where did you get those slippers?" The princess's gaze was fixed firmly on my blue slippers.

"Er," I replied, dropping my skirts to cover them. "Er, the cobbler in Carlieff Town?" I wished that it didn't sound so much like a question.

"I *must* have some, they're beautiful," the princess said. "*Too* beautiful for a countrified shopgirl."

"We can send someone to Carlieff Town for a pair at once, your Highness." A horse-faced woman standing behind the princess spoke up. "But first, let's buy the ribbon you wanted and return to the palace, it must be nearly time for you to dress for dinner." She sounded like a nanny trying to coax a spoiled toddler away from a toy.

"But I want them right now," Amalia said. "Give me yours."

"Princess Amalia, surely you don't want to wear the same shoes that a peasant girl has been wearing?" The horse-faced lady-in-waiting looked scandalized. I wondered how scandalized she would have been if I'd slapped her, and then her rude mistress.

"Maybe not," the princess said, never taking her eyes off me. "Maybe I just don't think it's fair that a peasant girl is wearing such fine slippers."

"You have dozens upon dozens of slippers," the lady-in-waiting protested.

"None like those," Princess Amalia said mulishly.

"Really, Amalia, this is childish," the duchess said, shaking her head in disgust. "If you deprived every person whose shoes you like of their footwear, half of the King's Seat would go barefoot. Let's buy those ribbons and return to the palace." She gave her attention to Derda once more. "I don't know what you mean, that it isn't good enough for me, Derda. If I like the girl's handiwork, then it clearly *is* good enough.

"Now, after you've made up that gray silk gown, let this girl embroider panels on the skirt and around the cuffs. I want something like this." She waved a hand at my gown. "Only all in shades of blue. That will go well enough with the gray, don't you think?"

Realizing that she had actually asked my opinion, I shook myself out of my stupor. "Very well, your . . . Grace." It had taken me a moment to think of the proper way to address a duchess. Fortunately my silly aunt's even sillier romantic tales were a good resource for such things. "I would be pleased to do it, your Grace," I added.

"Excellent. Amalia?" The duchess studied the princess, and then sighed when it appeared that Princess Amalia was ignoring all of us until she got her way. "Derda, please use as much of the ribbon as you deem necessary, and add it to the princess's bill." She gave another wave of her hand. "The pattern you showed us today will do very well. Now come along, all of you." And the duchess swept out, taking Princess Amalia and her entourage with her. I had just opened my mouth to apologize to Derda, and to find out why she was glaring at me in that way, when there was a shriek from the street outside, and one of the princess's burly guards came hurrying back in.

"Pippin! Pippin!" The man looked ridiculous, running around the pink-decorated shop snapping his fingers and calling that silly name.

"Here she is," I called. I had spotted a long silky tail disappearing under the cloth covering one of the refreshment tables. I reached under and pulled the little dog out. She was busily munching something she'd found on the floor. She licked my chin and I handed her to the guard with a grin that I couldn't stop.

"Thank you," he said in labored Feravelan, and left.

Derda rounded on me as soon as the door closed behind him. "How dare you leave the backroom to wait on a customer when you're dressed like that?" Her face was red with rage.

I gaped at her. "But—but the princess, she wanted the ribbon and I found it," I said helplessly. "I didn't know how to get anyone's attention, to have Marta or Alle come to get it." Did she want the princess to leave dissatisfied, and never return?

"That was the Duchess of Mordrel!"

Blinking, I shook my head. I had never heard of the Duchess of Mordrel.

"The Duchess of Mordrel is the cousin of King Caxel himself! Her husband, the duke, is second only to the king in wealth and influence," Derda ranted. "The duchess is one of our most important patrons, and now she will know that those designs are your own." She threw her hands in the air and stormed away in disgust. "Get in the backroom where you belong, girl!" she shouted over her shoulder. "I was doing a favor for Ulfrid by taking you in, but by the Triunity I will take that favor back if I have to!"

I stood staring at her as she lifted a discreet curtain and disappeared into some unknown quarter of the store. Alle gave me a scandalized look and began to clear up the mess that the princess had left. My hands clenched in my skirts, I started to stomp toward the backroom, when a hand on my elbow stopped me.

"She wanted to claim that the designs were her own," Marta whispered. "She always does. Says it's her right as our employer. Sewing embroidered ribbons around the necklines of gowns was my idea. And the kilted layers of skirts that are all the rage now? A local fashion where Alle is from."

Alle shot a terrified glance at Marta and moved farther away, as though not wanting to be tainted by association if Derda came back.

"Why don't you open your own shop then?" I asked, also keeping my voice low. My body was turning hot and cold and I wished with all my heart I was back in Shardas's cave.

"A shop? With what money?" Marta snorted at the idea. "I couldn't afford the rent on the shop and it would take years to build up a clientele." She shook her head. "The only hope for country girls like us is to keep our heads down and work for someone like Derda, and hope that we can save up enough money to go into business on our own before we're too old to care."

"You could attend the Merchants' Ball," Alle put in shyly, and then scurried into the backroom with an arm-load of cloth.

"Is it true that even an apprentice can go to the Merchants' Ball?" I picked up the spool of scarlet ribbon and another of gray, and Marta filled her arms with balls of embroidery yarn. My mother had told me that she had once thought of attending, before she married.

"The Merchants' Ball is a fool's dream," Larkin said as I stepped into the backroom. "I hope you have not been filling her head with such ideas, Marta," she said in a severe voice.

"Not me. Alle brought it up," Marta said with a toss of her head. "It's not like any of us would have a chance there. But who are you to decide what we can and can't dream about?"

I dropped the spools on the table with a clatter. "Will Derda attend?"

"Oh, no! Why would she?" Marta shook her head. "The Merchants' Ball is where people like you and me go to try and court a wealthy investor. Derda doesn't need an investor, and she would never gamble her money away on some unknown artisan. Anyone can attend, to try their luck." Marta wrinkled her nose. "The only catch is: you have to look presentable and have some really wonderful samples to prove yourself with. So what would I do? Go in this awful pink shopgirl's gown and show them some decorated ribbons?"

"We should be grateful to Derda for giving us this fine shop to work in and a good place to live," Larkin scolded.

I was starting to rethink my first impressions of these girls. Marta, though perhaps a bit of a flirt, seemed genuinely kind, while Larkin was striking me more and more as a wet dishrag, as Hagen would have put it.

"Grateful!" Marta rolled her eyes. "We do all the work, we invent the new fashions, and she takes all the credit and the money! If I had a fine enough gown, I'd be at the Merchants' Ball begging for a wealthy patron!" Her eyes roved over the shelves of brightly colored fabric. "There are times when I think about stealing some silk and making myself a ballgown," she confided to me.

"Derda and I both know the contents of this shop forward and back, miss," Larkin warned. "If enough silk went missing to make you a gown, we'd know before you had time to baste the seams!"

"Then why couldn't you find the scarlet ribbons?" she retorted. Marta stuck out her tongue and went back to the front of the store. As she went, I thought I heard her mutter something about a "two-faced little snake."

"What was it about your slippers?" Larkin gave me a mild look. "I could hear some of the conversation. The princess sounded quite taken with them."

"If by 'taken' you mean that she tried to force me to give them to her, then yes," I said with a snort.

"Why?"

I hesitated. I disliked calling attention to my shoes because of their odd origin.

"They're lovely," Alle said, coming around one of the rows of shelves, her chore finished. "Beautiful blue slippers, they are. A very strange style." She ducked her head at me in a shy gesture. "If they were mine, I would cut my skirts a little shorter, to show them off."

"She'll be cutting her skirts the same length as the rest of you," Derda said, smashing through the swinging doors. "I'm closing the shop. It's nearly time, and I doubt that we're fit to serve another customer.

"So!" She put her hands on her hips and looked me

up and down. "Take a bolt of the lightweight pink wool and start working on your dress. I don't want to see you in the front of the shop again until you have it finished." And with that she smashed back out.

"Gah," I said.

"You have no idea," Alle muttered under her breath. Then, seeing Larkin's dark look, she trotted out.

Numb Fingers, Itchy Feet

I had always loved sewing. Really, it didn't matter what kind: hemming sheets, tailoring my brother's tunics, or doing fancy embroidery. The idea of opening my own shop had glowed like a jewel in my mind. And yet, after just a day of working for Derda, I was starting to rethink my chosen career. Perhaps it was because I didn't really want to wear a pink gown. Or perhaps it was because whenever I worked on the gray gown for the duchess, Derda hovered over my shoulder inspecting every blessed stitch to make certain that it was up to her standard.

I had wondered how Derda and her girls could possibly wait on customers and get their work done, but that question was answered by the end of my first (very long) day. Fashionable ladies did their shopping at certain times: never before noon, because the morning was taken up with sleeping late and dressing languidly, and never after dusk, because that was when they had their social engagements. So Derda's shop, like any that catered to the wealthies (as Marta called them), was only open for four or five hours a day. Before and after closing, Derda supervised her employees as we sat around the large table in the backroom and sewed and gossiped and sewed some more. Derda had a small table of her own, where she worked on very special commissions, like the skirt with the scarlet ribbons for Princess Amalia.

So it was that within moments of nearly losing my employ for agreeing to sew for the duchess, I was cutting out the gray silk to make her skirt. Beside me lay a neatly folded pile of pink wool that would be used for my own shopgown. Marta told me that it seemed to go faster if you did things "all at once."

"Do all the cutting you have to do for both projects," she instructed me, sitting down to a large froth of pale golden silk that would soon be a ten-layered skirt for a countess. "Then do all the pinning, all the hemming, and so on. Trust me, if you only work on one gown at a time, you'll scream from boredom."

"If you find it so boring, you can find yourself another job, my girl," Derda said as she leaned over my shoulder and glared at the seam I was pinning. "Re-pin that," she barked.

With a sigh I removed the pins, straightened the two slippery pieces of fabric, and pinned them again. The ripples of gray silk reminded me of the pool in Shardas's cave that he used to talk to Feniul, and I felt a pang of longing for my quiet life there. I hoped that the migration would go well this year, and that Feniul was not bothering Shardas too much. It seemed like three weeks rather than three days since I had left him.

"Thinking of your swain?" Larkin raised her eyebrows at me.

I laughed aloud. "Oh, no," I told her, sobering at her startled expression. "I was just thinking of an old friend." A sudden vision of Shardas crouching in the street outside Derda's shop, knocking on the door with a claw, nearly made me laugh again, but I stifled it.

"Is your 'old friend' a prince?" Alle looked at me slyly as she embroidered a narrow sash.

I gave her a bewildered look. "No, why?"

"One of the kitchen maids told me that Ulfrid brought you here as a favor to Prince Luka," Alle answered, her expression eager.

"The prince was kind enough to direct me to Mistress Ulfrid's inn," was all I would say, no matter how Alle pried.

And she did continue to pry. There was nothing else to do while we sewed, hour after hour, than gossip. I, as the new girl, found myself being prodded for any gossip of interest from Carlieff Town (which wasn't much) or any variations on the same old stories they'd already told each other (which weren't many). A few days after I arrived, they were going around the table telling stories about sightings of goblins or dragons or trolls where they were from.

"Er," I said, when it was my turn. "There aren't any goblins or trolls in Carlieff."

"Then make something up," Marta urged me. "We've nothing better to do."

"You could sew," Derda said sharply from her table.

"Well, ah." I looked around the table, and they all looked back, expectant. "There is a dragon."

Larkin looked up at me sharply, and Alle giggled a little. Derda pursed her lips, but didn't interrupt again.

"The hills around Carlieff have lots of caves," I went on. "And it's rumored that there's a dragon living in one of them. Years ago he used to carry off children, sheep, goats, but no one's seen him now for generations and everyone thinks he's dead." I bit my lip. "Um, that's really all."

Disappointed, my audience looked back to their sewing, and I concentrated for a few minutes on the sleeve I was setting in my pink gown. Another day or two and it would be finished, and I would have the mixed blessing of being able to wait on customers.

"Our dragon is named Ama-something," Alle announced. "Amaracin, or Amacarin. Anyway, in my great-grandfather's time, the local laird challenged him to a duel, and Amacarin *ate* him."

"I don't know the name of the dragon my uncle claimed he saw," Marta said. "He just saw . . . something . . . go across the sky, and then later one of the older villagers said it must have been the dragon."

"The Carlieff dragon's name is Theoradus," I said, winking at Alle so that she would think I was spinning a yarn. "He's brown, with golden eyes and horns. He lives in a cave at the top of one of the highest hills. They say he has a pool of still water through which he can see and speak with other dragons."

"I wouldn't know our dragon's name," Marta said, laughing at my tale. "But he eats dogs, or something. If you have a really good dog anywhere near our village, it always disappears. My uncle, on my mother's side, claims to have seen something large and green carrying off our neighbor's new sheepdog once."

"Green, and likes dogs?" I laughed.

"Ridiculous, I know," Marta said with a shrug. "That's why I came to the King's Seat."

I laughed again, thinking of Feniul. "I came to get away from the dragons, myself," I told her with a grin.

She rolled her eyes at me and we both snickered. Derda cleared her throat, and we concentrated on our work.

It was the next day that my feet started to itch again. As if I didn't have enough to worry about, sewing for myself *and* a duchess, my feet had to bother me, too. But there I was, sitting between Marta and Alle, stitching away at the hem of my pink skirt, when I felt a sensation not unlike a feather being run across the bottoms of my feet.

"Hey!" I had pricked myself with my needle and a drop of blood fell on the pink cloth before I could catch it. I felt foolish for having pricked myself so many times in the last week. I had never been this clumsy at home; the fine fabrics I was working with now were making me nervous.

"What's wrong?" Marta stared at me, and then thoughtfully pressed her own handkerchief over the droplet of blood to absorb it.

"It felt like someone tickled my feet," I said, looking under the table even though I knew it was senseless. Who would be under the table tickling our feet? Besides which, the tickling had now settled into a constant itch that covered every bit of my soles. I paddled my feet against the floor and rubbed them back and forth, but nothing helped.

Larkin also ducked her head down to look at my feet. "I see that you are still wearing your blue slippers," she said in her soft voice when she straightened up.

"I have only one other pair of shoes, and they're just old sandals," I admitted. Then I threw an anxious look at Derda. "These blue slippers will be all right, to wait on customers, won't they?"

"I don't care what you wear on your feet," Derda informed me in a more good-natured tone than she had used with me since I was hired, "as long as you wear *something*. And they should be clean."

"Our skirts cover our shoes anyway," Marta said, after she spat a few pins into her palm. "So it hardly matters. Although the southern fashion for shorter skirts *is* catching on. . . ." She had raised her voice at this last comment, casting a hopeful look at Derda.

"My girls dress decently," was all Derda would say.

"Aaaah!" I dropped my work and ducked under the table, yanking off my shoes and frantically scratching the soles of my feet.

"Are you all right?" Marta's voice bubbled with laughter.

"I hope you don't have fleas," Larkin said with a concern that seemed feigned to my ears.

"Fleas!" Alle shrieked and jumped to her feet. "Fleas?! I'm itching all over, she's given us fleas!"

"I have not!" I yelled from under the table. Once I had gotten my shoes off, the itching subsided. "I think my feet are too hot. Or perhaps I'm not used to sitting so long. I did walk all the way here from Carlieff Town," I lied.

"I'm sure it's just your calluses or blisters healing," Marta said, helping me out from under the table.

"She looks clean enough," Derda said with a grunt. She frowned at Alle. "Now everyone get back to work."

Red-faced, I pulled my shoes back on, biting my lower lip as my feet began itching all over again. With an effort I returned to my work, speaking only when spoken to and giving all my attention to the seam I was stitching. I hoped that my diligence would be rewarded, either by taking my mind off the itching or by it going away entirely, but it was not to be. When I mounted the narrow stairs with the other girls, heading to our cramped rooms on the second floor, my feet were nearly as numb as my fingers.

Before I fell into an exhausted sleep, I noticed that the itching stopped when I took my slippers off.

"Shardas," I murmured into my pillow. "Why do my feet itch?"

"What?" Alle, on one side of me, raised herself up on her elbows. "*Do* you have fleas?" she hissed.

Marta, on the other side, reached across me and swatted Alle. "She doesn't have fleas, go to sleep."

"Shardas," I said into my pillow again. "I miss you." And I fell sound asleep.

A Plague of Royals

And I miss *you*," Shardas said in my dream. A laugh rumbled from his throat. "Who would have thought it? I haven't had a human friend since Jerontin's death. But truly, there is nothing that can compare to conversing with a human. Your brief lifespans give you such strange perspectives on life."

In my dream we were sitting beside his enchanted pool, sharing a bowl of grapes. I plucked several of the wine-colored globes from a stem and popped them into my mouth.

"How is Feniul doing with Azarte? Still having trouble?" I grinned.

"See for yourself." Shardas stirred the pool with one long claw, and I leaned closer to see.

There was Feniul, shaking a claw at the large, woolly wolfhound and scolding him for once again eating all the treats.

"Poor Feniul." I chuckled. "I don't think Azarte was meant for life in a dragon's hoard."

"Feniul's had worse trouble. At one point he had a hundred dogs. He used to just take whatever he wanted, we all did," Shardas said. "But since Milun the First, we have had to become inconspicuous." He sighed.

"I'm sorry, I guess," I said. "I mean, it's better for us humans I suppose. But it's not as good for you dragons."

"No," Shardas said, "it's better for all of us this way, if we cannot find a balance."

"I could help you find a balance," I offered.

The gold dragon gave me a look of infinite sadness. "Please don't."

"What?"

"You could kill us all," Shardas said.

"What do you mean? Shardas!" Everything was fading into a gray haze. "Shardas! I won't hurt you! I want to help!" I clawed at the haze, trying to see the dragon.

"Oi! Careful!"

Someone was holding my wrists. I twisted and writhed, trying to break free.

"Creel! What's wrong?"

I stopped fighting and stared up at Marta. She was crouched beside me in the bed, her strawberry blonde hair orange in the dawn light that was coming in through the open shutters. Alle was standing by the washstand, her mouth open in an "O."

"Who's Shardas?" Marta let go of my wrists. "We

couldn't wake you, and then you started scratching at the wall, crying."

"I was not crying. I just had a bad dream," I said, hastily wiping the tears from my cheeks. "Shardas is an old friend."

"I see," Marta said, but she clearly didn't. "Well, hurry and get dressed. If you don't get your shopgown finished today, Derda is going to start breathing fire."

"That doesn't scare me," I said with a private smile. "I've faced worse than a dressmaker who breathes fire."

I dressed and went downstairs to continue sewing. The kitchen maids served us tea and scones while we worked, and left towels and finger bowls next to the scones so that we could make sure our fingers were clean before we returned to our work.

"Mistress?" One of the maids came back in and bobbed a worried curtsy at Derda. "There's a lad here for to see Creel, mistress."

My eyebrows shot up. Who did I know in the King's Seat? Had Hagen followed me? Then my jaw dropped. It couldn't be. . . .

"You know that I don't allow such a thing," Derda huffed. "Send him away." She gave me a sharp look and I dropped my eyes to my hands.

"But, mistress," the maid said in a hushed voice. "This lad is a prince."

Alle dropped the shears she'd been using with a clatter, and Marta unconsciously put a hand to her curls.

"What did you say?" Derda rose to her feet.

"It's the young prince, Prince Luka," the maid clarified. "He's here for to see Creel." Her eyes lit on me, and I could tell that she was dying to know why a prince would want to speak to me.

"Well, girl!" Derda snapped at her. "I hope you didn't leave the prince standing there! Show him to a comfortable chair and bring him some wine!" She yanked off her plain working apron and ran to the little looking glass to straighten her hair. "I will chaperone you, of course," she said when she saw my puzzled face. "Now make yourself presentable. I will greet him while you do." And she bustled out, all smiles for the prince.

I gave Marta a helpless look. Presentable? I was dressed. . . . What more was there?

But Marta hopped to her feet and untied my apron with a single tug. Grabbing one of her own scarlet shop sashes from a hook, she whisked it around my waist and tied a large bow at the back. She pulled a comb from her pocket, untied my braid, raked the comb through it, and rebraided it much more loosely. She snapped her fingers at Alle. Giggling, Alle took a scarlet ribbon out of her dark hair and handed it to Marta, who tied it around my braid. Then Marta spun me around, pinched my cheeks hard, spun me back to face the door, and swatted me on the bottom.

I burst out laughing, too stunned by the rough handling to do anything else.

"Go," Marta hissed, giving me a push. "But we expect full details when he's gone!"

Still laughing breathlessly, I went out into the shop, where Prince Luka was sitting across from Derda. My employer was making awkward small talk with the prince, while his massive bodyguard loomed over them both. Tobin winked at me as I approached, and I rolled my eyes by way of reply.

"Your Highness." I curtsied, my eyes downcast. When I raised them, I found that Luka had gotten to his feet and was grinning at me.

"Creel." He gave me a polite bow, clearly amused at my overly formal greeting. "I wanted to know how you were getting on here in Mistress Derda's fine establishment."

"I am enjoying my work very much," I said, hoping that he didn't notice how red and pricked my fingertips were. "Mistress Derda is most kind."

"Excellent, excellent." The prince rocked forward on his toes and then back to his heels. We both looked at Derda, who was now standing between us, still all smiles and batting eyelashes.

"Well!" She slapped her hands together and gave a forced laugh. "I had better go back into the sewing room and make certain that the others aren't shirking in my absence." She gave a deep curtsy. "Your Royal Highness."

"Mistress Derda." Luka bowed.

"If you need anything, dear Creel, just ring for it," Derda told me with a fond smile, pointing to a small bell on the round table next to me. Then she went bustling into the backroom.

"Hmmm," I said, staring after her.

"Not usually 'dear Creel'?" Luka gave me a sly look.

"Hardly," I said, shaking my head. "Shall we sit down?"

"By all means."

We both sat in the ornately embroidered chairs and stared at each other for a minute. Tobin continued to stand behind his prince's chair, looking muscular and dangerous.

"Er, Tobin? Do you want to sit down?"

The mute bodyguard shook his head.

"He always remains standing, unless we're in the palace, or at Ulfrid's," Luka explained. He poured a glass of wine for me and then himself.

"Thank you, your Highness." I took a deep drink of the wine, feeling awkward.

"You can call me Luka."

"Are you certain?"

He raised one eyebrow. "Of course I'm certain. It's my name, after all."

I blushed. "I'm sorry, your . . . Luka."

"Your Luka? I think I like the sound of that," he mused.

I rolled my eyes, his teasing putting me at ease. "Oh, please!"

"That's better," the prince approved. "So, how are you settling in, really? Is Derda treating you well?"

"As well as can be expected," I said with reluctance. Should I tell Luka that she had planned to use my designs as her own? Marta had assured me that, as much as we both hated it, it was quite common for employers to do such things. It was frustrating, though, to think that the patterns inspired by Shardas's windows would be taken from me. "Sewing was always relaxing for me, before. You know, better than hoeing a row of potatoes." I made a face, thinking about how glad I was that I wasn't working on the farm anymore. "But now there's more pressure to make it perfect, and it's all I do all day. . . ." I trailed off. "Not that I'm complaining," I said quickly. "Because if you hadn't found me and if Ulfrid hadn't helped me get this job, I would be in deep trouble and I'm very grateful—"

Luka held up a hand to stop my rapid flow of words. "It's all right, I understand. When I was a lad, all I wanted to do was learn swordplay. I talked of nothing else, and if Ulfrid had let me, I would have slept with my toy sword. But then when I started to actually train. . . ." It was his turn to trail off, wincing and smiling at the memory.

"Sore muscles?" I hazarded.

"Sore everything, including my pride," he admitted. "I assumed that, since I was a prince and had thought of nothing else my entire life, I would become a great swordsman overnight." He shook his head. "Not even close to the truth."

I looked over his shoulder at Tobin. "Did he improve?"

Tobin made a gesture with one hand that clearly

said, "so-so," and I laughed. Luka pretended to be indig-nant, but then he laughed, too.

"Well, I suppose we'd better go," he said ruefully when we had stopped. "I only wanted to make certain that things were going well with you."

My eyes welled with tears at this kindness, and I jumped to my feet and fussed with Marta's sash to cover the emotion. The prince reminded me a little of Shardas, with his gallantry and his elegant manners. "Thank you, Luka," I said softly, my head bowed.

"It really is my pleasure," he told me. He took my hand and pressed it, and then he and Tobin left.

Somewhat dazed, I wandered into the backroom, where I was forced to recount the entire exchange, down to facial expressions, to Derda and the other girls. By the time they had analyzed every word and look, it was time for the shop to open and Marta was convinced that the prince was in love with me. Derda proclaimed this highly unlikely, but she still clucked over me like a mother hen, much to my annoyance. I was relieved when she and the others, save Larkin, put on their embroidered aprons and went out to open the shop.

"I wish I had royalty calling on me," was all Larkin said about it, her normally mild voice envious.

"Really, he's just a kind young man," I protested for the thousandth time.

"He is a prince of a royal house," she said primly, "the son of a king and brother of the king-to-be. Since the crown prince's betrothal, every young woman at court has been vying for his attention." She darted a disapproving glance at me, as though to say that I was unworthy of his notice.

I hadn't really thought about that, but now that I did, it made me feel self-conscious. I kept poking myself with my needle as I worked, and almost snipped one of my fingers instead of a loose thread.

"Cre-el," Marta sang out, coming into the backroom an hour later. "You're wanted in the shop."

"Why?" I put my sewing down and gave her a startled look. Larkin, too, stopped working and looked to Marta.

"Our very favorite princess is here," Marta said in her most sugary voice. "And she absolutely *must* speak to you." Marta rolled her eyes in sympathy. "You can wear one of my sashes again; I'm not going back out there while *she's* here."

She took the length of silk off a hook and I took off my coarse linen work apron for the second time that day. Marta helped me tie the sash in a tidy bow, and then sent me back out, this time without any giggling or swats, which was all right by me, since I was terrified of Princess Amalia.

She still wanted my shoes. I knew that could be the only reason she wanted to speak to me. She hadn't exhibited any interest in my work, and if it had been the Duchess of Mordrel who wanted to see me, Marta would have said.

Drawing a deep breath, I pushed out and went to

face the princess. The duchess was not with her, but the usual attendants, guards, and lapdog were. The little dog instantly jumped from her mistress's arms and ran over to me, dancing around me on her hind legs in excitement. I couldn't help but smile as I curtsied to the princess.

"What are you smiling about?"

"Er, nothing, your Highness . . . just . . . your little dog . . . she's very amusing."

"Well, that's not *nothing*, then, is it?" She arched her finely plucked eyebrows at me.

"No, your Highness, I beg your pardon." And I'd like to pinch you, I thought.

"Are you still wearing those shoes?" The princess did not waste words.

"Yes, your Highness. They are my only shoes," I informed her. That wasn't entirely true, as I did still have my old sandals, but Derda would never let me wear them to work in the shop, so I didn't feel they were worth mentioning.

Princess Amalia sniffed. "I am willing to pay you for them," she said. "More than enough to have some peasant cobbler make you another pair. A pair more suitable to your station, perhaps." She shook her head, making her curls bob. I had always been jealous of girls with naturally curly hair; it just wasn't fair when my own was so terribly straight. "Do you think it is right for a peasant to have prettier shoes than a princess?" Again up with the plucked eyebrows.

I just stood there and looked at her. Did she really want an honest answer? In fact, I wasn't even sure what a *dishonest* answer to this question should sound like. Was that what was bothering her so much? That she didn't think I deserved them because my family was poor? This princess was either spoiled to a degree that I had never seen before, or else she was a few berries short of a pie, as my mother would have said.

"Don't just stand there, girl, give me those shoes!" The princess stamped her foot with impatience. "I have other things to do this morning than wait upon *your* pleasure."

"I'm very sorry to hear that, then," I retorted, ignoring Derda's frantic looks and gestures. "Because I'm afraid that it is not my pleasure to give you my slippers."

"How dare you!" She lunged forward and slapped me.

I raised my hand to slap her back. Before I could, however, Derda grabbed my hand and dragged me into the backroom, calling apologies over her shoulder and screeching for the maids to bring Princess Amalia more cakes and wine.

"What are you doing, girl?" Derda had hold of my upper arms and was shaking me, making my teeth clack together. "You nearly struck your future queen!"

"She nearly struck the princess?" Marta's voice rose an octave on that last word. "Now I wish I had stayed out there!"

"Silence, you foolish girl!" Derda gave Marta a venomous look. She turned her attention back to me. "Just give her the cursed shoes, and I will buy you new ones myself! We cannot lose her patronage!"

To my embarrassment, I started to cry. "I'm sorry, but they were given to me by a . . . a . . . friend. I cannot part with them, I just can't!" A terrible, dark feeling had come over me. Amalia could not get the shoes, something terrible would happen, I knew it deep in my bones. "Please, Derda, please?"

Derda stopped shaking me, pushing me away in disgust. She marched around the table, picking up shears and spools of thread and slamming them back down again. She muttered angrily all the while, looking at me with a dire expression from time to time. After an interminable five minutes that felt more like five months, she came back around to face me.

"You would rather risk your livelihood, and mine, than give that snotty foreigner your slippers?"

"Yes, mistress, I'm sorry." I sniffled.

"Well!" Derda put her hands on her hips and surveyed me, her expression softening. "A gift from a friend, you say?"

I nodded, wiping my nose on the back of my hand.

"You cannot part with them?"

Again I nodded.

"Hmmm. Let me see these shoes that are so wonderful."

I lifted my skirt and showed her, my heart pounding. Would she, too, want to take them from me?

"I don't see what all the fuss is about," Derda declared. "But who can fathom the mind of a princess?" Her eyes narrowed in thought. "Did you show them to the princess today?"

"No, mistress."

"Larkin! Trade shoes with Creel. Quickly!" From the shop we could hear the sound of the princess becoming more and more shrill.

"Madame Derda," she objected. "What is your aim? The princess is not a fool; she will know that she is being duped. . . ."

"We shall do our best to brazen it out, Larkin. Now take off your shoes! I think you're about the same size," she said to me. "And, truth be known," she lowered her voice, "I think it's mighty high-handed of that foreign girl to come here and just demand the clothes off our backs and the shoes off our feet!"

Larkin was even more shocked by this admission, but she took off her plain brown slippers and I handed her my blue ones with great reluctance. I realized when I put on Larkin's shoes that my own were really terribly comfortable.

"She has come to her senses," Derda announced as we stepped back into the shop. "We are so sorry, your Highness. She is a new girl, and stubborn. Your Highness may take the slippers, with our compliments, and there shall be no charge."

With a great show of reluctance I sank down on a velvet-covered footstool and hiked up my skirts. I removed Larkin's brown shoes and held them out to the princess with downcast eyes.

"What is this?!"

I winced as Princess Amalia's shriek scraped my eardrums.

"These aren't the right slippers! They were blue! Beautiful blue slippers, not these rough peasant shoes!"

"But, your Highness," I lied in my most submissive voice, "these are the only shoes I own. Except for a pair of woven sandals. If your Highness wants those as well—"

"You liar!" Amalia grabbed my hair and yanked my head up so that I was forced to look her in the eyes. "You lying little prodo! I want those shoes!"

I looked her right in the eyes and thought about Theoradus and Amacarin, Shardas and Feniul. Any one of them could eat this horrid royal in one bite, as they could have eaten me. But they hadn't. I had faced them, I had bargained with them, and I had even become friends with one of them.

"These are the only shoes I own," I said in a level voice.

"You little—"

"Amalia!" The Duchess of Mordrel—*my* duchess—came sailing through the door and looked at the princess in shock. "What are you doing to that poor girl?"

Amalia released my hair, and I put a hand up to rub my stinging scalp. Tears were running from the corners of my eyes as a consequence of the pain, but I quickly wiped them away, not wanting to let her know she had hurt me.

"This horrible peasant is claiming that she doesn't

have those blue slippers anymore," the princess said. "I told her I wanted them, and I will have them!"

"Amalia," the duchess said in a stern voice. "I am well aware that in Roulain things are different, and your common people are treated, well, let's say more cavalierly than ours." The duchess folded her arms under her bosom and fixed the princess with an icy gaze. "But you are not in Roulain anymore. You cannot demand that this girl give you her slippers. You cannot threaten her, and you cannot pull her hair out by the roots. Come away at once. I think it's time you went back to the palace."

"But she—"

"I don't care. Stop acting like a spoiled little girl and more like the queen you may one day be!" And with that the duchess seized hold of Amalia's elbow and steered her expertly out of the shop.

"I shall be back tomorrow to see the progress on my gown," the duchess called out politely as they left.

"Woof!" I sagged lower on the footstool. Larkin's shoes fell from my hand to the floor with a double thump.

"That was very nearly the ruin of both of us," Derda told me in a curiously blank voice. "You had better prove to be the finest embroiderer I have ever seen, girl," she finished more strongly. "Now get back in there and get to work," she ordered.

I all but ran into the backroom, where a strange scene met my eyes. Larkin was lying prone on the big work table, and Marta and Alle were trying desperately to revive her.

"What happened?"

"We don't know," Marta panted, fanning Larkin with some silk stretched on an embroidery frame. "She put your slippers on and then her eyes went wide and she fainted!"

"Get my slippers off her!" Seeing the blue toes of my slippers peeping out from beneath the hem of Larkin's gray gown made a tide of rage stronger than the one I had just felt dealing with Amalia sweep over me. I yanked the shoes off her feet myself, and as soon as I did Larkin gasped and lurched to a sitting position.

"What's happening? What was that?"

"Larkin!" Alle fluttered around her. "You fainted!"

"I heard voices, horrible voices like rocks being ground together," Larkin moaned. "And my feet itched as though millions of ants were crawling over them!" She stared down the length of the table at me. I stood there with a blue slipper in each hand and stared back. "What is wrong with your shoes, Creel?"

"I don't know what you're talking about," I lied. I slipped the shoes back onto my own feet, ignoring the itching that started immediately, and sat down to sew. Had it been this bad when I had first put them on? I couldn't remember. It seemed to fade when I walked a lot. I hadn't heard any "voices like rocks being ground together" in my head, but I'd heard such voices before. Shardas. Theoradus. Amacarin. Feniul. I didn't know what it meant, but something told me it wasn't a mystery I wanted Larkin to unravel first.

"Would you mind getting off the table, Larkin?" My voice was cool. "You're sitting on my shopgown."

A Midnight Caller

W ith all the interruptions from various palace-dwellers, it took me another two days to finish the pink gown. I refused to talk about the incident with my shoes, no matter who brought it up. It was a measure of how badly she wanted to keep the duchess's patronage that Derda did not fire me over my surliness and troublemaking.

But she didn't, and in two days I was waiting on customers in the front of the shop, giving me a much-needed respite from the strange looks and comments of Larkin. Alle also gave me the eye from time to time, but it was less threatening coming from her, and Marta's sunny nature didn't allow her to dwell on the strange happenings at all.

When I wasn't out in the front of the shop, fetching and carrying lengths of cloth and ribbons, pinning hems, and telling very large middle-aged women that low-cut daffodil-yellow gowns made them look both younger and

slimmer, I was in the back, hard at work. The duchess's
gray gown was all stitched and I had lightly chalked in the
pattern for the embroidery. On my own poor gown I had
used whatever colors and types of thread I had with me,
but with the duchess's gown I had more freedom. Derda
kept a supply of every type of embroidery silk imaginable, in colors I had never even dreamed of, and for an important patron like the Duchess of Mordrel I could use
any of them that I fancied. The duchess had said that she
would prefer the colors to be shades of blue and gray, but
I branched out into lavender and violet, turquoise and
slate. I decided that I would outline each block of color
with silver bullion, to give the impression of silver leading holding panes of glass in place.

Larkin frowned at me as I embroidered a diamond-
shaped section of lavender next to one of deep blue.
When Derda circled the table to check on our work,
Larkin whispered something to her that sent Derda whisk-
ing around to my side of the table.

"This is for the Duchess of Mordrel," she stated.

"Yes, ma'am," I said, not looking at Larkin, who was
watching us avidly.

"She requested only blue and gray embroidery,"
Derda reminded me.

"Yes, ma'am, but when I am done, the colors will
blend together and make a beautiful pattern."

"You seem awfully sure of yourself for an apprentice," Derda said waspishly.

I did not reply that I was sure that I had a better

eye for color than most of our patrons and perhaps
even Derda herself. I merely bowed my head. "When the
dress is completed, if it does not please you, ma'am, or
her Grace, I will pay for the gown out of my own wages."

Derda snorted. "Of course you will. And with the
price of the silks you're using, it will take you a hundred
years to make up the debt, too!" But with that parting
shot she went to her own table to work, and I settled
down to embroidering the gown and ignoring Larkin.

It took weeks, but finally I was finished. And I could
say without any little pride that it was magnificent.
The gray silk gleamed and the panels of embroidery—
perfectly shaped like gothic arches—glowed like jewels. I
had been right about my choice of colors: the different
hues complemented each other perfectly, and the thin
lines of silver bullion created the exact effect I had
wanted. It looked like panels of Shardas's finest windows
had been transferred to the bodice and skirts of a beautifully fitted gown. The duchess stood before Derda's long
looking glass in silence for several minutes.

"You have a very great talent," she said finally.

"Thank you, your Grace." Feeling a surge of pride, I
hoped that the Triune Gods would let my mother hear
this from paradise, so that she would know I wasn't
squandering my talent or her training.

The women of Carlieff Town who had bought
Mother's work had always treated her as being merely
competent, sighing over the fact that she was their only
source for fancywork. But here I was in the King's Seat,

my mother's unofficial apprentice, being praised by a
duchess. My mother's handiwork was at least as good
as Derda's, if not better. I wished that Mother were
here. I wished that she were home, or anywhere, as long
as she was alive and I could throw my arms around her
once more.

I had to blink away tears before I accepted the
duchess's gracious praise again. Then she and Derda got
down to haggling about price while I folded up the gown
and wrapped it in linen. I think the duchess noticed my
tears, though, because before she left she patted my cheek
gently and pressed an additional silver coin into my hand.

After she was gone I offered the coin to Derda, not
sure what to do, but she gruffly told me to keep it. Marta
clucked at me as soon as we were safely out of our employer's earshot.

"How do you expect to ever save up any money if
you give it all to Derda?" She shook her head at me.
"Anytime a patron gives you a little extra for yourself,
put it in your moneybox as soon as you can!"

"I haven't got a moneybox," I told her, putting one
hand over the apron pocket that held the coin to make
sure it felt secure.

"Then that's the first thing we'll have to buy at the
market on our day off," she said, giving my shoulder a
little squeeze. "Everyone must have a moneybox."

The next day brought swarms of ladies to Derda's
shop and gave me hope that I would be able to fill a
moneybox of my own. It seemed that the duchess had

worn the new gown to a state dinner that same night, and now every woman who had been in the room was clamoring for a gown by Derda's new apprentice. My employer's mouth thinned until it almost disappeared at all the attention my design was getting, but she smiled for the customers no matter how much it grated, and promised such a gown to each of them.

I looked at Marta in despair. "How will I be able to make all those gowns?"

"We'll all have to help, of course," she laughed. "We'll sew the gowns and take care of the fittings, while you do the embroidery. I don't think I could ever figure out how you combined those colors to make it look so . . . shimmery."

Marta and I went to work immediately, taking down the fabrics and threads needed for each gown and placing them within easy reach. Derda joined us and announced that from now on I was to stay in the back-room, working on new designs and color schemes, since we couldn't insult the duchess or our other patrons by dressing them in the same gown. I felt like the walls were closing in on me. I had only had the freedom to move between the shop and the backroom for a few days, and already I was being shut in the back again. Larkin would be my only company during shop hours, and I wouldn't be in a position to receive any extra coins of gratitude from the patrons. It would take me twice as long to get my own shop, now.

As if reading my thoughts, Marta leaned in close and

said that) she would share her tips, as she called them, with me. I tried to refuse, but she shrugged me off, saying that if it weren't for my designs, she wouldn't be getting the tips, and I subsided gratefully.

"Don't your feet itch?" Larkin asked the question suddenly, making me fumble the reel of emerald-green ribbon I was carrying. It bounced onto the table and rolled past her. She reached out and stopped it, hard, with one hand.

"Beg your pardon?"

"Your feet. Don't they itch? If I wore those blue slippers all the time, my feet would always be itching."

"Um, no, they're fine," I lied.

The truth was that they did itch all the time. But by now I was used to it. In fact, until she had mentioned it, I hadn't thought about my feet all day. The itching grew stronger or weaker in surges and waves, and right now it was more like a subdued pulse that made me feel my heart beating in the soles of my feet.

"I thought I heard voices when I put them on," Larkin continued, ignoring my discomfiture.

"How odd," I said with a catch in my voice. "Perhaps you were overtired."

Larkin merely looked at me until I grew uncomfortable and went back to sorting silks. A young countess with dark hair would be dressed daringly in shades of red on a pale rose background, with the leading stitched in gold. A crocus-yellow gown for an earl's daughter would be ornamented with greens and blues, and the leading done with a green so dark it was nearly black. I laid out each collection of silks with care, positioning them atop the bolt of fabric that the gown would be made from. The red-on-rose reminded me of Shardas's *Lily Window*, bloodred lilies with green stems arching against a pale pink background. The yellow gown made me think of sunshine, and the blue-and-green embroidery would be eye-catching in patterns like ocean waves. I had never seen the ocean, but my memories of Shardas's *Ocean Window* would provide the pattern, with the fabric of the bodice rising over it like the sun. Enticed by the colors and the challenge of the designs, I set to work.

I was the last person awake that night. I had somehow found myself agreeing to cut out all the fabric for the new gowns I would be supervising, and was hunched over the worktable with a heavy pair of shears long after the others had gone up to bed. By the time I finished cutting the last piece of yellow silk, my eyes were dry and burning and the itching of my feet had deadened them until I could no longer move my toes.

With a huge sigh that made tears start in my eyes, I flopped back in one of the hard chairs and dropped the shears onto the table. "Oh, Shardas, how I wish I were back in your cave," I groaned, shaking out my sore hands. "How I wish I were sitting on a coil of your tail and talking . . . anything but cutting fabric!"

I was so tired that I couldn't even bring myself to mount the narrow stairs to the sleeping quarters. Instead, I slumped forward and pillowed my head on my arms. I closed my eyes and dozed off at once.

I awoke with a start. It felt as though my feet were on fire. I reached under the table and ripped my blue slippers right off, rubbing my stockinged feet back and forth on the bare wooden floor to try to soothe them.

The itching stopped immediately, which made the noise all the more obvious. There was a scraping sound coming from somewhere outside of the shop, accompanied by a weird rumble that reminded me of a dragon laughing.

With a jolt I realized that it *was* a dragon laughing, or sighing, or something.

I ran through the shop to fling open the front door, needing both hands to lift the heavy bar that secured the entrance at night. Running out into the street in my stocking feet, I nearly tripped over a coil of Shardas's tail. The huge gold dragon was crouched uncomfortably in the street directly in front of Derda's shop.

"Oh, Shardas! Dear Shardas, you're here!" I was half-laughing, half-crying at the sight of my friend. "I was so longing to see you!" And I threw my arms around one of his forelegs, the only part of him I could get my arms around, other than his tail.

"Of course I'm here," he said in his dry way. He huffed warm breath down the back of my neck. "How could I not come?"

"What do you mean?"

"Well," he began reluctantly, "you see, I—" He broke off. "Where are your shoes?"

"Oh, just inside there, they were making my feet itch so I took them off. Why?"

"They make your feet itch?"

"Yes, and I don't know why. I don't have fleas or anything. It was so bad right before I heard you that I thought I was on fire."

"I'm sorry."

I brushed aside his apology. "It wasn't your fault."

"Actually," he said, "I—No. Never mind. I came to see how you were getting on."

I realized that I was squinting, confused by his half-finished thought. "Er," I said, blinking. "Not very well," I confessed. Then I looked around. I thought I saw a movement in one of the second-story windows, but when I looked closer I couldn't see anyone. The shutter was ajar, however. "But someone might see you, you should go."

"I know a place where we can be comfortable," Shardas said. "If I may?"

He held out a claw to me. I stepped into it and he gently picked me up and leaped into the sky. A single flap of his wings and we had soared over the rooftops of the cloth-workers' district. A building with three fat steeples at one end of the roof loomed before us, and Shardas landed on it neatly. He curled up on the flat roof in the shadow of the spires while I seated myself on a comfortable section of his tail. Thus hidden from prying eyes, I spilled out my story.

"I know I should be grateful," I finished with a sigh. "But it's just that, well, I dreamed of coming here and becoming a famous dressmaker or some such. But I didn't think that most of my earnings would go to my employer, or that she would keep me in the backroom slaving away until my fingers bled!" I held up my reddened digits for his scrutiny.

"Come back with me, then," he offered. "You are more than welcome at my cave." He hesitated. "I must confess that I enjoyed having you there, and have found myself rather . . . lonely . . . since you left."

I blushed, flattered. Then I wondered if someday in the distant future Shardas would be telling another human about a girl named Creel, who had been his friend when he was a mere seven hundred and seventy years old.

"I would love that," I said. "But the truth is, I would feel like a failure if I gave up now and went with you. I came to the King's Seat to make my fortune and by the Triunity, I'm going to do it!" I pounded on his scales with one clenched fist.

"Yes, well, that's very noble of you," Shardas said with a rumble of laughter that rattled the slate tiles beneath us. "But please call on me if you decide that you've had enough." He raised his long neck and looked over the roofs. "It will be dawn soon, and I should go. But promise me one thing. . . ."

"What's that?"

"As soon as you have earned some money, please buy new shoes."

"What? What is it about my slippers?" I hopped to my feet. "Wherever I go these shoes stir up trouble. It's becoming ridiculous. You must know something; I can hear it in your voice." I remembered suddenly that I had forgotten to tell him about Larkin. "The other day one of the other girls put them on, and she fainted. Is that not strange?"

"She fainted?" Shardas sounded concerned.

"Yes, and she said she heard things, and that they made her feet itch, too." I shook my head, puzzled. "Please, Shardas, if you know something about them, I think I have a right to hear it. They are my slippers, after all."

Shardas leaned his long head in close to me. "They are not just any plain slippers. They are very old, and have a history to them." He looked at the horizon, where there was a faint hint of dawn. "I thought before that it might be better if you didn't know, but since they are making you itch and attracting attention, then perhaps it is time you knew. Those slippers come from—"

We both jerked as the sanctuary bells began to ring, heralding the first hour of the day. I gave him a panicked look.

"Derda's an early riser," I said.

Shardas spread one foreclaw and I jumped into it. He soared off the roof and back to the street where I lived now. He set me down gently, rumbled an apology, and took off again, unfurling his wings with a snap as soon as he cleared the rooftops. I whisked inside the shop and stood peeping out from between the curtains of the large front window, watching as a pair of King's

Guards marched down the street, on their way home after a night spent enforcing the curfew. After they had
passed I waited until the sun had risen fully for Shardas
to return, but he never came back. In the end I gathered
up my strange slippers and went upstairs.

Silver, Calfskin, and Pearls

W hy are we also weaving these sashes and embroidering silk scarves, on top of our other work?" I
picked up one of the offending scarves and shook it in
Marta's face. Then I tossed it down on the table, or tried
to, anyway. It wafted down in a less-than-satisfactory
manner.

It was supposed to be our day off, but we had so
much work that Derda had insisted we all stay in and sew
until lunchtime. If I wasn't worried about losing my job,
I would have rebelled.

Marta just laughed. "It's almost time for the Merchants' Ball. Some of the baker's girls from next door
have saved up so that they can attend. They can't afford
new gowns, but they want new sashes to refurbish the
ones they've got."

"Is it really necessary for them to dress so fine? Don't
the investors know that they don't have any money?
That *is* why they're at the ball."

"Thus the cruel irony of the ball," Marta said, holding up a finger. "One must have enough money to dress like a wealthy in order to successfully plead for more money." She shook her head again. "That's why I just want to save up enough to go home to my little village and open a nice country shop." She lowered her voice. "Just don't let Derda hear you say anything bad about the ball. That's how she got her start, you know."

"No! Really? Derda?"

"That's right," Marta whispered. "She saved for ten years and finally had enough to buy some pink silk and make herself a gown. That's why we wear this color in the shop, it's her signature, she says."

"If you had the right gown, wouldn't you do the same?" Alle plopped herself down on my other side with a sigh. "I know I would."

"Would you?" Larkin was looking across the table with intensity, but not at Alle. At me. "If you had a gown, would you go?"

"I—I suppose." I glanced around quickly to make sure that Derda wasn't within earshot. "It would be nice to have my own shop, and be able to pick and choose what I want to sew."

"Wouldn't it just?" Marta carefully folded the scarf she had finished embroidering and set it aside. She picked up another with an expression of distaste. "This is for that uppity little milliner's apprentice down the street," she said. "I can't abide her."

"You should admire her for having the initiative to strike out on her own," Derda snapped, coming around the shelves nearest the worktable with a bolt of ivory satin cradled in her arms like a baby. "That is why you will embroider that scarf as finely as you would for a duchess or a princess."

"Yes, mistress." Marta lowered her eyes to her work and busied herself with curved needle and silken thread.

"Well?" Derda tapped her foot.

I realized that she was looking at me. "I beg your pardon?" I looked up at Derda, confused.

"Larkin asked if you would try for a sponsor at the Merchants' Ball, if you had a suitable gown."

"Er." I felt red crawling up my cheeks. How was I supposed to answer? If I said "yes," would she think I was eager to get away from her and her shop? But if I said "no" . . . well, that would be a lie, and Derda was very good at spotting lies. "Well . . ."

"Yes?" Derda cocked an eyebrow, and the other girls were watching me carefully as well.

"Er. I suppose if I did have a proper ball gown, I might go." I tried to make it sound as offhand as I could. "I mean, who wouldn't take the chance to have her own shop?"

"Very true," Derda said, and I thought that she sounded vaguely approving.

"It's midday," Alle announced, putting down the sash loom she had been using to weave a long green-and-blue sash. She gave Derda a hopeful look.

"Oh, go on then, I shan't get any more work out of the four of you!" Derda clucked her tongue in irritation as she laid out the ivory satin for cutting.

We didn't need any further encouragement. Even Larkin was quick to put down her sewing, whip off her apron, and get out into the bright sunshine. Marta and Alle were going to take me to the market where they spent most of their hard-earned wages.

After we had gone a ways down the street, I looked behind us, thinking that Larkin was following at her slower pace. She was nowhere in sight, however. "Where did Larkin go?"

"Who knows?" Alle shrugged. "She never comes with us. I think she's afraid she might actually enjoy herself."

"I'm sure she goes to chapel and prays for our souls because we talk badly about the wealthies," Marta said. She paused in front of a shop that sold cookware and used the reflection in a large soup kettle to rearrange her curls.

"If we ever have a full day off, we should take Creel to the Boiling Sea," Alle said.

"What's that? A tavern?" I frowned at her.

Marta burst out laughing. "A *tavern?* Haven't you heard of the Boiling Sea?"

I shook my head.

"You've heard people swear by the Boiling Sea, haven't you?"

I started to shake my head again, but then I remembered. A few days ago I had overheard one of the serving maids telling Marta that her suitor had better propose soon, or "by the Boiling Sea, I will *make* him propose!"

"What's the Boiling Sea?"

"You can't tell from here, but the King's Seat is built above a cliff," Alle said. "The hill drops away behind the New Palace, and I've heard that from the southern windows you can look right out over the Boiling Sea and on to the Roulaini foothills."

"It's like some huge beast *ate* the back of the hill," Marta put in. "And at the foot of the cliffs is the sea, which is beautiful. The water is the exact color of that scarf you were just working on," she told me. "But it's boiling hot and poisonous to boot."

"You're having me on!"

They shook their heads. "It's true," Alle said. "We've both been. If you start early in the morning, you can get there in time to have a picnic by the shore, and still be back by curfew."

"But what makes it so hot?"

"Someone told me that it's the gods' bathwater," Marta said with a shrug.

"Or dragons made it," Alle put in.

Marta took my arm. "Next free day, we'll pack a lunch and take you. Then you can decide for yourself: the gods, or dragons."

We reached the booths and shops that catered to people like us. That is, people who worked hard, and had a little money to spend. There were lots of booths of fabrics and embroidery threads, but they didn't interest us. There was a huge book stand, but I hesitated to spend my few coins.

I hadn't thought to have any money to spend at all,

since I still "owed" Derda for my shopgown. But she wasn't completely without compassion. It seemed that she only took half of my wage, which meant that it would take me twice as long to pay off my debt, but in the meantime I was not without pocket money.

It was the thought of the Merchants' Ball that made me hesitate, though. The idea of it kept revolving round and about in my brain. What if I were to save up all my coins to buy fine silk for a gown so that I could go and convince some wealthy moneylender to bankroll my shop?

"If you don't want to buy a book, I know where we can borrow some," Alle muttered out of the corner of her mouth as I dawdled over the used books. The bookseller was glaring at us, no doubt wondering if we were ever going to stop touching the books and actually purchase one. "Neneh, the pastry apprentice across the way, has loads of books. She'll loan you one."

"Lovely," I said, and we walked away giggling at the bookseller's sour expression.

"I'll take you over today, if you like. I've been dying to read this new romance about a goose girl who—" Alle grabbed my arm, freezing in mid-sentence. "Oh. Good day, your Royal Highnesses," she squeaked.

I tore my attention away from the next booth, which was displaying some strange spiny fruit, and saw that Prince Luka and his brother, Crown Prince Milun, were standing in front of us.

Much to my embarrassment, I found myself blushing

and had to clear my throat twice before I could talk. "Hello, Luka, Tobin," I said. I gave a little bob to the crown prince, since he and I had never been formally introduced. "Your Royal Highness."

The crown prince gazed at me in amazement. "So this is the same girl?"

My blush faded as I looked from one brother to the other. "I beg your pardon, your Royal Highness?"

Luka laughed. "You're becoming quite famous around the palace. First as the would-be assassin of small, pampered dogs, then as the evil girl who refused to give her shoes to the poor, shoe-deprived princess. Amalia is more certain than ever that you are in the pay of some anti-Roulaini group."

"Oh, dear," I groaned. I didn't really care what Amalia thought of me, but what Luka thought? That was a different matter entirely.

"Don't worry about it." Luka patted me on the arm, making Alle gasp at the familiarity of his gesture. "We've tried time and again to explain to her that in Feravel we can't force anyone to give up their property, but I'm not sure she believes us." He shrugged. "We'll keep trying."

"Forgive my manners," he said abruptly. "This is my brother, the Crown Prince Milun, or Miles as we all call him. Miles, this is Creel Carlbrun and . . . ?"

"Oh, I beg your pardon!" I took Alle's elbow and guided her forward. She had been hanging back behind me with her jaw down around her feet. "This is my friend Alle, who also works in Madame Derda's shop."

"A pleasure to meet you both," Miles said with a stiff little bow.

"This is my bodyguard, Tobin," Luka added, seeing Alle's questioning look. Tobin grinned.

"Er, how nice," Alle stammered.

"Luka, you're frightening her," I teased the prince.

"I know, it's because I'm so commanding and kingly," he teased back. "Would you ladies care for some starfruit?" He nudged Miles with an elbow.

"Er, yes. Some refreshment." Miles held up four fingers to the fruit seller, and purchased four of the strange spiny things.

"Thank you," I said, accepting the exotic fruit with delight. "But what about Tobin?"

Miles looked confused.

"Doesn't he want one?"

"Tobin? But he's just a bodyguard," Miles said dismissively.

"And Alle and I are just shopgirls," I said as politely as I could. "And yet you bought one for me."

"Well, er, you—"

Tobin smiled at me and shook his head, then moved his hands in a strange, fluttering way.

"Tobin says 'thank you,'" Luka said in his cheerful way. "But starfruit makes him break out in a rash."

"Blech. That doesn't sound very pleasant," I said.

Tobin made a face and nodded.

"And you thought he was already scary-looking," Luka said as he tossed his fruit high and then caught it on the back of one hand. He rolled the spiny thing up his arm and across his shoulders, then down into his other hand. Alle and I applauded while Tobin rolled his eyes and Miles studiously peeled his fruit with a knife.

"I hope you two aren't getting up to any trouble," Marta said, at her most flirtatious as she joined us. "Our mistress will be very displeased if you have been fresh with any young men in the—" Marta broke off and went into a deep curtsy. "Your Highnesses."

"And this is Marta," I said, doing my best to keep a straight face.

Prince Miles looked around and frowned at the booths. "Lukie, why are we here? I doubt I will find anything to please Amalia in *this* market."

I was taken aback by his tone. Didn't he realize that this market was barely within our means?

"Why, Miles," Luka said, "I was doing you a favor by bringing you here! It would be impossible to find anything grand enough for Amalia at the shops around the palace. I thought that instead you could get her something simple yet heartfelt."

And with the rest of us in tow, Prince Luka made his way over to the booth with the glaring bookseller. He searched through the displayed books for a moment and then held up one, bound in calfskin, that was almost as thick as it was tall. He flashed his brother a triumphant smile.

"Aha! *The Compleat History of the Indigenous Peoples of Northern Feravel*," he read off the spine. "Just the thing!

As we are now her people, I think it would be very appropriate for her to acquaint herself with our, er, indigenous
northern peoples." Luka managed to keep a straight face
for another heartbeat, then he burst out laughing.

Miles bristled a little at Luka's teasing, but gave the
book a thoughtful look. "Amalia *is* interested in Feravelan history," he said, taking the book to flip through its
pages.

"Really?" I couldn't keep the surprise out of my
voice. I would have thought that Amalia would prefer
novels with lots of romance and clothing descriptions,
if she read at all.

"I need to purchase a suitable bride-gift for the
princess," Miles said. "And she is always hounding me
with questions about our history." He wrinkled his nose
at the book. "I'm not sure this is quite the thing, though."

Luka grinned and took the book back. "Well, if you
won't get it for her, I will. I think it's the perfect gift for
my future sister-in-law." He gave me a wink. "You have
plenty of time to find something else. Let's take these
three delightful girls to a bun shop and buy them tea and
sweets." He turned and started away.

"Luka! Wait!" I caught his arm, laughing. "You forgot
to pay for your *Compleat History of the North*, or whatever
it's called."

"Why, so I did!" He put a hand to his belt pouch.

"Oh, your Highness, please," the bookseller protested.
He was all unctuous smiles now that his customers were
royalty. "Please accept it as a gift, I insist."

"Oh, no, dear fellow. A fine book like this must be paid for." And Luka tossed him a silver coin. Half my month's wages, or what they would be when I was done paying for my shopgown. The bookseller's eyes gleamed.

"That's too much," I hissed out of the corner of my mouth.

Hearing me, the merchant glared evilly in my direction.

"Very well," Luka said in his breezy way. "Will that be enough to pay for a fine book for each of these three lovely ladies?"

The man gave a grudging nod.

I selected a pretty little edition of *The Lay of Irial*, an epic poem about the maiden Irial, who learned wisdom from a dragon only to have her suitor slay the dragon by accident. It was bound in calfskin, like *The Compleat History*, but ornamented with scrollwork that gave me an idea for an embroidery pattern. Alle took an adventure novel, and Marta, to everyone's surprise, chose a history of Lady Marita, the first apostle of the Triune Gods.

"What?" She was blushing at our stares. "I was named for her."

Luka and I laughed and talked our way through lunch at a nearby bun shop. Eventually Alle and Marta conquered some of their awe and joined in, but Miles's stiffness made it hard for them to forget he was the future king. After lunch we whiled away the rest of the afternoon looking at more booths. The Great Fair was just getting under way, and there was hardly a street that

wasn't lined with people from all over Feravel and beyond, hawking their wares. By the eve of the Merchants'
Ball, the climax of the fair, the city would be bursting at
the seams.

We all suggested increasingly outrageous items for
Miles to give to Amalia as a bride-gift. He seemed to like
one of my ideas, though. In a shop that sold strands of
pastel-hued freshwater pearls, I recommended that he
buy a few strands and a clasp to hold them together. The
pearls were locally caught, and it had been the fashion
since my grandmother's time to wear multiple strands
twisted together and held in place with clasps made of
native jasper, which was more pink than red.

Miles gave me a nod of thanks and considered several
strands with care before declaring that he would have to
think on it, and come back again. The shopkeeper also
gave me a grateful look, and promised me a real bargain
on my next purchase, if the prince should grace his shop
again. I thanked the man gravely, all the while thinking
that if I ever did have money to throw around, I still
wouldn't buy a necklace. I'd buy silk. Or a pair of slippers that didn't make my feet itch.

The two princes and Tobin walked us back to Derda's,
where she met us at the door, all smiles and offers of tea.
Luka and Miles refused with polite bows, and went on
their way. Giggling and gossiping, we made our way up the
stairs to our bedroom. Larkin was already asleep in her
little room. As the oldest apprentice she had her own
room across the hall. It was hardly bigger than a closet,

but at least she didn't have to fight anyone over the blankets.

I stripped down to my shift, hanging my old gown next to my new pink one. We snuggled into bed to read our new books. It was hours before I blew out the candle and we all wiggled into comfortable positions and went to sleep.

When I woke the next morning, there was a hideous ball gown of very expensive satin and velvet laid across the room's lone chair.

And, although I didn't notice at first, my blue slippers were gone.

A Gown Fit for a Princess

What is *that*?" Marta wrinkled her nose in disgust when she saw the gown.

"Gah! I have no idea," I said.

Alle just groaned and put the pillow over her head.

I lifted the strange gown and surveyed it. It was made of heavy velvet and satin, both in the same shade of antique gold. That in itself wasn't so bad. What was bad was that the seamstress who had made it appeared to have gone mad when decorating the gown.

It had a wide low neck, fitted bodice, and long tight sleeves. The skirt was full, and there were six layers to it: the uppermost of velvet, and the five underneath in satin.

But then there were the roses.

And the great swaths of satin that swooped between each fist-sized flower.

Alle took the pillow off her face, looked at the gown again, and groaned. "I thought I was having a nightmare," she said, her voice muffled by the pillow once more. "That's the ugliest gown I've ever seen."

"I agree," Marta said, lifting a sleeve to inspect the small rosettes that marched in a line from shoulder to wrist. "Who would wear such a thing?"

In addition to the line of rosettes along the sleeve, they also trimmed the cuffs and neckline, and a wide satin sash was draped from the left shoulder to the right hip, beginning and ending with a rose that was very nearly the size of a cabbage.

Larkin appeared in the doorway.

I held out the gown to her. "Have you ever seen the like? Isn't it hideous?"

Larkin frowned at me. "It's a dress suitable for a princess," she declared.

"The princess of what?" Marta's curls shook as she tossed her head and laughed.

"The Princess of Roulain," she retorted.

I dropped it back onto the chair as though it had burned my fingers. "I know that Derda is making one of her bridal tour costumes," I said, my eyes still on the dress. "But what is a ball gown of *hers* doing in *our* bedroom?"

"The Princess Amalia has generously given it to you," Larkin told me.

I was instantly on guard. Amalia was not the generous type. "Why?"

"Because she is great and noble," she said, her mouth twisted at my unworthiness.

"You've never actually met the Princess of Roulain,

that much is plain," Alle jeered, climbing out of bed at last. "She would never give anyone a gown out of the goodness of her heart. She doesn't *have* a heart."

And that was when I realized that my slippers were gone. For a moment I could only stare at the empty space on the floor where they had been. I suddenly knew exactly why the princess had had the generosity to give me a gown. She could afford to give away a gown, especially one as hideous as this.

But I couldn't afford to lose my slippers.

My stomach was somewhere down by my bare feet, and my heart was beating so slowly that I was sure my blood would congeal in my veins. It wasn't until Marta jogged my arm that I realized I hadn't blinked in several minutes.

"Creel? You're white as a statue. What's wrong?"

"She took my slippers. The princess took my slippers." Then I dragged my eyes from the floor to meet Larkin's innocent gaze. "No, not the princess. You. *You* took my slippers and gave them to her."

Grabbing Larkin's shoulders, I shook her hard. She writhed away, but I snatched at one of her braids and yanked it. She screamed and Derda came flying out of her own bedroom to see what the commotion was about.

"What is the meaning of this?"

"She stole my slippers!" I let go of the braid long enough to take hold of her shoulders and shake her again.

"Let go of her!" Derda herself hauled me away from Larkin, who was blubbering and slapping at me.

"When a member of a royal house asks for something,

you give it to her," Larkin screeched. "You never should have refused her your slippers. She was more than generous to let you have that old gown!"

Derda released my arm and stared at Larkin, her hands on her hips. "Is Creel's accusation true? You gave Princess Amalia Creel's slippers?"

"Of course I did. I do not deceive my betters!" Larkin attempted to straighten her gown. It was a gray gown, her best. Or at least it had been: I had torn it when I snatched her by the shoulders. The bodice would need clever stitching, if not replacing, I noticed with satisfaction. "You don't deserve the duchess's patronage," she added. "You have no respect!"

"So, you made a liar of me?" Derda's eyes were slits.

Larkin quailed. "No, mistress! I merely told the princess that there had been a mistake, that Creel hadn't understood which slippers her Highness was asking after." Then she straightened and glared at me. "I would never complain about serving a princess, like you and Marta. I think it's an honor." She tried to smooth her braids, which were tied with new silver ribbons.

My eyes narrowed. There were no ribbons like that in the shop's supplies. I wondered what else Amalia had given her. "Those were *my* slippers," I said, wanting to reach out and grab her by the throat. "You had no right—"

"I have every right to seek the patronage of whomever I choose," Larkin retorted. "I'm not a slave."

"Even *her* patronage?" Marta was indignant. "You know how horrible Amalia is!"

I felt as though a piece of me were missing. Waves of panic and rage and sorrow kept washing over me. It was almost as bad as when Mother and Father had died. "Larkin," I said with as much patience as I could muster. "I don't care if you serve Amalia or the Lord of Death himself. They weren't your slippers to trade. You have to get them back. Now."

"I can't do that." She shook her head adamantly. "She gave her word that you would receive a gown as payment and I gave my word that I would bring them to her. The deal has been made."

I turned to Derda. "You have to get my slippers back, please. Princess Amalia will listen to you. You're making one of the gowns for her bridal tour. Please?"

But Derda shook her head. "Are you mad? We've already lied to her once, and she knows it full well. If I try to get those slippers back, Princess Amalia could claim that I'm working with the anti-Roulaini faction that opposes the wedding. I don't fancy spending ten years in the dungeons because of a pair of shoes."

All I could do was stand there, clutching my hair and staring from Larkin to Derda in despair. I had bargained with a dragon for those shoes, and now they were gone. I had always known, deep inside, that there was more to the blue slippers than met the eye. They meant something, to the dragons at least.

To the dragons, and to one very spoiled princess.

"What am I going to do?" I whispered the question to myself, but Derda answered.

"You're going to buy yourself another pair of shoes, and then you're going to get back to work," she said in her most brisk voice. "I'm sorry that this happened, but it's over now, and there will be no more fighting or crying or screaming about it. Is that clear?"

I nodded, dumbfounded. I couldn't think of what else to do.

"Good. Now, don't you have a pair of brogues or something to wear?"

"Some old sandals," I mumbled.

"Hmmm. Marta, take her to a shoemaker and find her some shoes suitable for the shop. Larkin, you will pay half the cost."

"Only half?" Marta looked outraged. "But, Derda—"

"I said half! Larkin did trade with the princess for the gown, so Creel has been paid for the shoes."

"Then I shouldn't have to pay half," Larkin protested.

"You'll pay half because I've lost face and Creel's lost her only decent shoes," Derda shrilled. "Larkin, clean yourself up. Alle, get to work. Marta, Creel, get some shoes and be back as soon as you can."

Marta and I dressed in silence and made our way out of the shop and down the street. We headed for the same market square where we had spent such a pleasant afternoon the day before. Everything looked different now, in the morning light. Paler and sharper. The paving stones were hard and treacherous beneath the worn soles of my sandals.

Neither of us speaking, I followed Marta into a cobbler's small shop. The walls were lined with shelves bearing shoes, and that reminded me with sudden poignancy of Theoradus's hoard. None of these were as grand as the flowered, feathered, bejeweled, and embroidered creations that were his favorites, of course. They were mostly serviceable brown or black leather, the men's boots grouped on one side of the shop, and the women's slippers on the other.

In a hushed voice, as though I were ill or someone had just died, Marta told the cobbler that I needed new shoes, ready-made. He nodded his grizzled head, also speaking in a whisper. I realized that there must be something alarming about my appearance to make them act this way.

I stood in the middle of the shop, thinking of Theoradus's cavern full of shoes. Then that made me think of Shardas's beautiful caves, with their exquisite windows glowing in a double dozen colors, like all the jewels in the world put on display.

"I'm going to the ball," I announced abruptly.

The cobbler, who was just coming to offer me a pair of brown calfskin slippers, gave me a wide smile. "Of course you are, maidy," he said. His voice was slow, as though he thought I were simple.

Without looking at him, I raised my skirts above my ankles so that he could try the fit of the slippers. I looked at Marta instead. I could see that she knew what I meant.

"I'm going to take that cursed ugly gown and rework it, and I'm going to the Merchants' Ball," I said.

"I'll help you," Marta said. "On one condition."

"Which is?"

"When you get your shop, I want to work for you."

"Done." I looked down at the slippers I was now wearing. They were light brown, almost golden, with a slightly pointed toe and a low heel. They would match the golden gown well enough. I nodded at the shoemaker.

"Done," I repeated.

Wanting a Dragon, Getting a Prince

Derda made it clear that if I wanted to get that horrid gown reworked for the Merchants' Ball, I would have to do it on my own time. At first I was confused: she had seemed supportive of the ball before. But then I realized that she had hoped to get several years' worth of work out of me before I had enough saved to try for the ball. Also, I already had one prestigious client in the Duchess of Mordrel.

So, after sewing morning and evening, marking embroidery patterns on fabric and displaying them to the customers all day, I had to sit and sew some more. Derda didn't want me wasting her good candles on my gown, either, so I used the last of my wages to buy some of my own. That left me with nothing to spend on embroidery thread, and I needed to decorate the gown with my own handiwork to show it off.

"I'll pay for it," Marta offered. "If you're going to be my mistress, I had better start contributing."

"I don't want to take your money," I argued. "And I'm not sure I want to be your mistress. How about a partner?"

"Then as your partner," Marta insisted, "I have all the more reason to contribute. Give this money to Derda; she buys the finest embroidery thread in the King's Seat, so you might as well get it from her."

Later that day, when the shop was closed and I was sewing next to Marta, Alle nudged me. "I'll do your hair," she whispered.

"What?" I dropped my needle, startled.

"For the ball, I'll do your hair." She shot a look at Larkin. "It's not fair, what happened. Marta told me you want to try your luck at the ball. I do beautiful hair."

"Oh, thank you," I said.

To my embarrassment, tears welled in my eyes. Marta had also offered to loan me a silk shawl she had received from an admirer. It was cream-colored, and would go well with the gold gown.

I was touched by the support of the other girls. Except for Larkin. Larkin was ignoring me, wearing an expression that I could only describe as wounded superiority. She kept looking over my head and fiddling with the silver ribbons, smugly drawing attention to this sign of royal favor.

That night I sat in the cushioned seat at the front of the store, saving a candle by using the bright moonlight streaming through the large bay window to see my work. The others had all gone to bed, but I had too much to do.

My first impression of the gold gown had not changed: it was as if the dressmaker had gone completely and utterly insane. In my opinion, even one fist-sized rose on the skirt of a gown was too many. Sixteen of them was outrageous.

My mother had always called sewing her "thinking time," and now as I sat with my small knife and cut stitches to remove the decorations, I thought. Did I really want my own shop? Did I really want to go to the Merchants' Ball and woo an investor?

Well, perhaps. And perhaps not. As much as I balked at the thought of spending my life working for Derda—never being acknowledged for my designs, having room and board deducted from my wages—the idea of being on my own seemed even more daunting.

On top of building up a clientele, I would need to find a shop. I would have rent to pay, and there would be furnishings to buy. I would have to find a supplier for my fabrics and threads. And should I also hire maids to serve tea and cakes to my patrons?

It was almost too much to take in.

But what else was there? This was the only work I knew, the only work I had ever wanted to do. I supposed that I could go and live with Shardas. He had said that he missed my company. I could live with Shardas in his cave, keeping his windows polished and eating peaches by the bushel.

Thinking of Shardas, I remembered his insistence that he would hear me if I ever called his name. *Shardas,*

I thought, straining to project the words out beyond the walls of the King's Seat. *Shardas, please come. Shardas, I need you.*

But my gold dragon didn't come.

And he didn't come the next night, when I finished removing the last of the roses and the long swaths of satin from the gown. I held the velvet up to the moonlight and inspected it, my heart sinking when I realized that the roses had pressed down the pile of the fabric and removing the stitches had left tiny holes all over it. I would have to cover the dress in embroidery to conceal the damage.

There was barely a month left until the ball.

Marta offered to stay up with me the next night and help me design a pattern for the gold gown, but I refused her gently. I wanted to sit in my usual position in the window and call to Shardas with my mind.

If he didn't come tonight, I thought with despair, perhaps he would never come again. I had thought of little else for three days now, but there was no sign of him.

With a sigh, I lit one of my precious candles and set it in a wooden holder beside the wax tablet I had borrowed from Derda's supply. I drew the outline of the gown on the tablet, and pricked little dots to indicate where the worst of the stitch holes were. Thinking of Shardas and his gorgeous hoard of windows, I marked the skirt with great panels shaped like pointed arches. It was similar to the basic design of the Duchess of Mordrel's gown, but on a grander scale. The arched panels on the gray gown had reached only to her knees; these would extend all the way from the hem to the waist. But what to put inside them? Abstract blocks of color were too simple, and it seemed a waste to merely fill the panels with flowers. Something truly remarkable was needed. The Triune Gods? Ancient knights in combat? I bit my thumbnail and thought.

When the King's Guards marched by half an hour later I thought of Prince Luka. I hadn't had time to read much in the pretty little book he had bought me since that first night. The Lay of Irial would look beautiful done in glass, I mused.

Or in silk.

I picked up a knife and whittled the end of my stylus even sharper, then carefully tried to draw the shape of a maiden in one of the panels I had marked out on the gown design. The maiden Irial in one panel, the dragon Zalthus in another, with the tragic betrayal by her suitor in between, centered on the front of the skirt. And the three panels on the back could show other scenes: Irial playing her harp, Zalthus flying over a forest, the ill-fated hunt in which Irial fell from her horse and came face-to-face with Zalthus for the first time. My hands almost shook with excitement. It was audacious, but I thought I would be able to do it. The Lay of Irial, embroidered in thick segments of color like a stained glass window. Brilliant!

I fell asleep over the tablets (I had borrowed two more in order to draw my designs with greater detail). When I woke, it was dawn and Larkin was standing over me. Her expression was sour, as it had been since she traded my shoes to Amalia.

"Didn't the dragon come?"

I blinked at her, my head still in a fog of sleep. "Pardon?" I looked down at the tablets fanned across my lap. "Don't you know the Lay?"

"Not *that* dragon," she said. She pointed at the street in front of the shop. "The gold dragon that came to you before. Why hasn't it come again?"

I felt the blood drain from my face. Larkin, of anyone in the King's Seat, was the last person I would have wanted to see Shardas. With a sudden shiver I thought about the half-open shutter and the fleeting movement I had seen beyond it on the night he had visited. Had Larkin spied on us?

"I don't know what you're talking about," I said, keeping my voice steady with an effort.

"Princess Amalia was very curious about the dragon as well as the slippers."

"How did she know—" I stopped myself just in time and forced a disingenuous expression onto my face. "Why would she ask about dragons?"

"Because I told her that I had seen you talking with one," Larkin said, her expression perfectly complacent. She looked as if we might be discussing embroidery, or what to eat for breakfast, and not the possibility that a dragon had called on me. "Her highness is very interested in dragons." She looked down at my tablet. "As I see you are, too, whether or not you admit it."

I was saved by Derda, who came out of the backroom to complain that I was lingering over my personal work when I should be working for her. I gathered up my tablets and slipped past Larkin. Taking my seat beside Marta in the backroom, I set the tablets under my stool, covering them with the sweeping skirts of my shopgown. Marta raised her eyebrows, but I just shook my head, mindful of Derda's eyes on me.

When Larkin limped into the room a minute later, my hands were full of cool, slippery silk and I was hard at work. But inside my bodice my heart was hammering, and beneath my skirts my knees trembled. Larkin had seen Shardas!

When one of the maids came to announce that there was a caller in the shop for me, I almost stabbed myself in the palm with my needle. So preoccupied with Shardas was I, that for a moment I imagined Shardas crouching in the pink-draped shop, being offered tea and cakes by another maid.

"Prince Luka?" The girl looked at me like I was daft. "The second son? Of the king? He is here to speak with you."

"Luka?" I cleared Shardas from my head. "Oh, yes, I'm coming." I put down my work and got to my feet. Before I could step out of the backroom, however, Marta caught my arm.

"Are you mad? I don't care that you call him Luka, and that he buys you silly books! He's still a prince, you goose!"

And once more Marta straightened my gown, tidied my hair, and replaced my apron with a scarlet sash. "Much better!" she declared.

"Luka?"

The maid who had led me out to meet him gasped at my familiarity. I thought she was going to stand there and stare at us the whole time, but Luka and I both looked at her until she realized that she was gawking and scurried back into the kitchen.

Luka grinned, his hands in the pockets of his long coat. "Hello, Creel. I just came to see how—" His gaze sharpened. "Are you all right? You look tired. Here, sit down."

I sank into one of the overstuffed chairs. For a moment, I imagined falling asleep, and wondered what Derda would do if she came out and saw me snoring in one of her "patron chairs," a bemused prince sitting across from me.

"What's happened to you?" Luka studied my face, looking anxious. "You seemed happy the other day, shopping. Has something happened since then?"

"Princess Amalia stole my slippers." I didn't see any need to sugarcoat the truth. Luka knew me, and he knew Amalia. "She convinced Larkin, who works in the backroom, to bring them to her. In the night. She took them." Really, I hadn't noticed how tired I was until I sat down. I sat as straight as I could, keeping my back well away from the soft cushions behind me.

"Amalia had your shoes stolen?" Luka looked

astonished, then perplexed. "She has hundreds of shoes! Why would she steal yours?"

"You know, they were unusual, she wanted them." I waved my hand vaguely.

"I'll make certain that she pays you for them, if I can't get them back from her." His face clouded, and he lowered his voice. "In the meantime, do you have shoes? Other shoes? I know that a lot of people of your station have only one pair. . . ."

"Oh, Luka!" I let out a tired laugh. "You are very sweet. Especially for a prince. Derda made me go and buy another pair that morning. She made Larkin pay, but only half the price." I lifted my skirts and waggled my plain (but admittedly good quality) slippers at him. "Because Amalia sort of paid me for my slippers."

"She 'sort of' paid you?"

"She had Larkin bring me an incredibly ugly gown of hers as payment. So now I'm going to the Merchants' Ball. Which I hadn't planned on attending. And which I definitely cannot attend wearing a gown that ugly. Not if I want to find someone to invest in my dress shop."

Luka looked even more confused. "So, you *are* going to the ball?"

"Yes. Now." I glanced over my shoulder to make sure that Derda wasn't hovering in the doorway, eavesdropping. There was no sign of her, but I lowered my voice all the same. "I don't think I'm cut out for working for someone like Derda. I think I'll be a lot happier knowing that someone else isn't taking the credit—and the money—for my work."

He grimaced. "Well, I'm afraid that it *is* standard practice. When an apprentice creates something the credit is always given to their master, because the master taught them to begin with."

"But Derda didn't teach me to sew, my mother did!"

"I suppose that's true—" He hesitated. "I'm sorry, but there's really nothing I can do about that. But I *can* get your shoes back."

"You can?" I clutched at my pink skirts.

"Look, the situation with Roulain is a bit dodgy, there's no denying it. We need this marriage, and we need it badly. But if Amalia is going to be our future queen"—he made a face—"she really must learn to respect our people. I'll see to it that you get your slippers back."

A wave of relief washed over me. "Thank you, Luka! I'm sorry I was so angry about . . . things."

"I quite understand."

"I'll go and fetch her horrible gown." I hopped to my feet. "I'm afraid that I've ripped most of the ornamentation off it, but she can have it remade. Or burned, I don't care."

"No, no." Luka shook his head as he also stood. "You keep it. Make it over and wear it to the ball." He lowered his voice. "You're talented. You can find an investor and open your own shop. Leave Derda and get the credit you deserve for your designs."

I heard a noise and looked over my shoulder to see Marta coming out of the backroom. She was carrying a magnificent gown, another of the duchess's, held carefully across her arms. Alle was holding the door wide open for her.

"You remember Marta, don't you?" I asked.

"Yes, yes, of course." Luka smiled at her. "How are you?"

"Very well, Prince Luka."

"That's a nice gown," he said, nodding at it.

"Thank you," Marta and I said at the same time.

Luka laughed. "I take it you both worked on it?"

"Yes, for the Duchess of Mordrel," I said, fingering the green wool. Marta had done the sewing, but I had subtly embroidered the sleeves and hem in a slightly darker green. "It's for the royal wedding."

"Oh." Luka's face tightened.

"So," Marta said when she had laid the gown carefully on the counter, prior to wrapping it for delivery. "Did you tell his Highness about your slippers?"

"Yes." I clapped my hands in delight. "He's going to try to get them back."

"That should be easy enough. Just send *him* to collect them." She jerked a thumb at Tobin.

Tobin raised one sardonic eyebrow, his arms folded. He grinned at Marta.

"You don't scare me," she said, raising her chin. "But I can imagine that a Moralienin the size of an ox would strike a little fear in the heart of that uppity princess."

"What's a Moralien-in?" I hadn't thought that Marta had ever noticed Tobin, and now she was looking at him rather . . . *admiringly.*

"Moralien is a large group of islands in the Ice Sea," Marta lectured me. "It's ruled by a Council of Elders."

I gave Marta a speculative look, and she blushed. Interesting. Tobin grinned at me, but then ducked his head in an almost shy gesture at Marta. Very interesting.

"We'd best be going," Prince Luka said. "I need to see about getting your slippers back. And I have some other duties to attend to. I just wanted to come and see if you were well, and ask if I could meet you on your next day off."

"We're not really supposed to have young men calling on us," I told him.

"Another reason for us to have our own shop," Marta piped up.

Luka frowned questioningly.

"Marta is going to come with me, and be my partner," I explained.

"Capital idea," he agreed.

"But I wouldn't worry about *your* young man, Creel," Marta went on. "I believe that Derda has decided to make an exception in the case of *Prince* Luka here."

I blushed even harder. "Well, er, if you really must be going," I said to Luka.

He, too, was looking a bit red in the face. "Er, yes, we really must. Come along, Tobin." And they beat a hasty retreat.

"Marta!" I turned on her as soon as the door closed behind the pair.

She gave me an innocent look. "Yes, Creel?"

"When you're my employee, I expect—"

"Ah, ah! *Partners* can say what they like," she teased, and then we raced into the backroom.

Pearls, Not Glass

The next day a wooden box arrived for me, delivered by a footman from the palace. He placed it reverently into my hands, ignoring the curious looks of Alle, who had answered the knock on the shop door, and Derda, who had accompanied me. Then he bowed, as though I were a great lady, and left.

At Alle's urging, I set the box down on the long counter and opened it. Inside, on a velvet cushion, was a necklace of freshwater pearls. No, *three* necklaces of freshwater pearls. They had been twisted together in the classic fashion, and were held by a jasper clasp. One strand was faintly golden, another almost blue, and the third blush-colored.

"There's a note!" Alle was jumping up and down with excitement. "Read the note!"

I picked up the square of heavy linen paper and unfolded it. It was from Prince Luka. I had suspected as much, but it was strangely thrilling to see his small, neat handwriting.

Dear Creel:

The slippers are giving me more trouble than I would have guessed. Sorry. I thought these might look good with your gown, though. Best of luck, if I don't see you before the ball.

Luka

"What is this?" Derda's voice was sharp in my ear. She hadn't even pretended not to read over my shoulder. "You didn't tell the prince about your slippers, did you?"

"Of course I did," I retorted. "Luka is my friend, and he asked me why I was upset."

"By the Boiling Sea!" Derda hissed, grabbing my elbow and giving me a little shake. "Don't stir up trouble where there's already trouble in the works! That princess is spoiling for a reason to break off the betrothal, and if this sets her off, there could be war!"

"What?" I gaped at her.

"Don't pretend to be stupid. If I'd thought you were a fool I never would have hired you. What did you think when you heard of the curfew, and the stories of attacks on Roulaini in the streets? If the younger son takes sides against the Roulaini just because he likes your eyes, the Triunity alone knows what could happen!"

"Should I give the necklace back?" I longed to keep it, but if what Derda said was true maybe it would be better if I didn't.

"No, don't offend him. Just stop maundering on about those thrice be-damned slippers!"

"Yes, Derda." I bowed my head meekly.

"Now, put your pretty gift away and get to work! It's not the ball yet, and you still work for me!"

I took the box upstairs and hid it under my pillow, thinking that if Larkin laid a finger on it, I would be forced to throttle her. I didn't think even Derda would hold it against me if that were to happen.

While we sewed that day, the other girls talked non-stop about the necklace. None of them, it seemed, had ever received such an expensive gift. And they certainly had never gotten a present from a member of the royal family!

"That's not true," I pointed out, when Alle said this. "You and Marta both got books from Prince Luka the other day when we met him and Prince Miles shopping."

"Oh, books are all very well," Marta said, giving me a sly look. "But I think I would much rather have a triple strand of pearls. To honor the Triune Gods, of course," she said piously.

The others burst into laughter, while I turned red and hot and applied myself studiously to my work. This dress would have long spears of gladiolus, much like my old handkerchief, running up the skirt.

"Oh, so modest, are we?" Alle waited until Derda

had gone into the shop to retrieve something, then threw a spool of thread at me. "It's no wonder dear Prince Luka fancies you."

My face went even redder and hotter, if that were possible. Then Larkin spoke, and my blood turned to ice in my veins.

"Perhaps Creel is simply disappointed," she said in a sly voice.

"Disappointed?" Alle stared at her. "Are you mad?"

Larkin smiled. "Disappointed because she wishes it were colored glass, and not pearls," she said without looking up.

"What did you say?" It was hard to force the words through my numb lips.

"What are you talking about, Larkin?" Marta put down her work. "Why would Creel want fake jewels?"

"Not fake jewels. Stained glass windows, like the patterns she embroiders," Larkin clarified in her mild voice. "The most beautiful windows to have ever graced chapel or palace, gathered together into one magnificent *hoard*." She put heavy emphasis on the last word.

"*Have* you run mad?" Marta stared at Larkin, not understanding what the other girl was saying. Alle was also staring, mouth open in silent confusion.

"How could you know?" It was all I could say. I was still so very cold, my hands wrapped in the silk of the skirt I was embroidering, crumpling the costly fabric. "How could you know?"

"You're not the only one who has found favor with

the royals," she purred, and pulled up her gray sleeve to reveal a bracelet of gold filigree.

"Roulaini goldwork," Marta said, her voice flat. "What did you have to steal to get that? Or was it your reward for giving Creel's shoes to that horrid brat of a princess?"

"Shardas," I whispered.

"A magnificent animal, from what I have heard," Larkin agreed. "Did you know, Marta, that it takes only a few hours to get from the New Palace to Rath Forest, as the dragon flies? Or so dear Princess Amalia has just told me."

Without thinking I picked up the long shears sitting on the table beside me and, grabbing one of Larkin's braids before she could flinch away, I cut it off, very neatly, at the nape of her neck.

"What are you doing?" Derda had come back and looked at me like I'd lost my mind.

Looking at the plait in my hand, I thought perhaps I had. I dropped the hair and the shears on the table.

"I quit," I said in a voice that was surely too calm to be my own.

"Caxon's bones, girl," Derda said, hurrying to put her arm around Larkin's shoulders. The crippled girl was clutching at her shorn hair and weeping. "What have you done?"

"She deserved it," Marta said staunchly.

"I didn't do anything!" Larkin said, glaring at us through her tears.

"I will not work side by side with a spy and a traitor," I said in that same calm voice.

"Mind your tongue! That's a serious accusation," Derda snapped.

"It's the truth." I thought of Shardas and bile rose in my throat. "It's the truth." I glared back at Larkin.

"Larkin has worked for me for ten years, since she was only a slip of a girl," Derda said in a high, angry voice. "And you, you country bumpkin, come here and in two months you set out to ruin me!"

Without replying, I went to the large clothespress where the gowns in progress were kept. I pulled out the gold gown and wrapped it in cheesecloth. Marta had followed me, and she pulled out a basket full of the roses that I had cut off the gown.

"They're yours," she pointed out, her expression daring anyone to argue with her. "Maybe we can find a use for them sometime. And these are yours, too." She hefted the basket of embroidery silks she had purchased from Derda and the paper-wrapped packet of candles I had bought.

Nodding, I went up the narrow stairs to the small room I had shared with Marta and Alle. I packed my small bundle of things: my belt loom, my book, my old country gown and sandals, a wooden comb, a set of whalebone knitting needles, and Luka's pearls. It was a pitiful summation of my life, made even more pitiful by the fact that it fitted easily into the basket of discarded roses, with room for the candles as well. Marta put my carefully folded and wrapped gown in the other basket, with the embroidery silks, and walked with me to the door of the shop.

"Where will you go?"

"Ulfrid's inn," I replied, having just that moment thought of it. The sun was setting, and guardsmen would soon begin enforcing the curfew.

"Finish the gown there," Marta said, her voice barely above a whisper. Derda was standing a few paces away, glaring. "Go to the Merchants' Ball, like you planned. I still want to be your partner. You have a true gift." And she gave me a quick hug.

"Thank you," I said, feeling awkward, and not just because I had a heavy basket hanging from each hand. I looked over her shoulder at Derda, but could think of nothing to say. I turned on my heel and left.

Satin Roses and Golden Ale

Ulfrid took me in without a word. Over tea and spiced biscuits I told her everything: the theft of the slippers, the decision to go to the Merchants' Ball, Larkin's betrayal, the fear that something had happened to Shardas.

"Who was this?" Ulfrid looked confused at this last detail.

"A friend. A very dear friend. Amalia must want him for . . . something. I don't know what. But Larkin helped her to find him. She's been to his home, or else Amalia has told her about his home. Something terrible has happened to him, I just know it."

"First this princess took your slippers, then she took your friend?" Ulfrid was still perplexed. "This is strange indeed."

"Can we send a message to Luka?"

"Yes. I will ask him to come here tonight, and you

can tell him in person. But for now, I will have a girl show you to your room."

"So I can stay?"

Ulfrid, in her taciturn way, didn't bother to answer. She just pushed through the swinging doors into the kitchen, sending a maid out to lead me upstairs. Eyeing me oddly, the serving maid took me to the little room I had occupied almost two months ago, when I had first come to the King's Seat. I thanked her as I put my things down on the narrow bed.

"What's that?" She pointed to the gold satin roses spilling out of one of the baskets.

I made a face. "Oh, these?" I picked one up and held it out to her. "This gown that I'm remaking for the Merchants' Ball had all these ugly roses on it."

"Is this satin?" She stroked the rose with an admiring finger. "I don't think I've ever felt real satin before."

"Yes, it is." I looked at it, thinking that it was too big for her to wear in her hair. Or anywhere else, for that matter. Except. . . . "Here, let me see that again."

Taking the flower, I pulled a little pair of sewing scissors out of my basket and cut the threads that gathered the satin together. I tugged, and the rose unraveled into a long strip of cloth, folded in half lengthwise.

"I thought so," I said with satisfaction.

She looked at me with wide eyes. "Why did you do that?"

"There's enough here to put a border all around your apron," I told her, gesturing at the long white apron she wore. "It will go very well with your gown." All of Ulfrid's serving maids wore a rich shade of brown.

"Oh, thank you." She bit her lip. "But I've been saving for my dowry. I really don't think—I mean, that's very kind of you, but—"

I held up a hand to forestall her. "I understand." Then an idea struck me. "Well, I'll need to pay Ulfrid for my room and board somehow. I'll see if she won't let me decorate all your aprons in exchange."

Ulfrid agreed to this, but warned me not to be too generous. "You have only a few weeks to get ready for the Merchants' Ball," she reminded me that evening.

I was sitting in the kitchen eating a bowl of chicken stew. The serving maids rushed in and out, carrying trays of food and drink. Whenever the swinging doors opened, a rush of sound came from the main room. Gemma, the fat cook, handed me a slice of bread and cheese with one hand, and used a spoon to whack a slow-moving maid on the rump with the other.

"But this is the only way I can think of to pay you," I told Ulfrid. "I already owe you for the night I spent months ago, and for taking me to see Derda."

Ulfrid grunted. "Nothing to that," she said. "Favors owed, favors paid." She cut herself a slice of cheese. "I'm not saying that you shouldn't pay me this time, just that you need to work on your own dress first. Plenty of time after the ball to pay me." And she went into the main room to see to her patrons.

"Assuming I have any money after the Merchants' Ball," I said under my breath.

I had spent the day sewing. The hem of the velvet overskirt was so riddled with holes from the removal of the roses that it had started to tear beneath my needle. I had finally cut it off, hemmed it a hand's-width shorter, and frantically resketched my design to allow for the abbreviated overskirt. I was pleased with the way the satin underskirts now showed below the velvet, but it had set me back several hours while I trimmed and hemmed and drew. When I had been at Derda's I had concentrated on the bodice, practicing my stitches and experimenting with colors along the neckline and down the sleeves. Now I was ready to begin the most difficult part—the skirt—and my fingers felt stiff and clumsy. My whole future rode on this, and I didn't know if I was ready.

"Hello, hello!" The swinging doors flew open to reveal Prince Luka, grinning broadly. "Ulfrid sent a message saying that you were here." He plopped down on a bench across the table from me.

"Luka!" I reached across and clasped both his hands. "It's so good to see you!" He squeezed my hands in reply, smiling at me.

"Your Highness." With great formality, Gemma presented the prince with a plate of rolls, soup, and cheese, forcing me to let go of him and retreat to my side of the table.

"Ah, thank you, Gemma!" He scarfed down a roll as though he hadn't eaten all day.

With much less decorum, the cook threw a cheese roll to Tobin, who caught it deftly. He sat on a tall stool in the corner, and a serving maid handed him a mug of ale and a plate of fried onions and sausages.

"We can't stay very long," Luka said. He tugged at the collar of his blue velvet coat. "There's a state dinner tonight, y'see. But Ulfrid said you had something important to tell me."

"That's right." I pushed aside my own meal. "I'm sorry if you're missing a betrothal feast or something like that, but—"

"I wish," Luka snorted. "I could miss one of those without batting an eye. This is much worse: Amalia's father showed up yesterday."

"What? The Roulaini king?"

He nodded. "King Prilian arrived at the palace bright and early with his guards and his luggage and said that he just couldn't stand to be separated from his darling daughter a day longer."

I goggled at him as he downed another roll.

"The whole palace is in an uproar," he said through his mouthful. "I'm surprised you haven't heard. The kitchens are working day and night to prepare feasts to celebrate, but nobody has the stomach to eat them."

"Why not?" My voice was hardly a whisper. This, added to my news, made me feel cold all over.

Luka's expression darkened. "Something's going on. Amalia and her father spent most of yesterday and today holed up in her apartments. According to them, they're having some touching father-daughter talks, but it's obvious there's more to it than that." He shook his head. "Prilian brought two complete regiments with him as protection, all armed to the teeth and wearing full battle armor. We've had to move some of the King's Guard into the city to make room for the Roulaini men in the barracks. And let me tell you, that doesn't sit well with Father's master-of-arms. Father says it's a show of good faith to let the Roulaini have more men at hand than we do, but I can tell that it makes him uneasy. Frankly, it makes *me* uneasy."

"Oh, no," I whispered.

"Creel? What is it?" Luka pushed aside his mug and took my hands again.

"The reason why I quit Derda's, why I came here," I said, hardly able to think. "Larkin has a bracelet Amalia gave her. Amalia's done something to Sh—" I caught myself, swallowed. "Amalia is up to something. I'm not sure how, but somehow my slippers are involved, and something else." I bit the inside of my cheek, not sure what to say. "I think Amalia may have hurt a friend of mine."

"What?" Luka rose from his bench, still holding my hands across the table. Tobin got down off his stool and came over, concerned. "Who? Marta?"

Out of the corner of my eye, I saw Tobin gesturing with his hands. I shook my head. "Marta's fine. It's . . . another friend. He doesn't live in the King's Seat. Larkin has been helping Amalia, more than just giving her my shoes. My friend . . . he has a great treasure, hidden away, and Larkin somehow knew about it. I think Amalia has

been there, to his . . . house, and I think she may have
harmed him."

"I don't understand." Luka squeezed my hands even
tighter. "Who is your friend?"

"He's a—" Tears pricked my eyelids. "He's a sort of
hermit, you wouldn't know him." But I couldn't think
that Amalia would care two figs for Shardas's windows.
She must have wanted him for himself then. But why?
Because he could fly her wherever she wanted to go?

The cook opened the door to one of the huge ovens,
and the heat washed over us, making my forehead bead
with sweat. Heat. Dragonfire. It could destroy fields,
burn people to ash, perhaps even melt the stones of a
palace. . . .

"Creel?" Luka was patting my hand to draw me out
of my reverie. "Creel? Are you all right?"

"I don't know what Amalia is planning," I said, blinking to clear my vision. "But whatever it is, it's not good.
You should go back to the palace and tell your father."

Luka nodded. "Thank you. So Larkin is helping her?
Maybe someone should ask her some questions." He
and Tobin shared a look.

I felt a guilty little surge of satisfaction, to think of
Larkin being arrested for treason. To my surprise, Luka
came around the table and gave me a tight hug. "I'm sorry
about your friend," he said. "I hope that he's all right."

"Thank you." I hugged him back. "I hope this is all
a lot of nothing. Just Amalia being . . . Amalia." We
both tried to laugh, but it sounded false.

Tobin and the prince left, and I returned to my

room. I began the altered design of the skirt, my fingers shaking. It wasn't just Amalia being Amalia, I knew. Why would she want to hurt Shardas? And her father's sudden arrival was no coincidence.

Luka did not return to Ulfrid's. Two days later I received a note saying that things were too tense at the palace for him to slip away, but again he wished me the best at the Merchants' Ball. I put the note in the little box with my pearls and his other letter, and went back to work.

All day long and into the night I stitched away on my gown. The pictures were taking shape, the creased and hole-pricked velvet taking on new life. Whenever the color of the embroidery threads started to swim and swirl, I would set it aside and do a little "regular sewing": putting gold satin borders on the aprons of Ulfrid's serving maids.

For three weeks all I could do was pray and sew and hope that I would finish my gown in time for the Merchants' Ball. If there still was a Merchants' Ball this year.

We might just be having a war instead.

A Gown Like Stained Glass

Everyone was staring at me. I could feel their eyes running over me, over every inch of my gown and every braid of my intricately bound hair. If I had managed to eat anything at all that day, I'm sure I would have thrown it up then and there.

But I hadn't eaten, no matter how Ulfrid pressed me to have a bite of bread or a sip of tea, and so I didn't disgrace myself. Instead, I put my chin up and walked into the ballroom, doing my best not to gawk like a bumpkin at the marble columns like cold, white trees four times the height of a man, and the floor inlaid with jasper and malachite.

The Merchants' Ball was held in the Winter Palace, which had been built by Milun the First. The current royal family lived across the broad Jyllite Square in the unimaginatively named New Palace. The Winter Palace was used for public ceremonies, housing foreign dignitaries, and the Merchants' Ball. Amalia's father, King

Prilian, was in residence, though gossip said he would not make an appearance at the ball, considering it a vulgar custom. Ulfrid had told me that the royal wedding would take place in the Winter Palace's chapel, followed by a banquet in the same ballroom where I stood now.

The room was already aswarm with people. Along the walls were tables where some of the hopefuls displayed blown glass, paintings, cunning little clockwork toys, and other items. Knots of splendidly dressed nobles circled the room, talking to each other, to the artisans, asking to see their wares more closely or leading them into the figures of a dance. Music soared from a gallery high above the floor and thousands of candles blazed in crystal holders, making the room glow.

"You are exquisite," a rich voice said behind me, and I jumped.

Whirling around, I found myself face-to-face with the Duchess of Mordrel. She was wearing the gray-and-blue gown, the first I had made for her, and I felt a surge of pride at seeing my handiwork. It was beautiful, and the duchess wore it like she knew it.

"Thank you, your Grace," I responded, feeling shy. I made a small curtsy to her and her escort. She was holding the arm of a short, plump man with a friendly smile. He wore a darker shade of gray, to complement her gown, I noticed.

"This is my husband, the Duke of Mordrel," the duchess said. Her husband inclined his head to me, and I curtsied again, a little more deeply this time.

"Please turn around again, and let me have a look at that gown," the duchess instructed me. "I was feeling proud of mine, but you have truly outdone yourself with this garment." And she gestured at my skirt with her fan.

I didn't bother to repress the grin of satisfaction that settled on my face as I slowly rotated before the duke and duchess. For nearly a month I had sat in that little room at Ulfrid's inn and embroidered this gown. Every stitch that I sewed was a prayer: for success, for peace, for Shardas's well-being.

According to Ulfrid, I looked like a piece of gold and glass and something that she didn't know the Feravelan for. Marta and Alle had come to the inn that afternoon, bearing Marta's silk wrap. They had insisted on playing my handmaidens, and under their ministrations I had been bathed and scrubbed until I thought my skin would come off. They had combed, brushed, and combed my hair again, and then massaged lavender-scented pomade through it. Alle had plaited it into a bundle of braids, which she then arranged in a crown atop my head. And while she worked with my hair, she told me all the gossip: she had met a handsome baker's assistant in chapel, and he had left a rose and a love poem for her on the doorstep of the shop, to Derda's great annoyance. But the biggest news was that Larkin had suddenly disappeared a few days after I left.

"Good riddance," was all I would say to that, although inwardly I felt sick. She hadn't been "poached" by another dressmaker, as Derda feared, or gone into religious service as Alle half-jokingly speculated. She was in the Winter Palace with her new employer, Princess Amalia. I was sure of it.

Around my neck I wore the triple strand of pearls from Luka, and on my feet were my plain slippers, ornamented with some of the smaller rosettes from the gown. Marta's wrap went around my shoulders.

But it was the gown that was the real glory.

The great full skirt was almost entirely covered with six panels of embroidery telling the story of the maiden Irial and the dragon Zalthus in radiant hues of scarlet, azure, and violet, with leading of a mellow gold thread highlighting each block of color. The tight bodice had more abstract embroidery around the neckline, and the long, fitted sleeves were decorated down the outside of each. While it wasn't the fashion for ball gowns to have sashes, I wanted to show off my skill with sash-weaving and, as Marta had pointed out, I was creating my own style anyway. So I wore a sash of azure and violet and scarlet silk yarns, woven in the most intricate pattern I knew. I had wrapped the sash twice around my waist, and then let the ends hang down my left side, in military fashion. I thought it went well enough with the straight, snug fit of the bodice, and the stiffness of the heavily decorated skirt.

"My dear, you are magnificent," the duchess said at last.

I had made at least three revolutions in the meantime, and we had attracted quite a crowd. There were a handful of men of all ages giving me admiring glances and not,

I realized with surprise, simply because of my gown. There were several older women as well, looking thoughtful and more than a touch envious. One or two people, however, wore sour expressions, and I recognized them for my fellow hopefuls. I gave one young woman in a beautiful sky-blue gown a small smile, but she made a rude gesture with her fingers and turned away.

"Would you care to dance?" The duke was standing at my elbow. "My wife has spoken to me of you and your work, and I would like to discuss your plans, should you gain a sponsor."

The duchess was looking on and smiling in an encouraging way, so I said that I would love to dance. I hoped that the duke was a good dancer, since I was terrible at it. I knew all the country dances of the north, but Ulfrid had been trying to teach me (with Tobin's silent help) the more courtly dances performed in the King's Seat. In her post as royal nanny, she had sat in on Prince Luka's dance lessons, and was an able instructor. Even more surprising: her brother was a skilled dancer. She informed me that any good sword fighter should be, which made sense, in a way.

At least, with my long skirts, no one could see my feet if I forgot the steps.

The duke and I moved through the stately passes of the alutine. It was a slow and easy dance, and the duke was a fine dancer, putting me at ease immediately.

"All the dances are like this," the duke explained, as though sensing my relief. "It's easier to conduct business if one isn't hopping up and down and panting with exertion."

"Very sensible." I couldn't think of anything else to say. What was wrong with me? After weeks of sewing and planning and learning to dance and getting my hair painfully pinned up, my mind had gone blank. I should have made Marta put the dress on and come in my stead. She was never at a loss for words.

"Do you sew as well as embroider?" The duke took the lead, fortunately.

"Yes, but my real talent lies in the embroidery, and the designing of patterns," I babbled with relief. Marta and Ulfrid had told me to go ahead and boast about my skills, everyone was expected to. "But I have a partner," I went on. "She's even more skilled than I at dress-making, and is responsible for the current trend in low, decorated necklines."

"Well, I'm sure that gentlemen all over the King's Seat thank her for that." The duke chuckled.

I snorted, then tried to turn it into a ladylike giggle, but gave up and just snorted again.

"So, it sounds like you have a good plan for your shop," the duke said in a leading tone.

"Yes," I said with firmness. Since I had quit Derda's, Marta had been sneaking over to Ulfrid's inn so that we could plan. We would mostly specialize in what my mother called fancywork: aprons, sashes, scarves and shawls, the occasional ball gown. At least at first. Then, once we started making some money, we wanted to hire apprentices so that we could branch out and start doing more gowns. I related our ambitions to the duke, and he seemed impressed.

"You have clearly taken the time to think about your future, young mistress," he said.

"Thank you. Marta and I have been planning hard," I replied.

"My only hesitation is that the political situation is rather dodgy at present." He went on, looking thoughtful. "My wife always insists that we attend the ball, but this year I hadn't planned on investing too deep."

I knew a lot more about the "dodgy situation" than I should, so I swallowed my own doubts and brazened on. "I should think that a royal wedding would be the perfect time to open a ladies' shop," I said. "I understand that there will be balls all summer, and parties, and of course the ten feasts surrounding the ceremonies."

"If the wedding takes place, yes," the duke said in a low voice.

"What?" I stumbled, and he had to haul me upright. "But, I thought that the arrangements had been made."

"I know that you are a friend of Prince Luka's—he speaks very highly of you, and made me promise to seek you out tonight—so you must have an inkling that things aren't right. King Prilian of Roulain is here right now, you know. These days our king isn't as enthusiastic about this marriage as Prilian, and now Roulain is making more demands for the marriage settlement."

I blew out my lips. "Then why is his majesty going

along with it? Why not just send them back to Roulain?"
I couldn't keep my outrage hidden.

"We'd like to, my dear. Oh, how we would like to!
But we would benefit from any alliance with Roulain,"
the duke told me. "Our nation is far wealthier, but they
have the best ports. Better port access, relaxed tariffs,
they would be invaluable to us."

I was very pleased that the duke was talking to me in
this frank way, as though he thought me an equal, or at
least an intelligent human being. "Of course. I've been
wondering what we're supposed to gain from it, other
than a rather shrill future queen."

"Our Feravelan velvet and furs exported across the
sea without having to pay the Roulaini tariffs," the duke
said, a smile playing at the corners of his mouth at my
description of Amalia. "And, most important: a cessa-
tion of hostilities along the border."

"I didn't think our border was all that hostile," I said,
puzzled. "Since King Milun defeated the Roulaini—"

The duke was shaking his head. "Milun's, er, un-
orthodox methods . . . were successful, but they made
the Roulaini very bitter toward us. We've been trying to
smooth things over through a royal marriage for centuries. Prilian was the first king to even consider it."

A jolt went though me. "Why?"

"What do you mean?"

"Why after all these years would the Roulaini suddenly agree to this marriage?" A voice in my head snickered that he was trying to send Amalia as far away as

possible, but I stamped it down. There was something odd about this.

Pursing his lips, the duke's feet slowed, and then we scrambled to catch up with the dance before the couple to our left stepped on us. "We thought it was because Prilian was more peaceable than his ancestors. And Miles and Amalia are much of an age, so it would be a good match for them." He nodded, thoughtful. "But in light of recent events, it does seem . . . odd." He opened his mouth, then glanced around and closed it. "State secrets," he said with a shake of his head. "You are a very clever girl. I will say this, though: lately King Caxel seems to think that something is afoot. . . ." His voice trailed away and we danced in silence for a moment.

"Who will inherit the Roulaini throne?" I had never heard anything about a crown prince.

"A nephew. But the boy is barely old enough to—"

The duke never finished his sentence, because that's when the roof was ripped off the ballroom.

As I watched in shocked disbelief, a great golden dragon head snaked down through the gaping hole where the roof had been and a long tongue flickered out. All around me, women and men fainted dead away and the screams of others scratched my ears like rusty nails. The candlelight gleamed on his crown of blue horns, but his eyes looked cloudy and didn't reflect the light as they usually did. I stepped forward, rather than back, ignoring the duke's shout to take cover. He pulled at my arm and I shrugged him off.

It was my dearest friend looming above us, my own Shardas, but something was terribly wrong.

"Shardas! Shardas, what are you doing?" My fists clenched, I shouted up at him, but he didn't acknowledge me.

His nostrils flared as he sucked in a great breath. Horrified, knowing what was coming next, I ran for one of the tree-trunk-like pillars, dragging the duke with me. We barely made it to safety before Shardas unleashed a great gout of blue dragonfire.

Tears coursed down my face as I looked out at the chaotic scene and listened to the heightened screams of people trying to flee the attack. "Why would Shardas do such a thing?"

"You know this dragon's name?" The duke, white with horror, was staring at me as though I was the one who had just set fire to the ballroom.

"He's my friend." My voice came out in a sob. "He's always gentle, not a killer! Not a killer!" I wrapped my arms around myself, rocking back and forth in my plain slippers.

The ballroom was in flames. Where dragonfire hadn't set the tapestries alight, candles tumbled from their holders by falling pieces of the roof had done so. Tables bearing the wares of other hopefuls had been shoved out of the way by escaping dancers or started on fire as well. My stomach lurched as I saw still figures who hadn't escaped the fire.

"Come with me," the duke urged. "This way."

I didn't want to go. Shardas needed me! And the duchess, where was she? "But, your wife. . . ."

"I saw her run out the doors on the far side. We'll look for her outside," he said in a trembling voice. "We must get clear of all this, and then we'll have to talk."

I felt faint, but forced myself to follow him. I craned my head over my shoulder as we went, searching for another glimpse of gold scales. "How could Shardas do such a thing?" I kept repeating the question as we hurried through the maze of pillars and made our escape through a servants' door half-hidden behind a smoldering tapestry.

"It isn't in the nature of dragons to attack us in this way," the duke agreed. "It's been rare enough to *see* a dragon since Milun the First's time."

"Something's happened to him," I blubbered. "He was not himself. His eyes were clouded, as though he were asleep, or under some sort of a spell. . . ."

The duke stumbled and the hand on my arm tightened painfully. "What did you say?"

I extracted my bruised arm, but didn't slow my steps. "He's under a spell," I said with greater conviction. "Shardas would never do such a thing."

"Or an alchemical enchantment," he said. "A dragon attacking humans, like they did during the last Roulaini war." His voice was hardly a whisper. "The Triunity protect us."

"Do you think that Amalia is an alchemist?" The idea was ludicrous, but somehow she had found Shardas's lair, had told Larkin about it, and now this.

"An alchemist?" The duke shook his head. "She wouldn't need to be, to control the dragons."

"That's ridiculous! Dragons don't just take orders from humans!" Shardas in particular, I thought, would not bow to the will of someone like Amalia.

"Not if they can help it," the duke said hoarsely. "But it seems, my dear Creel, that someone has found Milun's dragonskin slippers."

"What?" I stopped dead in the middle of the little passageway I was following him down. "Were they blue?"

A Council of War

The Duke of Mordrel led me down one passageway and then another. Other survivors stumbled after us, but the duke kept us ahead of them, his eyes warning me to silence after my outburst. I realized at one point that we were in an underground tunnel. It was faintly damp-smelling, and cold, and lit by weird blobs of glowing moss that were positioned too regularly to have grown there by nature.

When we had ascended into a fresher-smelling passageway, lit by candelabra, I stopped again and asked where we were.

"In the New Palace," the duke said. "It is . . . convenient . . . for members of the court to be able to get from one palace to the other without having to cross the square." Then he took my arm and continued to lead me along, motioning for those behind to follow.

At last we arrived in a wide and very well-lit hallway, ending in a large set of doors embossed with a golden sun. I hesitated. Every child in Feravel knew that the golden sun was the symbol of our kings. I was in the New Palace, the home of my king, and those were the doors to some intimate chamber inhabited by royalty. I shouldn't be here. The people following us took another, smaller door to one side, and I made to go with them.

"No, no, I need you," Mordrel said, gripping my arm even tighter.

He knocked on the massive doors, and a guardsman with drawn sword opened them from the other side before the duke had even lowered his fist. The guardsman glared at us, and the duke glared back.

"Step aside, man! I must see King Caxel at once!"

"Who's this, then?" The guardsman pointed his chin at me.

"She needs to see his majesty as well," the duke said coolly. "Now let us pass."

"Mordrel, is that you? Let him through, Sergeant," said a proud voice from behind the guardsman.

The guard saluted and stepped aside. On the arm of a duke, I entered the presence of my king.

It was disappointing to say the least. The two princes must have gotten their looks from the late queen, for their father's features weren't exactly the stuff of maidens' daydreams. Balding beneath his crown, stomach stretching his fine velvet robe, and with a frightening beak of a nose, he surveyed us from the depths of a massive gilded chair, his long-fingered hands clutching the carved arms. Knots of people crowded the room, some of them as soot-smudged and tattered as we were.

"Who is this girl?" The king's voice came out like a bark, making me jump.

"Creelisel Carlbrun, your Majesty," I introduced myself, making the deepest curtsy I could manage without falling on my face.

"Who?"

"Creel! The Triunity be thanked!" Luka rushed around the map-strewn table to me, wrapping his arms around me and giving me a rather painful squeeze. I hadn't noticed him there, and gave another startled jump when he grabbed me.

"I was afraid you had been burnt to a crisp by that dragon," Luka said.

"Mistress Creel keeps her wits, even when faced with dragonfire," the duke explained. "She saved my sorry hide as well, Sire, pulling me behind a pillar just in time to avoid a scorching."

"And for that she is to be privy to this council?" King Caxel was not pleased.

"She knows the dragon that attacked the Winter Palace," the duke said.

"Creel? You know a dragon?" Luka looked incredulous. The whole room looked incredulous.

"His name is Shardas, your Majesty," I said in a hesitant voice. "He's really very gentle, I don't know why he's behaving this way. Something's happened to him." I glanced at the duke. "His Grace said something about . . . some slippers?"

"Mordrel," the king said in a warning voice. His eyes flicked toward the gaggle of other people in the room, all watching us avidly. "That is not something that I wish to discuss in front of an audience."

Still standing close to Luka, I saw his face go chalky with shock. He stepped away from me. "*Your* slippers? The slippers Amalia stole? They were. . . . Where did you . . . King Milun's slippers! Caxon's bones," he swore. "Why didn't you tell me?"

"Luka!" King Caxel snapped. "Not here!"

"I didn't know. I still don't know." Trembling like a newborn foal, I looked from prince to king to duke. "What is this? What about King Milun's slippers? Someone please tell me what is going on!"

The king's face was purple. He pounded a fist on the table. "Privy council only!" he shouted. "The rest of you, out!"

All but a handful of the others hurried from the room. Luka moved close to my side again, and gave his father a stubborn look when the king tried to send us away as well. As the room began to clear I noticed the crown prince sitting on a window seat. He came forward, but not to leave. Instead, he took a seat at the table on his father's left hand, giving me a brief nod by way of greeting.

"King Milun the First controlled the dragons through a pair of magic slippers," Luka said to me.

If he had spoken in Roulaini, it would have made more sense. What did Shardas—my Shardas!—tearing the roof off the Winter Palace ballroom and burning dozens of people to death have to do with the long dead king's slippers and my slippers . . . if they really were the same?

The Duchess of Mordrel came in looking pale. Her husband greeted her with an explosion of relieved breath and a kiss on the cheek.

"This is a matter for the privy council," the king told her, though with greater respect than he had shown anyone else.

"Forgive me, your Majesty, but I just now overheard someone mention Milun the First's slippers." The duchess's expression was troubled. "I know something about them."

"It seems that everyone does!" The king threw his hands in the air.

"Does *she* have them?" Luka's face was still white.

"Yes." The duchess knew exactly whom he meant. "I saw them before Amalia left this morning. Her new maid was carrying them."

"New maid?" I raised one eyebrow. "This new maid doesn't walk with a limp, by any chance?"

The duchess looked startled. "Why, yes. She limps quite badly, in fact." She went on, still giving me a puzzled look. "I wasn't certain what they were then, but there is no other explanation. Princess Amalia has the slippers. And from what I've been hearing, she stole them from Creel."

"Larkin, the girl with the limp, used to work at Derda's shop with me. She stole the slippers and gave them to Amalia." I tried to clench my fists in my skirt, but the embroidery made it too stiff.

"How did a mere seamstress come by King Milun's

slippers?" King Caxel pinched the bridge of his nose with one hand, looking pained.

The way in which he said "mere seamstress" made me bristle—my mother had been a "mere seamstress"!—but I fought the urge to sass the king and thought about my answer. I had spent months avoiding telling anyone where I had gotten my slippers and what had inspired me to leave Carlieff Town.

Then the memory of Shardas tearing the roof off the ballroom of the Winter Palace came rushing back. It was time to tell the truth.

"The slippers were given to me by a brown dragon named Theoradus, your Majesty," I began. And then I unwound the whole tale. My aunt, Theoradus, the long trek to Rath Forest, how Shardas had saved me. I paused there. "I don't understand why Shardas would act this way, why he would attack the palace."

Luka took my hand. "It's the slippers, Creel. Whoever wears them controls the dragons. *All* the dragons. Milun used them to win the Roulaini War, but the slippers were lost not long after the war. I suppose this Theoradus found them somehow."

I understood now what had made Shardas drop the window and carry me to safety. Good as he was, it hadn't been altruism. It had been the coercion of the slippers.

All eyes were on me: the king's and crown prince's, Luka's, the serious gazes of the privy council. I swallowed and continued my story of arriving in the King's

Seat, getting lost and stepping on Amalia's lapdog, being hired by Derda, and Amalia's demand that I give her the slippers.

"The princess recognized them at once?" The king steepled his fingers and focused intently on them, as though his fingernails held the answer.

"I don't really know. I thought—well, I hoped—that she just wanted them because they were pretty." I felt very foolish for not listening to the nagging voice in my head. I had suspected from the moment I'd seen Theoradus's reaction that there was something unusual about them. It wounded my pride to have to say that, yes, the obnoxious Princess Amalia had known more about them than I who had worn them every day for months. I just hoped that they made Amalia's feet itch as badly as they had mine.

Feet itching . . .

"The itching!" I blurted out, startling everyone. "Er. They made my feet itch, and Larkin put them on once and said that her feet itched, and she heard voices. Was that—was that part of the alchemy?" The question sounded ridiculous, once I blurted it out. Why would King Caxel care that they made my feet itch?

"And you didn't think to wonder why?" King Caxel's face was a thundercloud. "The itching was to alert the wearer that a dragon was trying to communicate with you! And you did what? Scratched your feet and ignored the voices?"

Luka gave me a comforting smile. "How could Creel

have known? It was one of the best kept secrets of the royal family."

All the same, I hung my head and blushed, embarrassed at my stupidity. Why hadn't I listened to my gut and tried to find out more about the slippers?

"I'd like to know how the Roulaini knew about Milun's secret to begin with," King Caxel said, turning to Miles with a hooded expression. "Our family has kept the means of his control over the dragons in strictest confidence for centuries. Who told her?"

Miles paled. "I never, sir, I swear."

"The Roulaini have been trying to turn the tables on us since their defeat," Luka said, coming to his brother's rescue. "If you ask me—"

"I didn't," the king interrupted.

"If you ask me," Luka brazened on, "Amalia was sent to discover the secret, or to map out our weaknesses. The marriage was a ruse all along."

Heads nodded in agreement all over the room. I looked at Miles, wondering if he was disappointed that Amalia had only been using him, but he was nodding as well, looking more thoughtful than anything.

"From the day she arrived, Amalia's been asking questions," he said. "She claimed to be fascinated by Feravelan history."

The king shook his head. "Prilian's no fool: I can't imagine him sending the princess as a spy. She has no training in . . . anything other than shopping, as far as I can tell."

"Making her perfect for the job, Sire," the Duke of Mordrel said. "Who would suspect shallow little Amalia?"

The duchess put in, "I can attest that, while her personality is somewhat grating, she is nevertheless quite intelligent. And her constant questions looked like nothing more than a very heartening interest in her future people."

The king groaned. "The Triunity protect us," he muttered under his breath, then he turned his attention to me. "What did *you* intend to use the slippers for?"

"Pardon?" I shook my head. "I'm still not sure I understand what the slippers . . . do . . . or what they are. Are you saying that I'm a spy?" My knees shook. Would they lock me in a dungeon?

"No, no," the duchess assured me, slipping an arm around my shoulders. "My many-times great-grandfather—I'm Caxel's cousin, if you didn't know," she explained with a nod at the king. "My many-times great-grandfather Milun was looking for a way to end the war with Roulain and unite Feravel, which at the time was little more than a loose collection of counties, as I'm sure you know."

I nodded my head to show that I did. As I had told Shardas, the schoolteacher for the poor children of Carlieff Town had thought Milun the First the greatest hero Feravel had ever produced. Behind her back we had joked that she was in love with him.

"Milun made friends with a female dragon," the

duchess continued, "who I believe was a leader of their kind, and asked for her assistance. Since the dragons rarely unite for any cause, she told Milun that they would have to be forced and gave him the slippers."

"I see." I stiffened, remembering Shardas's harsh words about King Milun. "The dragons tell it a bit differently," was all I could think to say. The king terrified me, and I didn't want to insult him by calling his ancestor a liar.

We all stood or sat in silence, staring at one another. Then the king got to his feet and looked around the room, studying the face of each person present.

"We are at war," he announced. "The Roulaini have attacked without warning. The betrothal of Crown Prince Milun and Princess Amalia of Roulain is hereby dissolved." He pounded his fist on the table three times. "General Sarryck." He pointed to a gray-haired man with a military bearing at the end of the table. "You are dismissed to gather our forces and prepare our defense."

"It will be done, your Majesty." The man stood, bowed deeply, and marched out of the room.

"Sarryck has mustered the King's Guards," the king said, turning to Mordrel. "There are bowmen on the roof, standing ready. Mordrel, you will command them."

"Sire," Mordrel murmured, nodding in acquiescence.

"Shardas," I murmured, half to myself. "So you'll shoot him, if he attacks the New Palace?" I asked the king.

"They'll shoot him if they see a gleam of a scale, whether he's attacking, or taking tea with a friend," the king said. "This is war, young woman."

I closed my eyes against the cold horror and pain in my chest. "He prefers peaches," I mumbled.

"Creel." Luka took my hand. "I know that this is hard for you. You cared for Shardas, and I'm sorry. But he's no longer the dragon you knew. With Amalia controlling his mind, he wouldn't hesitate to kill even you."

"I know," I said with a shiver. "I saw him at the Winter Palace. He was not himself."

"He'll likely never be himself again," the king grumbled. "Now, since you have experience using the slippers, I'm going to keep you close," he instructed me. "Mora, take charge of her. I want her to sleep in your apartments," he said to the duchess, who inclined her head in agreement.

"But I really should get word to Ulfrid," I said to Luka, feeling trapped by the king's decision and the knowledge that I could not refuse.

The duchess assured me that she would see to it that word was sent. Since I was no longer needed, she and I took our leave of the king and his councillors. The duke excused himself to see us safely to their apartments before he took command of the palace defenses. Luka looked like he wanted to come, too, but his father barked for him to sit down and stop twittering. With a grimace, Luka bade me farewell. The door closed on the sound of the king giving the order for a map of the Feravel-Roul border to be brought in.

The Duke and Duchess of Mordrel walked hand in hand ahead of me down a wide gallery. I was a pace or two behind, studying the portraits that hung on its walls of every queen since the third century.

That was when the second attack came.

An Unusual Messenger

It wasn't Shardas. I had never seen this dragon before, its scales pale red mottled with brown. The thought brought a surge of relief, even as I ran for my life alongside the duke and duchess.

There was no time to seek out the secret tunnels. Instead the duke all but pushed us out the nearest first floor windows, and we picked ourselves up and ran along with everyone else lucky enough to have escaped. Blue-white dragonfire lit the sky, and everywhere there was screaming and the sound of falling bricks. Windows shattered from the heat, and the roar of the dragon was only silenced by the roar of its flame as it burned the New Palace.

As we stumbled across the Jyllite Square, the duke, duchess, and I couldn't help but look back over our shoulders. The roof of the palace had been ripped away, and not one, but two dragons were busily setting fire to the interior. The square was flooded with sobbing, running, fainting people. Some were wealthies, some servants in livery, and some looked to be bystanders who had come to gawk at the damage to the Winter Palace and been caught in this new attack.

The King's Guards were lining up in the square as best they could, considering the number of people running through their ranks to safety. The bowmen the king had positioned on the roof had either fled or been killed, and now more bowmen were taking aim, trying to find a clear shot at the dragons through the smoke.

As we turned into a relatively quiet side street, the panting duchess yanked on her husband's arm, pulling him to a halt. "Where are we going?"

"I'll take you and Creel to safety, then return to organize the guards." He turned and would have kept going, but she stopped him again.

"But *where* exactly? We can't run all the way to our country estates!"

"Ulfrid's inn," I gasped, my hand pressed to the stitch in my side. "It's a ways east, but I think we can make it, and we'll be safe there."

With me in the lead, we fought our way through the crowded streets toward Ulfrid's inn. Some of the people we pushed past were terrified, others strangely resigned. We passed houses where men with rusted swords, no doubt inherited from their grandfathers, stood guard, and shops where white-faced apprentices were hastily nailing boards over the doors and windows. Dragonfire would easily burn through such defenses, but I did not stop to tell them that. A woman screamed in my ear and then stumbled to her knees, I pulled her to her feet and she slapped at me as she staggered on.

It seemed forever before we arrived, but at last I was pounding at the thick oak door, shouting Ulfrid's name. I heard a muffled sound on the other side, as though something was being pulled back from the door, and then Ulfrid's voice came faintly, asking who we were.

"It's me, it's Creel!" I pounded again. "Please let us in!"

There were exclamations from inside, and then the heavy bolts were drawn and the door swung open. Ulfrid stood there with a sword in her hand, Marta beside her clutching a dagger in a shaking fist.

"Creel!" Marta tossed her dagger down on the table and yanked me inside. She threw her arms around me and gave me a huge hug, which I heartily returned. "You're safe!" Her cheeks were tearstained. "We were sure that you had been eaten by that awful dragon."

Ulfrid ushered the duke and duchess inside, then closed and bolted the door behind them. She sheathed the sword in the scabbard hanging at her waist with a smooth motion: she had used a sword before.

"Tobin?" Ulfrid was looking to the Duke of Mordrel, whose presence didn't seem to awe her. After all, she had raised a prince.

"We have not seen him," the duke said. "But the king often sends him scouting when there is trouble."

Ulfrid nodded, satisfied by this.

"Creel, what's going on?" Marta's voice shook. "They say that dragons attacked the Winter Palace."

"Yes," was all I could say for a moment. I sank down on a long bench, and one of Ulfrid's serving maids brought me a cup of hot tea. "It was my slippers," I said after I had taken a sip. "The slippers that Larkin stole once belonged to King Milun the First. They can be used to control dragons, and Amalia is doing just that." I took another, longer sip of the tea.

"What?" Marta clutched at her apron. "Why?"

"To start a war." It was the duke who answered her. "A war they know they can win, because they have turned our greatest weapon against us."

The duchess sat beside me, patting my hand. The girl offered her tea as well, and the duchess took the thick mug with graceful thanks, as though it were the finest palace china. The duke, meanwhile, told a wide-eyed Marta and a silent Ulfrid the rest of the story.

"I'd like to black both her eyes," Marta said in a fierce voice.

A movement caught my eye, and I turned to see Tobin standing at the door to the kitchens, his head back in his silent laugh. Marta blushed scarlet, and looked down at her clenched hands, relaxing them with an effort.

"Ah, Tobin!" The duke slapped one hand on the table. "What news?"

I thought this a rather odd question, considering that Tobin couldn't answer, other than to make faces or maybe a few signals with his hands. Tobin began to make a series of quick and complex gestures. I had seen him do this before, but hadn't realized the extent of his "vocabulary," or that anyone besides Ulfrid and Luka understood it. The duke, Ulfrid, and even Marta followed the motions with nodding heads, as though it made some sense to them.

"So Prilian has delivered an ultimatum?" The duke stroked his chin and squinted. "What is it he wants?"

More gestures from Tobin, a gasp from Marta.

"No lack of ambition, eh?" The duke gave a mirthless chuckle, his expression dark.

"What did he say?" The duchess prodded her husband's arm, her brow creased.

"Prilian is demanding no less than the throne of Feravel. He marched into the council chamber with an armed guard just after the dragons attacked the New Palace. Apparently the Roulaini army has been mobilized for weeks: they've been trickling toward our border a regiment at a time, moving only at night, and now they've crossed over in full force. If we don't surrender, what the dragons don't burn the Roulaini army will."

"I can't believe it!" The duchess chewed her lower lip. "It's madness! What are they planning to do, burn us all to death? What would they have to gain?"

"A very large country of very submissive peasants," I said bitterly.

"Yes, but why?"

"Because Prilian wants what every king of Roulain

has wanted since Milun the First's crushing defeat: Feravel," the duke said. "They aren't content with taxing our furs and gold and other exports. They want them for their own, and—" The duke broke off. "What's that?" He rose, and we all followed suit.

There was a scratching sound coming from the inn door.

Tobin and Ulfrid had their swords out before I could blink. Tobin glided over to the door and pressed one ear to it, holding out his free hand in a "stay" gesture to the rest of us. The maids all squeaked and pulled out carving knives and small daggers, and Marta had her dagger in hand as well.

"It sounds like—" I began, but was hushed by the duke.

"What is it?" he whispered to Tobin.

The noise continued: a scraping low against the door. It put me in mind of something. My first thought was dragons, but then it was replaced with a memory of my uncle's old bird hound, begging to come in from the cold at winter.

"It sounds like a dog scratching!" I hissed.

Tobin shot me a look, then unbarred the door and peered out. First he looked up, then down, and gave a whoosh of surprised breath. He opened the door just a tad wider, and a tall but very narrow dog came slinking in.

He was white, with large black patches, and a long snout not unlike a dragon's. He rushed to me at once, and licked my hand, leaning his considerable weight against my thighs.

"Azarte?" I laid a tentative hand on his head and he wagged his tail. "Is that you?"

"A friend of yours?" The duchess looked amused.

"He belongs to—" I stopped myself, then realized that they knew everything anyway. "He belongs to a dragon I know," I finished. I sighed. "Poor Feniul. He's quite harmless, sort of like a dithering old uncle. He doesn't deserve what the Roulaini are doing."

I scratched Azarte's head and then moved down to his neck as he closed his eyes and let his tongue loll out of his mouth with happiness. My fingers encountered a wide collar of woven tapestry-work, and I scratched beneath it. Something slipped out of the collar and fell on the floor with a soft smack.

"What's this?" Marta put down her dagger and picked up a folded square of paper.

She opened it to reveal a large, ragged sheet of parchment. Block letters the size of my hand had been printed on it in smudged charcoal.

"What does it say?" The duke leaned over, curious.

FOLLOW THE DOG.

"How odd! Who do you imagine wrote it?" The duke took the parchment from Marta and frowned at it.

"Feniul," I breathed. Azarte's tail wagged, pounding against the side of the table. "Feniul? Did Feniul send you?" More wagging. "Where's Feniul, Azarte? Where is he, boy? Go find him!"

Grinning his toothy grin, the dog bounded to the door, woofing with joy that I had understood. I went after him, my heart pounding. Feniul!

"Wait a moment, there!" The duke, alarmed, hurried over to stop us. "We don't know for certain who wrote this. That dog could be leading you into a trap!"

"But I know this dog," I protested. "I'm sure that he was sent to help us. A dog can't be manipulated with the slippers; I'll wager Feniul sent him for help."

Tobin gestured to me and Azarte, seeming to indicate that he was coming along, then opened the door for us to exit. Azarte, needing no invitation, leaped out the door. I followed, with Tobin just behind.

The street was eerily quiet. It was nighttime, but compared to the noise and panic of before, the stillness was jarring. The windows of the shop across the street had been boarded up, but the ale house next door looked abandoned: the door left open wide and one window smashed.

"Hey! Who's there?"

Azarte had run right into someone who was standing in the street outside the inn. Tobin stepped forward, sword drawn, then relaxed. It was Luka, tunic torn and face smeared with soot and dirt. I felt weak and the blood rushed in my ears to see him standing there unharmed.

"Tobin? Creel? Everyone all right?" He was leading a pair of horses.

"We have to follow that dog!" I pointed at Azarte, who had run a little way down the street and was now doubling back, prancing with impatience.

"What?" Luka gave me a concerned look, then glanced beyond me to Tobin. "Is she all right?"

"I'm fine," I assured him. "But that dog belongs to a dragon I know. He had a note on his collar and he's leading us to the dragon. I have to follow!" I reached out and took hold of the reins of one of the horses.

Tobin made some gesture that I didn't pay attention to as I talked soothingly to Luka's horse. I didn't know how I was to ride in my stiffly embroidered skirt, but I would have to: walking the entire way was out of the question.

"Here." Marta, who had followed us out the door, anticipated my need. She came forward with her dagger drawn. "I'm sorry," she said, and then she slashed open my outer skirt in the front and back, cutting neatly between the panels of embroidery. I felt faint at seeing all my hard work ruined, but pushed the feeling aside. More important matters were at hand. Marta offered me the dagger and I tucked it into my sash.

"Your Highness?" The duke came striding out of the inn. "Is King Caxel well?"

"He's been taken to the caverns," Luka said. Seeing the questioning look on my face, he explained, "The hill beneath the King's Seat has quite a few natural caves. There are tunnels leading down from the palace to the caves, to hide the royal family in times of war. It's stocked with enough food and water for three months." He made a face. "Father tried to refuse, of course, but the council forced him to go down. We'll still be able to get word to him, through the guards."

"And the crown prince? He is with your father?"

"No." Luka turned to the duke, his expression grim. "Miles and his escort started for the caves after you three left. But word came just as my father was entering the tunnels that he never reached the caves, and his guard was found dead in a side passage."

"The Roulaini," the duke breathed. "They've kidnapped Prince Milun?"

"So it appears," Luka agreed bleakly. "I slipped away to find Tobin. I thought that we could do some scouting, since I have no stomach for sitting idle underground." He wrapped the reins of his horse around a clenched fist, then loosened them when his fingers started to turn dark.

"I need to follow that dog," I said, feeling frantic. Azarte was pacing back and forth, making little yips from time to time. I understood his impatience completely.

"From what the scouts say, it appears that all the dragons are controlled by the Roulaini," Luka said, putting one hand out to stop me as I tried (not very gracefully) to mount his horse.

"I don't think this one is," I insisted. "I think he sent this message because he needs our help, or can help us. I have to go."

"Then I'm coming with you," said Luka, and boosted me into the saddle.

"Fine, fine," I said, distracted. Azarte had started down the street again and was waiting at the corner for us to catch up.

Luka swung up behind me and Tobin mounted the

other horse. In the glow of burning buildings and the silver moonlight, the Duke and Duchess of Mordrel, Marta, and Ulfrid bade us farewell, and we rode off after the leggy dog.

Feniul

It was daybreak when we arrived at the outskirts of
Rath Forest. Shardas's cave was deeper within, and I
did not know the way there. Nor did I know where Feniul lived, for I had only seen him in the enchanted pool.

But it was not long after we had followed the dog
into the cool darkness of the forest that our tired horses
began to whicker and balk. The temperature rose, and
a gust of wind brought the odor of sulfur to my nose.

"Feniul?" I slithered down from the saddle, looking
around eagerly. Azarte was standing nearby, wagging his
tail and looking pleased with himself. "It's me, it's Creel."

"Azarte! Good boy!" Feniul's voice boomed and
crackled from behind a tight cluster of aspens, and
Azarte gave a bark of delight while the horses whin-
nied and rolled their eyes. Then Feniul's great horned
head emerged from the trees, and the horses went berserk.

Tobin and Luka dismounted quickly, but there was

no way to calm the beasts. While Feniul dithered and apologized and Azarte romped and barked, the horses screamed and reared. Finally, Tobin and Luka simply let go their reins, and the horses tore off in the direction of the King's Seat.

"Really, I am so sorry," Feniul said. "I didn't mean to alarm your horses. I just wanted to talk to Creel."

"Feniul!" I ran forward and laid a trembling hand on the end of his snout, ignoring Luka's shout of warning. "I'm so glad you're all right! I can't believe that you aren't under the slippers' power, like Shardas . . ." My voice faded away. "I saw him, in the King's Seat," I forced myself to say.

"Yes, yes, it's horrible!" Feniul's head shook back and forth, and I noticed that he wore a strange sort of woven collar around his neck, just behind his head.

Luka came a little closer, but I could see that he was still tense, one hand on his sword hilt. Tobin held his naked sword in one hand, his eyes fixed on Feniul.

"How do we know this isn't a Roulaini trick?" Luka asked with narrowed eyes.

"A trick? But I wouldn't do that!" Feniul sounded genuinely shocked at the idea. "I'm not in league with the Roulaini! Oh, my, no!"

I could see that his eyes were clear of the dullness caused by the slippers' coercion. His bearing, his speech, everything about him was unchanged. "How is it that you are not affected?" I asked.

"Well, for two days I felt very strange," Feniul said,

his words tumbling over one another. "Like I *needed* to fly east, but why would I do such a thing? There are too many humans in that direction! I tried to bespeak Shardas, but he didn't answer, so I resisted the urge to go east and went to Shardas's cave instead. When I left my caves, I saw other dragons flying toward the human city in broad daylight. It was very strange.

"Shardas was gone, but he had left a message in his pool for me, something I didn't understand, about that alchemist who used to live in his caves, and you, and your shoes or some such. I was so upset, I could hardly follow it."

"How was it that you managed to avoid the call?" Luka's hand was on the hilt of his sword, but he had not yet drawn, as Tobin had.

"I almost didn't," the dragon admitted. "But I never fly in the daylight anymore, it's much too dangerous," he told the prince with a self-deprecating expression. "I suppose my fear was even greater than the power of the slippers. I would be embarrassed, but I am too relieved. The message also said for me to put on this collar." He blew smoke fretfully through his nostrils and a claw came forward to indicate the woven band around his neck. "Once I put it on, I didn't feel the urge to fly east anymore. So I sent Azarte to the King's Seat to find Creel. That was in the message, too."

"Let me see the collar," I said, and Feniul obligingly lowered his head.

It was similar to the collar Azarte wore, only on a

much larger scale. The threads of red and blue and gray and green had been clumsily knotted and woven: there were many mistakes in the pattern, dropped stitches, and knots. But there was a beauty to it, all the same. The threads felt sticky, and when I raised my hand to my nose I caught the odor of sage and thyme, and other sharper things I could not name.

"What is it?" Luka came up beside me, still uncertain of the dragon, but close enough that he could see the collar, too.

"I don't know. I think it's some sort of alchemy. A charm to counteract the slippers, maybe."

"Are there more of these collars?" Luka, his expression intense, looked from me to Feniul and back.

"No, I didn't see any others," rumbled the dragon. "But then, Shardas's cave is rather a mess."

"What? Shardas is neat as a pin," I said, startled.

"I know, but . . ." Feniul trailed away, his tail curling around a young tree in a nervous movement. "Something happened. The windows . . ."

I felt my heart stutter in my chest. "The windows?" I whispered. "Were some of them . . . broken?"

"This collar was carefully hidden," Feniul said, avoiding my gaze. "And there's a message for you in the pool. I'll show you."

"Feniul—"

"I should just . . . just show you."

I steeled myself. "All right." I grabbed hold of the collar, using it to pull myself up onto Feniul's neck. He was not as big as Shardas, but still much larger than a horse, and the spines running along his neck were sharp. I heard one of them catch my satin underskirts and tear them. All the work I had put into making this hideous dress presentable and it was ruined after only one night. I heaved a sigh.

"Er, Creel, is that a good idea?" Luka's hand was still on the hilt of his sword. Both Feniul and I looked at him, my expression determined, Feniul's . . . draconic. Luka swallowed. "I'd like to come as well," Luka said tentatively. He was looking at Feniul as though there were nothing he would like *less*, but his jaw was set.

Tobin sheathed his sword and stepped up, pounding his fist to his chest in a gesture that clearly said: If my prince goes, I'm going, too. Feniul exhaled a breath that rattled the leaves on the trees, and both Tobin and Luka jumped back, making me snicker.

"All three of you may ride," Feniul said with great dignity. Then he leaned down to Azarte. "Run to Shardas's cave, boy! Run! Run to Uncle Shardas's cave!"

Laughing aloud, I helped Luka up behind me, and Tobin hopped up after him as though he'd been riding dragons all his life. Azarte took off, racing through the trees with his tongue hanging out the side of his long muzzle.

Feniul leaped into the sky, his great wings fanning out once he had cleared the treetops. I held on to the woven collar, my head thrown back, looking up at the early morning sky in delight. Behind me, I heard Luka swear by the Boiling Sea.

Seeing the brightness of the sun, now that we were

no longer in the shadow of the forest, sobered me. Feniul, dear, fearful Feniul, so paranoid about the human migration to the King's Seat, able to resist the pull of the slippers only because his phobia of being seen was so great, was now flying in broad daylight. We were on the very fringes of Rath Forest, where countless tinkers and bandits lived, and where travelers on the road would spot us if they only looked up. These were dire times indeed, for Feniul to risk such a thing.

The sun was rising high when we reached Shardas's hollow hill. Feniul landed and we slithered off his back and clambered down the grassy side of the hill to the entrance to the caves.

"So this is a dragon's cave," Luka mused as we stepped inside. "Not very tidy, was he?"

The floor of the first cavern was covered in mud, twigs, and leaves. There were loose scales and what looked like a broken sword. I almost couldn't believe that it was the same cavern.

"Shardas is very tidy," I informed Luka, looking around with concern. "He isn't responsible for this."

"I think that the human who has the slippers came here. With armed men," Feniul said, clicking his fangs together nervously. "They probably thought they would find gold."

"They didn't?" Luka looked surprised.

"Of course they didn't," I snapped, upset at the destruction of my friend's home. "Shardas doesn't collect gold. I told you: he likes glass."

Which made me very afraid to look in the next cavern.

"Oh, Shardas," I breathed, when I stepped through the doorway. Tears welled up in my eyes and spilled down my cheeks. "Oh, my dear Shardas, I am so sorry."

It wasn't one or two windows that had been broken, it was all of them. The floor was covered in literally thousands of pieces of brightly colored glass, chunks of wooden frames, and brittle segments of leading. Wires hung askew from the ceiling, the windows they had borne now lying in ruins beneath our feet. The mirrors that redirected the sunlight to shine through the windows had been smashed or knocked over so that the cavern was only dimly lit. A mercy, considering the terrible, sick waste that surrounded us.

The sheen of something that was not glass caught my eye and I turned to look at one of the broken frames. A scrap of ribbon had caught on the jagged wood. A scarlet ribbon of the finest silk.

"Amalia did this," I said with conviction, plucking the scrap of ribbon free and crumpling it in my hand. "And when I get my hands on her, I. Will. Make. Her. Pay." I pounded my fist into the opposite palm. It was worse than the way I had felt when Larkin admitted to giving my shoes to the princess. Seven hundred years of collecting beauty in the form of glass windows, and Shardas's treasure was destroyed in a matter of what? An hour?

"All right," Luka said. He seemed a little alarmed at my vehemence, but I could see by the stunned expression on his face that he understood some of what had been lost here.

Tobin reverently picked up a large piece of glass that still carried the delicately shaped face of a woman, and set it out of the way where it would not be stepped on. When he saw me watching him, he gave me a look of deep sympathy, and nodded.

"Show me the message, Feniul," I said, my voice coming out strangled.

"Over here, in the pool."

I went and stood beside him, looking down at our reflections in the still circle of water. At Feniul's instruction, I bent and touched my finger to the surface. The ripples that spread from my fingertip spread across the pool and then Shardas's face appeared.

"My dear Creel," he said.

"If you have received this, then some horrible fate has befallen me. I should have told you when you were here with me, or at least tried to make you leave those slippers behind. Your blue slippers are made from the hide of Velika, the last queen of the dragons. She befriended Milun the First, and he repaid her friendship by slaughtering her and using her skin to make those slippers. Through them Milun controlled my people, using them to fight his war and spreading the lie that she supported him freely—that all the dragons sided with him. My alchemist friend kept me safe from manipulation by use of his arts. When the turmoil was over and I had returned to my senses, I helped Jerontin sneak into the palace and take the slippers.

"I could not bear to destroy them—they were all we

had left of our beauteous queen—so I gave them to The-oradus, hoping to hide them in plain sight among his many shoes. Thus they came into your possession. I do not know how you lost them, I can only hope that you were not harmed.

"I have tried to re-create the charm Jerontin used to protect me, and have left it for Feniul. I trust that you will be able to make more, and I beg you to help free my people from this horror. May your gods pro-tect you."

"Feniul," I said, tears coursing down my cheeks. "I don't understand. Why couldn't he destroy the slippers, for all your sakes?"

"Ah." Feniul's tail whipped through the broken glass on the floor. "He . . . ah . . . took the betrayal of our queen very hard. His . . . allegiance to her was great and he was . . . quite grief-stricken." His agitated tail swept the shards against a wall, breaking them into smaller pieces.

"Oh." I swallowed, feeling guilty that Shardas thought the slippers had been taken from me by force, when really I had just been tricked by a spoiled princess and her spy. "And I don't see why he didn't wear the collar himself."

"In my message he said that he felt strong enough to resist the compulsion, that it was there but it only nagged in his head. He thought that it would be better if there were two of us free instead of just one," Feniul explained, distressed. "The messages were only in case

he couldn't fight it off. He was going to come to my cave
with the collar, but then I suppose *she* arrived before he
could. Up close, the strength of the slippers was too
much, I think."

"Oh." I stared at the pool, which now showed
only our two reflections once more. Dashing aside my
tears, I turned away. "Show me where you found the
collar," I said.

Feniul led us into the alchemist's cave. The shelves
had been rifled, jars broken or left unstoppered on the
long work table. But it didn't look like the work of the
intruders. It looked more like something done in haste,
as though jars had been dropped and there was no time
to clean up their contents. I thought of Shardas trying to
handle the delicate glass jars with his huge, slick claws,
and understood.

"It was up above the shelves," Feniul explained, "in
a crack in the rock. Dragons have very sharp eyes;
Shardas had written my name with the faintest bit of
charcoal. I saw it at once."

There was a square of parchment on which Shardas
had listed several herbs and scented waxes that were to be
smeared on the yarn or knotted into the weave of the collars. A few hanks of wool spilled out of a box on one of
the shelves, but it looked like barely enough to make one
more collar.

"Oh." I looked helplessly at the alchemist's formula,
my eyes still blurry. "There're instructions here for more
collars," I said to Luka and Tobin.

"What needs to be done?" Luka touched my elbow gently.

"We need to gather the things on this list, pack them up, and take them somewhere safe." I looked at the box of yarn. "We'll also need a lot more of this," I said, holding up a tangled skein.

Laying the list down on the table where we could all see it, I began sorting through the jars. Tobin found a box and Luka offered his tunic to cushion the jars so that they wouldn't break during transport. I gathered up the yarn that was left and tucked it around the jars as well, then we covered the box and started back through the caves to the main entrance.

"Feniul." I laid one hand on the dragon's foreclaw. "I know this is a very great favor, but it's very important that we get back to the King's Seat as fast as we can. Could you please fly us there? I need to start making more collars like yours, so that we can stop this war. Or at least help the dragons who are being forced to fight in it. Like Shardas."

Feniul hesitated, rocking from side to side for a moment, then he swung his head up and down. "All right. I'll do it."

"Thank you, Feniul."

"I have a family obligation to Shardas, you know," Feniul said.

"I know. And I know that he would do the same for you," I told him gently.

"If he could take us to the Duke of Mordrel's country

estate, instead," Luka said, after conferring with Tobin. "I think we would be safe there. Then, if it looks clear, could Feniul go to the King's Seat and bring back the duke and duchess?"

"Yes, I think that would be all right. Feniul?"

He nodded his great head, and we walked out of Shardas's cave with our box of alchemical oddments and a faint glimmer of hope.

Hope Strung on a Loom

"What makes you think the dragons are just going to bow their heads and let us collar them?" Luka put down the yarn he was coating with herb-infused beeswax and looked over at me.

It was a week later, and we were in the large sitting room at the back of the Mordrel country manor. It was a spacious room, beautifully decorated, but looking rather untidy at the moment. Bundles of herbs and cones of wax cluttered the small tables and skeins of yarn were draped over every available surface. A large table had been brought in to hold the duke's maps and the scouting reports that were still pouring in.

"Feniul's going to help us," I said.

I continued to work my belt loom. It was fastened to the back of a chair instead of my belt, though. It made it easier to work with. When it got too long, I would just scoot my stool back to maintain tension. Marta was sitting on a stool beside me, her loom fastened to the same chair.

"Er, no offense, Creel, but Feniul doesn't strike me as the most awe-inspiring member of his kind," Luka replied. "I know he means well, but is that going to be enough?"

"Probably not," I said placidly. "But there's little else we can do now, is there? Your father is in hiding, your brother is a hostage, and the King's Seat is besieged by mad dragons. We have to take the dragons away from Amalia so that the Roulaini are forced to fight fair. That means collaring as many as we can. But if you have any better ideas, I'd love to hear them."

"I can't believe you're talking to a prince like that," Alle, who was seated on my other side, hissed out of the corner of her mouth.

Looking up, I saw that Luka had heard her all the same. "Oh," I said in a light, disparaging tone, "he's just a younger son."

"Has anyone ever told you that you are covered in freckles?" Luka picked up a small ball of beeswax and lobbed it at me.

My hands full of yarn, I hunched my shoulders and let it bounce off one of them and onto the floor. It rolled under the table, and Marta bent down to retrieve it.

"Children, these things are very precious," the Duchess of Mordrel reprimanded us. "Please stop playing with them." She took the wax from Marta and frowned at it, then picked off a bit of lint it had collected on its way under the table.

"How, precisely, will your friend Feniul be helping us?" The duke spoke up from where he stood on the other side of the room, consulting with Tobin and Earl Sarryck, the Commander General of Feravel's army, about the war. They were marking positions of armies on an enormous map of Feravel and Roulain.

In the past week the situation had gotten more dire, if that was possible. The Roulaini army was on the march, Prince Miles was a hostage, and messengers were able to get only limited information to and from the hidden King Caxel. Most of the king's privy council were dead or hostages; the Duke of Mordrel, the Earl Sarryck, and Prince Luka were the only ones able to communicate freely with the army.

"Feniul and I have some thoughts," I said, feeling shy under the scrutiny of the earl. "One is to gather things that the dragons hoard. You know, wave around a—a shoe or what-have-you, until we get their attention and they try to get the object."

"And what if they simply burn you?" Luka was frowning at me, concern written large on his face.

"If they did, they'd destroy whatever it was we were offering them," I explained. "So they wouldn't do that. They'd have to come down and talk to us, or at least face us, and then we could get the collar on.

"Feniul also thinks that the others may *want* to be collared," I continued, "so that they don't have to feel the compulsion to fight anymore. It's demeaning for them, you know, and he thinks that if they are offered the chance of freedom, they'll take it. We just have to get their attention first."

"This is all hinging on a lot of ifs," Earl Sarryck grumbled. "Not to mention relying on the word of a monster."

"Feniul is not a monster," I retorted. "Your Lordship," I added after Marta nudged me.

As the men went back to their maps and plans, the duke exhaled with a sigh. "We just don't have enough soldiers to take back the King's Seat unless we surrender our border to Roulain." He grimaced. "Of course, now that Prilian is there leading the army in person, we don't have much of a border left."

"We need to get my father out of the caves and free Miles," Luka said. "There're over a hundred soldiers in the caves as well."

"We don't have the manpower, and the city is guarded by dragons," Mordrel said, ticking the points off on his fingers. "We need to get rid of those dragons, and Creel's plan is the best we have to offer." He gave me a slight smile, which I returned, and then he directed the earl's attention back to the map and the latest news from the border.

I concentrated on my own work. We had been weaving collars for days, and I was exhausted. After Feniul had brought us to the Mordrel estate, I had flown back to the King's Seat with him to help convince the others that he wasn't under Roulaini control. It had taken us five trips to pick up the duke and duchess, Ulfrid, Marta, Ulfrid's bar girls, Derda, and Alle. None of the trips was what you might consider restful. The Roulaini-manipulated dragons were patrolling the skies, and Feniul had gotten his tail toasted by none other than Theoradus, my old friend from the Carlieff hills.

It had been Ulfrid's idea to fetch Derda and Alle, and it proved to be very good advice. The waxed yarn was difficult to work with, and knotting the dried herbs into the pattern was, as Alle rather crudely put it, like trying to shove an egg back into a chicken.

The herbs were brittle, and if too much of them broke off, it ruined the charm. Or so the alchemist's notes indicated. I had finished one collar, and set it down on the table, when Alle accidentally knocked it to the floor and half of the rue crumbled to dust. I had to unravel the whole thing and start over with a new bundle of rue. I swore like a tinker until I saw that Alle was biting her lip to hold back tears. Chastened, I gave her a hug and admitted that it had not been her fault.

Despite this, tempers were short and all of us were vowing that we would never wear—let alone weave— another sash as long as we lived.

"There!" Marta smiled with triumph as she finished the collar she had been working on. With great delicacy she cut the collar free of the loom and laid it, loosely coiled, on a large sideboard. There were half a dozen other collars already there, all waiting to be wrapped around the necks of dragons and fastened with a knot of scarlet silk.

With much less fanfare, Derda also rose to her feet, cut loose the collar she had been working on, and put it on the sideboard. She picked up some skeins of yarn from the table, and a bundle of herbs. The yarn was silk, from her own backroom. The stout dressmaker appeared aged by the shock of the dragon attack. She was no longer brusque and blustering, but quiet and prone to starting at any noise. Her plump cheeks sagged, and she barely ate. Ulfrid sat up with her at night, offering tea and her particular type of comforting silence.

"Creel, are you ever going to be done with that one?" Marta plopped down on the stool next to mine with an armload of yarn and began stringing her loom for another collar.

Feeling guilty, I looked down at my work. Marta had caught me unraveling the last handspan I had woven. There had been a flaw in it, and I wanted to correct it.

"We don't have time to make them perfect," the duchess pointed out. Alle and Marta were teaching her to weave so that she could help us, and the one collar she had finished so far was what we politely called "a good effort."

"Look at Feniul's," Marta agreed.

"I know," I mumbled. "But I was thinking of using this one for Shardas."

"Oh." Marta let the matter drop, and so did the others.

I had been trying to capture the color-block style of stained glass on the narrow collar, and it wasn't going very well. But even if it was for his own good, the thought of collaring Shardas like a dog made the bile rise in my throat. I was salving my conscience by trying to make his collar as beautiful as possible. I hoped that it would work. For both of us.

"How many dragons have been reported?" It was the earl again, pulling at his lower lip while they studied the map.

"At least a dozen," the duke said.

Tobin made some signs with his hands at me, but I still couldn't get the hang of the gesture-language that he used.

"He says that there's only one gold dragon, and that it is your friend," Marta whispered in my ear.

"How do you know what's he's saying?" I looked over at her, surprised.

She flushed deeply. "I . . . have a cousin who is deaf. Tobin uses similar signs." She blushed even darker and went back to work.

"It's all very well for you to make a special collar for your friend, dear," the duchess said. "But we shall need five more collars as soon as possible, and you are the best weaver here." She gave me a kind smile. "Perhaps you could hurry just a little?"

"You'll need to hurry a lot," Earl Sarryck said, coming away from the table to frown at us. "We've been gathering things from that list the dragon provided. We want to try collaring the dragons around the King's Seat right away. If it doesn't work, we need to know so that we can mount a better defense." He shook his head. "We had no idea that their army was so large, and I'm getting reports that dragons are raiding cities as far north as Carlieff."

I went pale at this, thinking of Hagen and my relatives. "Carlieff?"

The earl nodded, grim. "And it's still not certain if the Roulaini are holding Prince Milun for negotiation, or if they're going to execute him."

"They won't hurt the crown prince," the duke argued.

The earl snorted. "Even if they're trying to eliminate the royal family so that they can annex Feravel?"

"That seems a bit extreme, don't you think?" The duchess gave the earl a severe look.

"Half of the King's Seat and nearly all of the court are in line for the throne, one way or another," Luka put in. "There are dozens upon dozens of us. They'd have to—"

"Burn the King's Seat to the ground?" Earl Sarryck's voice dripped acid. "I believe they've already gotten a good start on that, your Highness."

Silence greeted this remark. The earl, no matter how unpleasant, was right. The King's Seat lay in ruins, the king was in hiding, and the roads were flooded with soot-covered people fleeing the city. Things were desperate, and this plan of ours was risky in the extreme.

Bending my head over my work, I began to weave for all I was worth, carefully working the herbs into the silk and telling myself sternly that the pattern didn't matter. It was hard to keep myself from continuing the pattern I had already begun; my fingers had fallen into a rhythm. So rather than turning my energy to breaking the pattern, I forced myself to ignore it if my fingers fumbled and I knotted a thread three times instead of twice, or slipped a stitch. Shardas would understand if his collar was not perfect, I told myself.

At least, he would understand once I had the collar on him. Assuming I *could* get the collar on him, and that it had been made correctly. Sweat slid down my back as I thought of what would happen to Shardas if it didn't work.

And what would happen to me, if I were standing nose to nose with a dragon controlled by Amalia.

As though reading my thoughts, which both he and Marta had the disconcerting habit of doing, Luka came to my side and crouched down. "Creel, don't worry. It will work. And you will help Shardas put his cave back in order. I promise." He laid one hand on top of both of mine, stilling my frantic movements.

"But if it doesn't?" Tears pricked my eyes and my nose started to run, much to my embarrassment.

"It will," Marta said firmly, and passed me her handkerchief. It was snowy white and embroidered with roses.

As lovely as it was, I used it to blow my nose, then gave them both tremulous smiles. I would make it work. For Shardas's sake.

Collaring Dragons

Here I was, being sacrificed to a dragon yet again. My aunt would be thrilled. Well, perhaps not. She *would* be thrilled, though, to know that I was guarded by a prince, a duke, an earl, and two dozen strapping soldiers. She would pack her things and move to the King's Seat right away, in order to help negotiate wedding plans with any one of them.

That was assuming, of course, that I survived the next hour.

I was standing in a field a league or so east of the King's Seat, with a pile of ancient scrolls and hand-illuminated books around my feet. Hanging over my left shoulder was a wide, stiff length of waxed silk woven with herbs that made my nose tingle. My guards and the assorted nobles were all carefully concealed beneath loosely piled hay or overturned wagons, leaving me to the fate I had volunteered for. I had experience with dragons, I had argued when Earl Sarryck tried to put one of his soldiers in my place. I didn't flinch when a dragon approached me, and I was less threatening than a soldier.

Plumes of smoke rose here and there from the King's Seat, but it was gray smoke, which signaled cooking fires. Half the New Palace was gone, but the other half still stood, ragged and proud and stained with smoke. The duke's scouts said that the intact parts of the palace were occupied by the Roulaini ministers, already settling into their new apartments, despite the rubble and the dragons circling overhead.

"Cheeky mugs," the duke had said upon receiving this news.

"Here, dragon-dragon-dragon," I said to myself now, thinking of how my mother used to call our barn cat to the kitchen door for scraps.

I prayed to the Triunity that my mother was so busy enjoying paradise she couldn't see me standing here, waiting to try to fasten a collar around the neck of a fire-breathing beast the size of our old house.

"Here they come," one of the hidden soldiers called out.

The sweat slicking my forehead and back turned cold and then froze, and I started to shake. Looking up into the brittle blue sky, I could see two forms swooping toward me like very large eagles, or the black omen-clouds that were said to have descended upon the god Caxon and his lover, shortly before she was slain by—

No, don't think of that, I told myself firmly. Just think about the here and now.

"You mean the dragons swooping down on my head?" I said aloud, my voice rising with panic.

"Beg pardon, mistress?" I thought I saw a man raise his head from behind a nearby hay bale.

"Nothing," I shouted back, over the sound of flapping dragon wings.

And then the dragons landed: first Feniul, who had led the other here, then our prey.

It was Amacarin, Theoradus's friend whom I had spoken with in the enchanted pool back in the hills above Carlieff Town those long months ago. Feniul had told us that Amacarin was rather small for a dragon, and might be an easy catch to try first. He collected old books and scrolls of poetry, and so the Duke of Mordrel had been persuaded to loan us a portion of his own treasured collection.

The duke had looked nearly as blue-gray as Amacarin at the thought that the priceless manuscripts might be burned to ash by the dragon, should things go badly. I felt much the same, thinking about what would happen to me in that situation.

Feniul and Amacarin had landed, one on each side of me and my hoard of books. Feniul had his wings neatly folded and was looking calm—eerily calm, in fact, considering that Feniul was usually dithering and fidgeting about *something*. Amacarin's head moved sharply as he tried to read the spines of the books, watch me, and keep a lookout for danger at the same time. It was reassuring to see that he *was* smaller than Feniul, though still the size of a small cottage.

"Greetings, Dragon Amacarin," I said politely. "You probably don't remember me—"

"By the First Fires! It's that human maid of Theoradus's!" Amacarin reared back his head, gazing down at me with loathing. "Do you have any idea of the trouble you have caused? I'm being forced—*forced*—to do the bidding of some irritating human maid. And why? Because you tricked those slippers away from Theoradus!" He snorted a gust of steam at me, but I stepped out of the way. "And now, in the capricious and foolish way of your kind, you have just given them away, causing no end of suffering to my people. And yours as well, might I point out!" Amacarin fanned dust at me with his wings to underline his displeasure.

Coughing, I shook my head to clear away the grit and thought fast. Flattery and offering him the books seemed senseless now. He knew who I was, he knew what was going on, it made better sense to just be honest.

"Amacarin, put this collar on," I said, taking the charm off my shoulder and holding it out to him. "It will make you immune to the slippers. You won't have to fight anymore; you can go home to your cave and read poetry."

"Do you really think that I'm going to listen to you?" Amacarin's voice was quite rude. He reached for the manuscripts with his foreclaws. "These are very nice, and you don't deserve them. I shall take them."

Feniul's foreclaws scratched the ground. "No, no! You must put the collar on!" He looked helplessly at me.

"I'll do nothing of the sort. I'll take these and—"

"And what?" Luka had left his concealment and now strolled up to stand beside me, making Amacarin lash his tail in surprise and fear. I had been startled myself, but covered the "eeping" sound I made with a cough. "You'll take the manuscripts and go back to the King's Seat? And there you'll wait for the next time Princess Amalia commands you to go out and burn something, or chase someone, until eventually you get fired on with a hail of arrows and plummet to your death?"

"That's a rather vivid picture," I said out of the corner of my mouth. I thought I saw him wink, just barely.

"It's really none of your business, human, what I do," Amacarin said. He swung his head back and forth, sniffing the air. "How many of you are there here?" he hissed.

"Enough to riddle your soft underbelly with arrows before you can blink," Luka said in a conversational tone. "Now put on the collar."

"No, I must get back." Amacarin spread his wings. "She is wondering where I am, I can feel it. I must get back." His eyes were wide and the swinging motion of his head now looked mechanical and unnatural. "I must get back."

"Creel," Luka whispered. "Do it now."

Everything I had felt standing outside Theoradus's cave with Hagen whispering in my ear came back to me. My trembling knees locked, my breath whooshed out of my body, and the sweat thawed and began to pour from my brow and back once more. I made a small whimpering sound from between stiff lips.

"Creel! Do it now!" Luka poked me in the ribs.

Amacarin cupped his wings, preparing to take flight. His eyes looked glazed, and his head was still moving in that stiff way.

I lunged just as he jumped into the air. The collar slapped around his neck; I grabbed the dangling end as it came swinging underneath his throat, and clung to the trailing scarlet cords as he flew off with me hanging down his chest like a pendant.

It's no easy thing to tie two pieces of cord together when you're hanging from them. Particularly if you are sweating, and the cords are made of silk. I could feel myself slipping, and knew that I hadn't a chance in this life or the next to tie a knot. But I had a sudden blaze of inspiration: did the collar have to be knotted, or simply closed?

With my eyes squeezed shut and a prayer to all three gods on my lips, I kicked out with my legs, hitting Amacarin squarely in the chest. The force of the kick caused me to swing wildly, and I twisted my body as I went.

As I spun around to face away from the dragon, the cords I was holding twisted together, closing the collar into a loop. Amacarin gave a great shudder and we began to plummet downward. I couldn't help myself, I screamed for all I was worth, even after I felt my feet hit the ground with a painful jarring.

It wasn't until a huge hand clapped over my mouth

and an arm like a band of iron encircled my waist that I stopped screaming. My eyes were still closed, but I went limp and let whoever it was half-carry me away from Amacarin. When the hand moved away from my mouth I opened my eyes and saw Tobin looking down at me with concern. I gave him a faint smile.

Then I leaned over and threw up.

One hard hand patted my back while another held my braid out of the way. When I felt better, Tobin offered me a large handkerchief. It seemed that I was always accepting other people's handkerchiefs these days.

"That was amazing!" Luka came running over. "Are you all right?"

"I can't do that again," I said, my voice shaking and my eyes watering.

"That's all right; we can take care of the rest. Now that the men have seen a freckled slip of a girl do it, I think they'll manage the others," he told me. "You were incredibly brave. I don't think many men would have had the courage to do that."

"That wasn't courage, that was blind fear and stupidity," I said. Then my knees buckled and I collapsed to the ground, Tobin's handkerchief still clutched to my mouth. The soldiers had burst from concealment and were cheering and chanting my name, making Amacarin lash his tail nervously.

"Whatever it was, it worked," the duke said, coming over to join us. "You are a wonder, Mistress Creel. Do you think you can pull off that stunt a few more times?"

"What?"

"I have just been speaking with these two dragons," the duke said. Then he gave a small laugh, shaking his head in disbelief. "I never thought I'd say *that*, did I?"

I would have laughed, but I was too busy shaking.

The duke must have sensed that the rest of us were not as amused. He sobered, and glanced back over his shoulder at the dragons.

"The dragons have agreed that you are the best choice to collar their kind. They would like you to keep doing it."

"No, no, no!" I shook my head, putting my hands over my ears. "I am never doing that again."

"I think you should feel flattered," Luka said, trying to jolly me out of my terror. "It's not every young lass who has a pair of dragons admiring her."

"They can bloody well admire you and Tobin. I am not doing that again."

"My dear girl, we do need you." The duke squatted down beside me. "You have more experience with drag-ons than anyone else living. With the possible exception of Princess Amalia," he amended. "What you did was heroic and dangerous, and we need you to do it just a few more times."

"I could have died!"

The duke put a hand on my arm, his face grave. "Creel, I hate to manipulate you in this way, but I'm afraid I must."

I stared at him, dreading what I knew he was going to say next.

"You were there with me in the Winter Palace. So many people died, and have died since, because of the attacks. We must stop them, or even more will die. We desperately need your help."

I sighed so deeply that when I exhaled I blew Tobin's handkerchief out of my hand. It caught on the crushed wheat beside me, and I fixed my eyes on it. I thought about the dragons. About Shardas. Did I really want anyone else trying to put a collar on my friend? Could I really walk away from all this, knowing that innocent people were dying in the fires of dragons? The dragons themselves were besieged—forced against their will to become the fiercest, most ruthless warriors in the Roulaini army. Could I turn my back on my country, and let Amalia and her father take control?

I sighed again. "Bring out those tapestries," I said. "Tell Amacarin and Feniul to look for a large dark green female. She's the one who likes tapestries."

"Thank you," the duke said sincerely. He stroked my hair in a gentle, fatherly way and then stood up, groaning as his knees creaked, and walked over to the dragons.

"Don't worry," Luka said with a grin. "By our last count, there're only eleven more."

Shardas

After Amacarin, I thought that surely things would get easier. After all, we had two dragons on our side now, and some experience. We knew the collars worked, we knew that luring them with the things they collected worked. Simple, right?

Perhaps it had occurred to some of the others, and they just didn't want to worry me. I'm quite embarrassed to say that it failed to cross my mind: but it would be rather difficult not to notice if a dragon suddenly went missing, wouldn't it?

The large green female, whose name was Niva, landed beside me not a quarter of an hour after Amacarin had been sent to get her. He had told her that someone fleeing the King's Seat had dropped an heirloom tapestry in a field and she, being released from duty for the moment, had come to see. Much shrewder than Amacarin, she bartered with me for the tapestry.

"But don't you want to be free of the Roulaini?" I clasped my hands and gave her a pleading look.

"Of course I do," she retorted. "But how do I know that being under your power will be any better?"

"But you won't be under my power," I protested. "You just won't be controlled by the Roulaini. The collars block the pull of the slippers, nothing more."

"So *you* say," Niva said. "But how do I know for certain?"

"You make a very good point," I said, after a moment's thought. "So, if it will put your mind at ease, you may take one of these tapestries." I indicated the three gorgeous wall-hangings spread out around me. "They belong to the Duke of Mordrel, but I'm sure he can spare one for your fine collection."

"How do you know it's fine? You've never seen it." She eyed me sharply. "Have you?"

"No, but Feniul told me of it, and described how beautiful it was."

"I doubt that." She snorted smoke. "Feniul's as colorblind as his dogs, and cares for little else. I'm amazed that he even noticed what I collect."

"All right, I was only assuming that it would be a magnificent collection," I admitted. "It's just that I've seen two—well, three—dragon's hoards, and they've all been very impressive in their own way."

"And who has been letting a human maid peek at their hoard?"

"Theoradus of Carlieff, which started this whole

mess," I told her. "He let me take the dragonskin slippers made by Milun the First."

She shuddered. "That fool! Theoradus never should have been entrusted with a power as great as those slippers!" She clawed the ground angrily. "Shardas should have destroyed them. It was his responsibility. What was he thinking? Madness!"

"Shardas? Why should it be *Shardas's* responsibility?"

Again the sharp look. "How do you know Shardas?"

"He saved my life. He's my friend. These collars were his idea. I've seen his hoard, it's the most gorgeous thing I've ever seen," I found myself babbling. "Look," I spread out my skirt. "I used his windows as a pattern for my gown." I was wearing a green gown salvaged from Derda's shop. The embroidery was only half-finished, but I doubted the young countess who had paid for it would ever know, if she was even still alive after the attacks on the city.

"So Shardas is behind the collars, eh?" She stretched her wings, then refolded them neatly. "Well then. I'll take all three of those tapestries, and in return you can collar me. I'm starting to feel the pull from that whinging human brat again. Then take me to see Shardas, I want to know his plans."

Picking up the collar at my feet and moving to toss it over her neck, I shook my head. "I'm sorry, but we haven't collared Shardas yet."

"What?" She drew back. "Then how did you get these? I thought you said that this was Shardas's idea?"

"Shardas gave his only collar to me," Feniul said, arching his neck forward to show her. "So that I could be his messenger. He thought he would be strong enough to resist, but alas. . . ." Feniul shook his head.

"He had a friend who was an alchemist," I said, "four centuries or so ago, who developed the spell. He left a message and instructions for me, so that I could help Feniul."

"I see." Niva stretched out her neck again. "Collar me quick, and then I'll help you locate Shardas. I saw him attack the King's Seat at the first, but I haven't seen him since. That's why I assumed he was working with you."

I tossed the collar over her neck and knotted the dangling cords firmly under her chin. When the ends were joined, her scales rippled and she fanned and folded her wings again.

"That feels marvelous! You should have just sent Feniul or Amacarin to tell me that Shardas had provided a way to fight the power of the slippers."

"Is Shardas a friend of yours?" I asked as Luka and the duke approached to introduce themselves.

"I would hardly presume," Niva said in a formal voice.

This made me shake my head in confusion. Why did this dragon regard Shardas with such reverence? "I'm sorry, I don't quite understand what you're talking about." Something she had said a moment ago struck me. "Why is it that Shardas is the one who should have destroyed the slippers? Why not Theoradus? Or any of the rest of you?"

Niva snorted loudly, setting a small clump of wheat on fire. Luka was quick to stamp it out. "Because Shardas the Gold is our king," the dragon said deliberately, watching me closely to gauge my reaction. "Velika Azure-Wing was his mate. As our king it was his duty to dispose of those awful slippers."

The world began to spin around me. Shardas was the king of the dragons. I had been wearing shoes made from the skin of Shardas's mate. *I had lived with the king of the dragons, eaten peaches with him, ridden on his back, and waved those accursed slippers right under his nose!*

I thought I might be sick again.

"Creel? What's wrong?" Luka came over and touched my shoulder, concerned.

But I didn't take my eyes off Niva. "We have to help him. We have to get him free of *her*," I said vehemently.

"I haven't seen him since he was first sent to destroy that palace," she said. "But I will find him. Feniul and Amacarin can help me. Do you have one of these"—she gestured to her collar with a foreclaw—"for Shardas?"

I nodded and bowed my head. It would be even harder to collar Shardas now, knowing that he was a king.

"Creel made a very beautiful collar just for Shardas," Luka said softly.

Niva lowered her head and looked at him. "Are you the younger prince?" she asked.

"Yes. Prince Luka of Feravel at your service . . . Madam." He bowed to the dragon.

I squinted toward the King's Seat. "Were we expect-ing another dragon?"

"No!" Luka turned and began to shout to the men. "Take cover, take cover!"

Niva swiveled her head around and looked up at the approaching dragon. "It's Shardas." Her voice was flat. "You can see the gold of his scales in the sun."

"And someone's riding on him," I said, shading my eyes with one hand. Rage bubbled up in me. I knew pre-cisely who it was. "May I?" I took hold of Niva's collar and raised my foot, ready to climb up onto her back.

"Please," she said, leaning down to make it easier for me. "Are we fleeing, or facing them?"

"Facing, I think." I was now an expert at riding drag-ons and had myself comfortably seated between two neck ridges, with my skirts spread around me, before Luka or the duke even noticed what I was doing.

"Creel, come down from there! Take cover!" Luka was pointing at an overturned wagon, as though that would protect anyone from dragonfire. It wouldn't even withstand regular fire, for Jylla's sake!

"You take cover, I want to talk to Amalia," I retorted.

"I'm coming with you!" He started to reach for the collar as well.

"My prince, it's too dangerous! We cannot risk you!" The duke took hold of one of Luka's arms, and Tobin took the other. "I'll go instead," the duke said as he reached for the collar.

Luka fumed for a second but then turned away,

shaking off Tobin's restraining hands. He slunk toward the cart with anger visible in every line of his tense shoulders and taut spine.

"It's very rude to mount a dragon without permission," Niva said in frosty tones, moving out of the duke's reach. "You may ask Feniul or Amacarin, if you like." And then she sprang into the air.

Hanging on for dear life, I looked back down to see the stunned duke running to Feniul and gesticulating. I couldn't blame Niva for being curt with him, she had been through a great deal in the last few days, and disliked being treated as a mindless animal.

On the other hand, the duke was kind, and it was just that he was accustomed to having his way. And we humans had all been through a great deal, too.

There was no further time to think about it, though. Straight ahead of us, his scales gleaming golden in the summer sun, was Shardas. A rider in scarlet sat on his back, her hair streaming in the wind created by the dragon's flight. Niva curved right, Shardas left, and they were gliding in circles, nose to tail. There was no sign of recognition, or even intelligence, in Shardas's eyes.

"What are you doing with my dragons, you ugly country cow?" Amalia had to shout to be heard. "They all belong to me!"

"They aren't *your* dragons, you spoiled brat," I retorted.

"They are now." She raised the hem of her scarlet skirt (the one that Marta and Alle had worked on, with the scarlet ribbons I had found on my first day at Derda's). The blue slippers almost glowed in the sun, a beautiful contrast to Shardas's scales. A tide of rage washed over me, leaving me shaking.

She dug her heels into the sides of Shardas's neck, as though he were a horse. "Shardas, burn them!"

"Shardas, I shall fight back if I must," Niva warned.

"If you must," Shardas said. His voice was thick and slow, not at all like the warm, rumbling tones I had grown to love.

"I did not give you permission to speak," Amalia shrilled. Then she pointed a finger at Niva. "And I didn't give you permission to leave! Shardas, I said to burn them!"

Niva's wings snapped wide and she hurtled upward, with me clinging like a burr to her collar. Looking back, I saw a sluggish tongue of fire curl through the air where we had been. We could no longer hear Amalia, but she was waving her arms and clearly shrieking like a mad thing. Below them, approaching with great caution, was Feniul with the Duke of Mordrel on his back.

Another, more spirited burst of flame came from Shardas, narrowly missing Feniul, who swerved just in time. As it was, the tip of his wing had been singed. He spiraled slowly to the ground.

"What should we do?" My question was lost in the wind as Niva circled high above.

Shardas dove after Feniul, and a gout of flame tore across the ground, scattering the men, who appeared no bigger than ants, and causing the hay bales and wagons that had concealed them to explode.

Dragonfire is very potent, and very quick. In a matter of minutes, it seemed the entire field was ablaze. The men who had managed to escape were mounting their horses and galloping for their lives. Feniul and Amacarin had flown for the cover of the forest, and Shardas was now making slow circles over the destruction.

"Shardas!" Niva's voice roared out, making my legs tremble where they clasped her neck. "Fight her! Fight the pull of the slippers! Think of Velika, think of this human! Fight it!"

Shardas turned and headed straight for us. I saw his mouth open wide, and forced myself not to put my arms in front of my face or close my eyes. "O Regunin, Caxon, Jylla," I prayed, "protect us. Protect Shardas from the slippers. Please."

Fire roared from Shardas's mouth, blue and gold and scarlet flames. I could feel the heat even from a distance, and my sweat-slick hands nearly lost their grip on the collar as Niva dove to avoid the flames. I kept my eyes open, my gaze fixed on Shardas.

Then, at the very last second, Shardas raised his head. It wasn't much, but it would have been enough to direct the flame safely over my head, even if Niva had not made her move.

"Thank you, Regunin, Caxon, Jylla," I breathed.

With Amalia still astride his neck, ranting and waving her arms, Shardas was now flying back to the King's

Seat. Niva swooped over the ruined field to the small wood where we had seen Feniul and the others take cover.

"Thank you, Shardas," I said as we landed, and Luka ran out to meet us.

The New Palace by Night

Luka and the Duke of Mordrel had both escaped, but many of their men had not. After we had gathered anyone who was left to gather we returned to the duke's country estate. I rode Niva, and Feniul and Amacarin flew back and forth, watching for Roulaini-controlled dragons.

"There's no help for it," Earl Sarryck said when we were once more ensconced in the sitting room with the maps and stacks of herbs and yarn. "We will have to destroy the remainder of the beasts. Particularly this gold-colored one."

A horrified gasp came from Marta, who gave me a quick look of sympathy and reached out to pat my hand. I shook her off and rose to my feet. I wasn't shocked, I was even more filled with rage than I had been at seeing Amalia riding Shardas.

"They are not beasts," I said in a carefully controlled

voice. "They are not rabid dogs or lame horses, and it is not for you to decide that they must be slaughtered." I folded my arms and glared at the startled earl. "And furthermore, I'd like to see you try."

"What's that?"

"I'd like to see you bring down one dragon, let alone ten," I clarified. "Their scales deflect arrows, they can breathe fire, and they can fly. How, precisely, were you planning to destroy them?"

"The same way Milun the First did," the earl said grimly. "Ambush. Spears, archers, swords to finish the job."

A brittle laugh burst from my lips. "Yes, let's all follow Milun's example: butchering a thinking, feeling creature who called him friend, using her hide for his own purposes, and lying about it to cover his perfidy. Gave him the slippers out of friendship, indeed!"

"King Milun did what needed to be done—"

"King Milun was a—" I began, but Luka interrupted before I could say anything shocking.

"Some of these dragons are our allies," he said, putting his arm around me. "Creel is right: we should be working *with* them, not executing them for actions they cannot control."

"That gold dragon destroyed a field and killed twenty men as well!" The earl pounded his fist on the table, sending a map slithering onto the floor. "I believe that could be considered a crime in this country."

"He was being controlled by Amalia," I protested.

With an effort, Sarryck reined in his temper. "Our border is completely open now, patrolled by Roulaini soldiers. Prilian is leading his army straight to the King's Seat, with dragons flying overhead to prevent any attack we might stage. We don't have time to win the creatures over to our side, one by one. We need to eliminate them, and concentrate on moving our men into position around the King's Seat."

"But with the dragons working for us," I protested, "we'll have the extra edge over the Roulaini."

"Three will have to be sufficient," the earl countered. "Because unless you can think of a way to get every dragon out of Amalia's control by tomorrow, young woman, I can see no alternative." His face softened. "Maybe it isn't the fault of the dragons, as you say, but they're dangerous all the same. A danger we cannot afford to have loose." He picked up the latest reports from the scouts and shuffled them into a pile. "I'm giving my remaining men the extermination order." He strode out of the room.

In my head, wheels were turning. My thoughts and feelings churned and tumbled over each other. There had to be a way to free the dragons en masse. Amalia commanded any dragon within at least two hundred leagues, thanks to those wretched slippers.

"Luka," I said, my eyes fixed on a diagram of the New Palace that lay on the table. "How long will it take the earl to organize his men?"

Luka looked to Tobin, who held up his thumb.

"They're standing ready, but it's dark now, so they won't be able to move out until tomorrow morning. Dawn probably."

"Good." I got to my feet, shaking out my crumpled and now rather stained and ragged skirt. "I'm going after the slippers myself. By the time he's organized his ambushes, I'll have them back on *my* feet and our problems will be solved."

The duke raised his eyebrows. "And how do you propose to do that?"

"Easily," I said, hoping that my voice wouldn't tremble. "I'm going to have Feniul fly me to the palace, and then I'm going to find Amalia, punch her nose, and take them back. Niva and Amacarin are collared, Prilian has, what, three dragons with him? That means five fewer dragons guarding the palace." I tried to snap my fingers, but they were shaking too badly. I would not let Shardas and the others be "exterminated," even if I died on this fool's errand.

"I'm coming with you," Luka said.

"Absolutely not." The duke stood up and put his hands on his hips. "Neither of you is going anywhere tonight. I will not allow a royal prince to endanger himself in this way, Luka. And Creel." He turned to me. "You're an intelligent young woman: think! What chance do you really have at succeeding? Even if Feniul can get you to the palace without a hostile dragon seeing you, how will you find Amalia? I've no doubt she's heavily guarded. How will you get the slippers and escape?"

Luka sagged back in his chair, glum, but I didn't waver. "I would rather die tonight trying to help my friends, then stand by tomorrow as every one of Sarryck's bowmen opens fire on them. Besides, as the earl himself keeps saying: we can't afford to spare any more men. How many of the archers will die tomorrow, trying to kill the dragons? Their arrows will be little better than kindling."

Now it was the duke's turn to sag. "I know. And Sarryck knows. But we don't have any experience with this: last time we fought the Roulaini, the dragons were on our side."

"Let me go," I said levelly. "Feniul knows me. He'll listen to my orders, he'll protect me. And, just like the Roulaini sending Amalia in as their spy, who would suspect that you would send a young girl to steal the slippers?"

The duke stared moodily at the fireplace for a long time.

"You'll have to lock me up to stop me, you know," I said a few minutes later.

"I know." He ran his fingers through his graying hair. "Just . . . try to be careful."

"I will." Impulsively I stood on tiptoe and kissed his cheek. "Don't worry."

He snorted at that. "At least Prince Luka has some sense," he said, indicating the morose prince, slumped in the chair beside us. Luka grunted.

I went to ask Feniul, who was somewhere in the

gardens with the other dragons. I had just stepped onto the gravel path that led to the herb garden when Luka came out of the manor behind me and grabbed my arm.

"I'm going with you," he said, his voice low and tense. His free hand gripped the hilt of his sword.

"Fine," I said, hiding my relief at not having to go it alone. "Just don't get in my way."

We found Feniul in the duchess's herb garden, trying not to trample anything. I told him what I wanted, and he dithered.

"You are Shardas's cousin," I reminded him. "You have an obligation to him."

"All right." He sighed reluctantly.

"All you have to do is drop me on the roof of the palace. You can fly back here, and I'll climb down into a window. Your part will be easy."

Feniul gave another sigh and stopped beating the lavender plants with his tail. He bent down for me to mount.

I climbed up Feniul's shoulder and took my place between his neck ridges, just behind the collar. Unfortunate though it was that they were even necessary, I found the collars to be very handy for dragon riding. Luka asked Feniul's permission to come along, but Niva stepped forward and offered to let him ride.

"I have business to conduct in the King's Seat," she said, and neither of us dared to ask what it was. Luka scrambled onto her back, and I gave Feniul a pat on the neck.

"Go, Feniul!"

We flew to the King's Seat at a faster speed than I had ever gone before. I had to keep my eyes shut for some of the trip, and was heartily glad that I had been too upset to eat supper. It certainly made me swallow my earlier delusions concerning my dragon-riding abilities. I came to realize that on my previous rides the dragons had been going slow to spare my delicate constitution. But Niva had no time or patience for human weakness. She set the pace, and Feniul struggled to keep up with the larger dragon, with me clinging to his back like a nauseated burr.

When we approached the King's Seat, things looked even worse than they had before. Much of the city was on fire, and a number of the manors surrounding the palace had been reduced to rubble as well. Several of the larger houses that still stood had lights in their windows, and the wind carried the sound of men shouting drinking songs. The earl's scouts had reported that more regiments of Roulaini soldiers had arrived in the past few days, but I don't think even he realized how many there were. I counted at least five mansions that had been turned into barracks.

By tugging on Feniul's collar and pointing broadly, I managed to direct both dragons to land on the top of a chapel. It was the same flat-roofed building with the squat steeples where Shardas and I had enjoyed a midnight talk weeks ago. I slithered off Feniul's back, and Luka joined me.

"What now?" He looked at the sky nervously, but there was no sign of a dragon patrol.

"We can't land on the roof, like I planned," I said. "There are far more soldiers than I counted on. Luka, you know the palace best. How do we get inside, and find Amalia, without being caught?"

He blew his breath out, stirring my hair. "That could be a problem. I was hoping that you had a better plan."

"No, I was too upset to think of an alternative."

"Well, all my family's apartments have broad balconies. If Niva and Feniul could drop us onto a balcony, our best bet would be to sneak through the family quarters and make our way to the council rooms. I don't think there was a light in Miles's rooms. . . ." He scanned the skies again.

"But what if we run into Shardas, or one of the others?" Feniul dipped his head and spoke in the dragon version of a whisper, which nevertheless vibrated my back teeth. "We'll have to fly straight across the square. Anyone, human or dragon, might see us."

"True," I agreed. "What if they dropped us at the far end of the gardens, and we snuck in ourselves? Through a kitchen door or some such place?"

"The palace is crawling with Roulaini soldiers. They'd catch us long before we got within a hundred yards of Amalia," Luka predicted, shaking his head. "First we'd have to get across the gardens, then into the palace, and then through the halls. Not possible."

"Back to the balcony then?" I twisted my fingers nervously in my sash.

"I don't like it," Feniul said.

"Neither do I, but there isn't another option," Niva

put in. "I'll take them both myself: one dragon is far less conspicuous than two. I'll fly in, drop you on a balcony, and fly away as fast as I can. You'll be on your own once you dismount," she warned.

"Understood," Luka said, his voice tense.

"But what about me?" Feniul sounded close to tears. "What if something happens to you? I promised Shardas that I would keep you safe."

I put a hand on his muzzle. "Dear Feniul, you have kept me safe and been braver than I could have imagined. Thank you for that. I know Shardas will be proud when he hears about all you've done. But for now, I need you to go back to the Mordrel estate. Keep an eye on things there, and follow the duke's orders. All right?"

His tail swept around and curled briefly around my legs, wrapping me from ankle to hip, and then uncurled. "All right," he said finally.

"Good man . . . er, dragon," Luka said.

I patted Feniul's nose and then stepped aside. With a final bob of his head and lash of his tail, he leaped into the sky and glided away.

Niva shook her head. "He is rather strange," she said.

"He has a good heart."

"True."

And with that, Luka and I mounted the green female dragon. In silence she took off from the roof of the chapel, and in silence she flew to the New Palace. She checked her speed when the dark form of another dragon flapped between two of the chimneys that still stood. But the patrolling dragon continued on, and Niva soared in the opposite direction, to where a stone balcony jutted out above the rose gardens.

Luka leaned close over her neck. "That's Miles's bedchamber," he whispered loudly.

Niva's head dipped, and she maneuvered until she was just above it. Without stopping to think, I slithered off her back and dropped to the stone floor, Luka a heart-beat behind. Niva wheeled in the air and flapped away, leaving us alone and exposed in the moonlight.

Luka drew his sword and I pulled Marta's dagger out of my sash. We exchanged a look, and then he pushed open the glass doors and we stepped into the crown prince's bedchamber.

A Visit to the Kitchens

I'm not sure who was more startled: Luka and I, or Larkin. Luka swore and I took a step back, but Larkin dropped the gown she was mending and shrieked. That gave Luka just enough time to stride across the room and clap a hand to her mouth.

No one came to answer her shriek. I peeked into the adjoining dressing room. It was knee-deep in shoes and cast-off gowns—Amalia had clearly taken over—but there was no sign of her or anyone else. The only light in the entire apartment came from a trio of candles on the table near Larkin. I turned my attention back to the traitor.

"Larkin!" I wanted to shake her until her teeth rattled. The duchess had been right: she had come to work for her precious Roulaini princess. "How can you sit there and mend *her* clothes! Do you realize what she's done—what you've done?" I waved a hand at the balcony doors, although the pretty view of the gardens outside belied what was happening in the city all around us.

Larkin just gave me a defiant look over Luka's hand. I took a step toward her, but Luka warned me away with a shake of his head.

"Larkin," he said in a much calmer voice, "where is Amalia? If I take away my hand, will you tell us?"

She shook her head, still glaring.

"Larkin," I said, making my voice as calm as Luka's, "do you realize who this is? This is Prince Luka. Of Feravel. The son of *your* king. And if the Roulaini have killed Prince Miles, *he is your future king.*" I saw with great satisfaction that her eyes were wide and the color had drained from her face. "Now tell us where Amalia is."

She shook her head.

I had never seen Luka's face look so cold. He kept staring around at the room that had once belonged to his brother. Amalia had redecorated with a vengeance. It was all pink hangings and boxes of sweets. Shawls and scarves were draped over most of the chairs and crystal vials of perfume cluttered the dressing table.

Leaning in close to Larkin, Luka said, "Do you know what the penalty is for spying? Or conspiring with the enemy? Or kidnapping a member of the royal family?" He whispered something in her ear that made her go even whiter. "But if you cooperate," he said in a normal voice, "I will see to it that some leniency is given." He slowly removed his hand.

Larkin's spine stiffened and she gave him a haughty

look. "Princess Amalia isn't here," she said. "His Majesty King Prilian just arrived by dragon. She's gone with him to the caves where your father was hiding like a coward. Your father is dead, and you are the heir of nothing." She laughed, a mad cackling sound, and then drew a deep breath. "Gua—"

Before she could finish, I stuffed a stocking into her mouth. Luka grabbed one of her hands and I grabbed the other, and we tied her to her chair with a pair of embroidered sashes. I took off the gold filigree bracelet Amalia had given her as a reward for the slippers. I put it on my own wrist and pretended to admire it, ignoring her glares, and then slipped it off again.

"I wouldn't want to wear traitor's gold," I said, and walking to the balcony doors, I pitched it out. "How do we get to the caves?" I asked Luka, pointedly not looking at Larkin's frantic struggling.

"Through here." Luka led me into the little dressing room, shoving aside mountains of clothing.

The back of one of the wardrobes opened with a hidden latch, and we slipped into a narrow passageway between the walls. Seeing how dark it was, I returned to the bedchamber and fetched a lamp, while Larkin glared at me and drummed her heels on the floor.

With the lamp held high, Luka led me deep into the bowels of the palace. Other tunnels and stairwells crossed ours, and from time to time we passed another secret door, but Luka never wavered. Neither of us said anything: we didn't want to give Larkin's words any credence.

King Caxel could not possibly be dead.

One of the little doors to our left rattled open, and we froze. I took the lamp, and Luka unsheathed his sword. A shaved head tattooed with blue dragons poked through the door: Tobin.

He grinned, and gestured, and we both sagged with relief. We stepped out of the hidden passage and into a dimly lit corridor.

"He says that Amacarin told him where we'd gone," Luka translated, "and he came here after us. He heard from some guards on his way in that Amalia and Prilian had gone to the caves, and figured that's where we were headed."

"So he's been backtracking to find us?"

Tobin nodded, and gestured again.

"Yes," Luka translated, "but he's also been trying to figure out how the Roulaini even got to the caves; the lower passages have been collapsed."

"Did the dragons do that?" The lower levels of the New Palace had looked intact; how could the dragons have gotten to the hidden tunnels?

"No, my father did." Luka didn't need to ask Tobin. "It's part of the defenses. Some of the tunnels are rigged to collapse as a last defense."

"But how will they get out?"

"There are two other escape tunnels," Luka explained. "They lead right under the palace grounds and even I am not sure where they come out. We'll have to figure out a way to—"

"You there! Drop your weapons!" A Roulaini soldier with a thick mustache to match his thick accent
came around a corner. He carried a barbed spear, and it
was aimed right at Tobin's heart. More guards followed,
until that end of the corridor was completely filled.

"Creel," Luka said very softly. "Run."

"No."

"Creel, follow this corridor until you come to a green-
painted door."

The Roulaini soldier snarled. "I said to drop your
weapons, fools!"

"The green door leads to the kitchens. Go through
the kitchens to the gardens. Now."

"No." I held my little dagger in one shaking fist, the
lamp in the other.

"Creel, I command you," Luka said.

I looked at him. It was quite possible that he was
now the king, and at that moment he looked it.

"Attack!"

The Roulaini soldiers leaped forward. I threw my
lamp at their leader, turned, and ran. Down the endless
miles of corridor I went, twice bumping into Roulaini
soldiers. They shouted and tried to follow, but their armor hampered them. With my skirts hiked up above my
knees, I burst through the green-painted door and into
the kitchens.

I suppose it should have occurred to me that someone would be cooking for the palace. Late as it was, there
were a number of cooks and maids baking bread for the

next day. They all scrambled about for a moment and then froze, staring at me in amazement. I stared back.

Then I gave them all a smile, trying to look as inno-cent as I could, and started across the room to the door at the back that led to the gardens. The head cook stepped into my path holding up a large wooden spoon like it was a sword.

Doing my best imitation of Amalia's accent, I said, "What ees thees? I must to thee gardensss!" And I tried to brush past her.

One of the kitchen maids had come up behind me and grabbed my arm as I stepped around the head cook and her spoon. I twisted as best I could, trying to stomp on her feet, but her gown was so long that I couldn't reach them.

"Let me go!" I writhed free, backing away from both the cook and her helper.

And then I got a good look at the helper.

It was a man, dressed in a gown and wearing the apron and head scarf of a cook. He could almost have passed for a woman—a very ugly woman, mind you—if it weren't for the scattering of stubble on his cheeks.

"By the Boiling—" was all I managed before he put a large hand over my mouth.

"Shh," he whispered.

"She's not Roulaini," the cook said, coming closer. "And she's not dressed fine, like the limping one."

I pushed the man's hand away. "I'm with Prince Luka. I need to get to the caverns under the palace," I said. "I won't tell anyone that he's a . . . that you have a man in here." I shook my head over this. Why was he dressed that way? I noticed that his hands were hard and calloused—definitely not the hands of a cook—and that his right hand hovered near his hip, as though feeling for a sword. "Are you a soldier?"

The man and the cook exchanged looks again.

"I told you," I said impatiently, "I'm here with Prince Luka."

"My brother is in the King's Guards," the head cook said finally. "I've been hiding him since the Roulaini took control."

"Cara!" He frowned at her.

"Excellent!" Now it was my turn to grab *his* arm. "Guide me to the entrance to the caverns at once. I'm going to find Princess Amalia and wring her scrawny neck!"

"I can't," he protested. "The entrances are hidden."

"But you're a palace guard; you must know where they are!"

"I did know a few, but some of them are burned out, and some have collapsed."

I tapped my foot in irritation. "So how did Amalia get down there?"

"She took one of them dragons. There's a big sink-hole at the southern end of the palace grounds, caused by all this dragon-work, reckon they went down thataway."

"If we could get to that sinkhole, could you help me find the way down into the caves?"

A shrug. "Supposing we could get there, yes. Trick is, kitchens are on the north end. Besides that, it's a straight drop down that hole into the caves."

"That won't matter. Come with me." I wheeled around, heading for the garden door.

Behind me, I heard the swishing and fumbling of clothing coming off. I glanced back to see the guard casting aside his apron and gown. Underneath he still wore the green breeches of the Guard, but a plain white shirt. The head cook produced his sword and belt from a cupboard and smiled in approval as he buckled them on.

We slipped out, craning our necks from side to side to look for Roulaini guards. In the middle of the kitchen garden I stopped, put my fingers to my lips, and whistled, hoping my hunch was correct.

The guard gave a start and clutched my elbow. "What are you doing?"

"We're going to fly around to the sinkhole," I explained.

Niva had said that once she dropped us off we would be on our own, and I believed her. She was a plainspoken, haughty sort of dragon.

Feniul, however, was a different beast entirely.

With a whoosh of air and a flap of his wings, Feniul landed beside us. The guard cursed and fell on his rear.

"Can this guard ride with me around to the southern side of the palace?"

"Of course."

I scrambled onto his back. "You were supposed to

wait at the estates," I teased him as I held out an impatient hand to the guard.

"I'm sorry." He ducked his head. "I was worried
about you."

"Feniul, I adore you," I said. "You can disobey my instructions anytime." I grabbed the guard's shaking hand
and yanked.

Grunting and biting his lips, the guard struggled up
behind me. He wrapped both arms around my waist in a
way that would have been highly inappropriate had the
man clearly not been terrified. He was shaking and I
thought I felt sweat drip onto my neck.

"Ugh. Feniul, hurry," I said.

The dragon obliged. To avoid notice, the lithe Feniul
wove between the turrets of the palace, sometimes almost scraping the roof with his claws. As we cleared the
building and looked down onto the gardens, it was plain
where the entrance to the caverns was: there was an enormous hole, blackened around the edges, gaping in the
middle of what had been a smooth and verdant lawn.

"That hole is big enough for me," Feniul announced
after circling it twice. "I shall carry you down."

"Be careful," I warned, but he was already diving for
the opening.

With my eyes squeezed tight, I kept myself from
screaming as we shot through the narrow sinkhole. I told
myself that dragons larger than Feniul had fit into the
space, but I was still half-convinced that I was about to
die. The guard must have thought the same, for he was

whimpering and shaking until I had to grip his hands at my waist to prevent him from slipping off.

When Feniul's speed slowed, I dared to open my eyes. He had tucked his wings in close, and was coming to a gliding stop in a large passageway deep beneath the earth. It was a natural tunnel, with strange luminous rock formations, and I was heartened to see that it was more than big enough for Feniul to accompany us.

"You can let go now," I told the whimpering guard. "Let's get down and walk."

"Thank the Triunity," he said in a hoarse whisper. Letting go of my waist, he slithered off Feniul and onto the floor, where his knees buckled and he sagged to a crouch.

"Are you well?" Feniul tilted his head to inspect the shaken guard.

"Yes, thank you, dragon . . . sir," he mumbled.

With just a trace of smugness, I swung myself neatly down and started to walk along the passage. "Coming?" I said over my shoulder. I heard a groan from the guard, and the scrape of Feniul's claws on the stone.

Although we were deep under the ground, there seemed to be illumination coming from somewhere ahead of us. We finally turned a corner, and found a tunnel that looked as if it had been carved by human hands. Every ten paces there was a burning torch set into a wall sconce, though some of them had gone out. Feniul relit them as we went along, puffing little spurts of flame from his nostrils.

When the tunnel forked, the guard took over, leading us down the right-hand branch. There were more burned-out torches this way, and some had burned so low that Feniul couldn't get them to light again. I took one of the better ones, and the guard took another. There was an ever increasing sound of running water that, combined with Feniul's bellowslike breathing in the cramped space, made conversation impossible. All we could do was trudge along and hope that we found what we were look-ing for before our torches went out.

Instead, we turned one corner, then another, and found ourselves in a very well-lit cavern. Glowing moss covered the entire cavern ceiling, bathing the scene below in a weird greenish light. Because of the fey lighting it took me a moment to register what I was seeing. When at last I was able to make sense of the scene before me, my mouth dropped open and I gave a little squeak.

The source of the sound we had been hearing proved to be a massive underground waterfall that roared into a pool at one end of the cavern. The rushing water had muffled the sound of the battle that was raging here under the New Palace. Our enemies had penetrated Fer-avel's last defenses and now only half-a-hundred Ferave-lan guards stood between the king and the Roulaini invaders. King Prilian himself stood atop a boulder and shouted encouragement to his men. If King Caxel were killed, Prilian would declare himself king here in this cave beneath the New Palace.

And where was King Caxel? I searched the surging,

clashing mass of men and swords and pikes. In the middle of a knot of Feravelan guards I spotted a stout grayhaired man slumped on the arm of an elderly gentleman in physician's robes.

"It's the king!" I jostled the guard's arm and pointed. "The king lives!"

"My king! I must go!" And the guard went racing away to engage the first Roulaini man he came across.

Feniul hung back in the shadows behind me, and I stayed in the mouth of the tunnel, looking on in shock. I had come down here thinking that I would find Amalia and a few guards who would be easily intimidated by Feniul, and then I would take back the slippers. Instead I found myself witnessing Feravel's last stand.

A glimmer of something silver caught my eye, and I turned my head and looked up. There, on an outcropping halfway up the wall of the cavern, stood Amalia. She was clad in a beautiful gown of gleaming gray silk, leaning over the edge of a natural balcony to look down on the battle. At the back of the ledge was a small tunnel leading who-knew-where. I backed a little farther into my own tunnel, to make sure that I couldn't be seen, and put a hand on Feniul's neck.

"Can you get me up there?" I said, pointing to the outcrop, but the roar of the waterfall and clash of swords swallowed my words. "Can you get me up there?" I shouted this time, and Feniul nodded. He extended a foreclaw, and I climbed up. Sensing that I wanted to surprise the princess, he backed up a few steps to get a running start and then propelled himself out of the tunnel, soaring straight for Amalia.

The Roulaini princess clapped her hands to her cheeks in dismay when she saw us coming. She began to slink down the smaller tunnel behind her, but she didn't get far. Feniul swerved when we reached the ledge, barely checking his speed, and I took the hint. I leaped from his shoulders and rolled onto the rough stone.

I was so tired it was all I could do to scramble to my feet and set off after Amalia. Fortunately, the princess was not a very fast runner. I caught her easily, flinging my arms around her and bearing her to the ground with my weight. I pinned her arms to the stone above her head.

"Give me the slippers," I grated.

"No!" She spat at me, but I turned my face aside. "Help me!"

"I don't see your bodyguards, your Highness," I said. "It seems that they've abandoned you." I kept my voice level. "Now. Give me the slippers, and I'll let you choose whether you are punished by human justice, or by dragon." I curled my lips in a snarl. "After what you did to Shardas's cave, I'd choose human."

"I didn't do anything," she protested. "Shardas did it all himself. He's nothing more than a dumb animal." A sly look flitted across her face. "Of course, I may have made a suggestion. . . ."

With a wordless scream of rage I released one of her hands and punched her in the nose. She shrieked and I drew back for another punch, but stopped when I saw something in the shadows.

"Help me," Amalia sobbed, her nose bleeding freely.

She wasn't calling to her bodyguards. Waiting in the darkness to carry out its mistress's commands loomed a large gray dragon.

Beneath the King's Seat

Shocked, I released the princess as the dragon snatched me up. One wing was folded awkwardly by its side and seemed to have been broken, but it looked like an old wound. The dragon was certainly fit enough to hold me several paces above the stone floor, in a grip so tight that I could hardly breathe.

Its voice rumbled from deep in its throat, boiling out like breaking rocks. "Shall I kill it, mistress?" There was no expression in the rough tone.

"Yes, at once!" Amalia got clumsily to her feet, brushing dust off her gown.

The dragon was holding me level with its breast. What I saw on its chest made me stop wriggling and stare. There were strange marks, long slashing marks. The scales there were smaller, as if they had formed a kind of scar tissue. And although the light in the tunnel was dim, I could see now that the dragon was not gray, as I had initially thought, but blue.

The same blue as the slippers.

"Velika?" I gasped the name, and the claw holding me gave a convulsive jerk, slicing through the sleeve of my gown and cutting into my upper arm. "Queen Velika? Is that you?"

It was a rather stupid thing to say to a dragon, I thought as soon as the words left me. "Is that you?" It seemed such a common way to say it, like I was greeting an old friend who had a bizarre new hairstyle. But as I stared in shock at the scars on the dragon's breast, I knew it to be true.

It seemed that Milun the First had lied about more than just how he came by the slippers. The queen of the dragons was still alive. And under the thrall of the slippers that had been made from the very scales of her breast. Tears leaked out of the corners of my eyes. It had been a horrible day, and this, for me at least, was the last straw.

"Oh, Shardas will be so happy," I blubbered. "I know he will! All the dragons will! Niva spoke of you with such awe; I know that they would all be thrilled to know that you are still alive. Especially Shardas!"

By now the claw holding me had lowered so that my feet in their plain slippers touched the uneven floor of the tunnel. The dragon's neck was bowed, her head nearly resting on the ground before my feet, and she was not looking at me or anything else. Her blue eyes were cloudy but she twitched whenever I said Shardas's name.

"What are you saying?" Amalia flapped her hands

at us. "Eat her, dragon. Or burn her to cinders, I don't care. Just do it now!"

"Velika, I know it's you," I said in a lower voice, getting a grip on myself. "Please don't do this! You must fight the power of the slippers. King Milun was evil to do this to you, and all your kind. You have to fight the betrayal! Please? For Shardas?"

"Kill her," Amalia ordered again.

The ravaged queen dragon raised her head, but again she hesitated. And in that moment of hesitation I heard another sound: the rasp of claws on stone. And it wasn't coming from Velika.

A long golden snout entered the tunnel, followed by the rest of Shardas. We all froze—Amalia, Shardas, and myself—and looked at Velika. Her head still drooped near the ground, and her grip on me had not slackened.

"Creel?" Shardas's whisper blew a hair across my nose and I sneezed. "Is it truly her?" The anguish in his voice broke my heart. "Is it . . . my Velika?"

I couldn't speak, and Velika gave no reply either. Instead, her claw loosened and I fell to the ground. Her whole body was trembling, and now she threw back her head and keened in what sounded like pain or grief or both.

"Dragon!" Amalia's voice was near hysteria. "Kill them all! Burn them! Do it now! I command you!"

Shardas moved closer, pushing me out of harm's way with a gentle claw. I stroked one folded wing, and then stepped aside as he advanced toward his mate.

Velika was swaying back and forth, her eyes half-closed. Shardas was whispering something, a throaty rasping purr that was in a language no human could voice. After a moment I recognized the tongue of the dragons. He was pleading with her, from the sound of it, pleading with his mate to—what? Fight off Amalia? Attack the Roulaini princess? Or was he simply begging her to remember him, to look at him, to speak to him?

The scarred queen dragon backed down the tunnel, moaning. I went after her, walking beside Shardas. We went slowly, while behind us Amalia screeched and stomped her feet. Shardas continued to whisper and croon in the dragon language, and I found myself adding more pleas for Velika to stop, please, to let us help her; I would be her friend, too. . . .

The tunnel widened and we were in a large cavern. Patches of luminous moss growing up the walls cast a faint green illumination. There was a musty-smelling hollow padded with dried moss and leaves, and claw marks scarred the floor.

"This must be her home," I whispered to Shardas, and tears pricked my eyes. I thought of the airy, clean lair where Shardas lived, with its many rooms and the beautifully displayed windows. And all this time, his mate had been hiding away here. Or not hiding, I realized, but trapped by Milun's cruel alchemy, locked away to keep his horrible secret safe. There was no sign of a hoard, unless she had hidden it somewhere else or the moss was what she cultivated. But I doubted it.

She turned now, moving faster, and went through an opening at the far end. We followed, and I had to drop back to walk alongside Shardas's spiked tail, since the opening was so small.

The tunnel was not long. It turned sharply to one side, and then we were blinking in the light of dawn, standing on a wide natural terrace that jutted out from · the cliff on which the King's Seat stood. The ground sloped steeply down into the Boiling Sea.

The waters of the Boiling Sea bubbled and steamed, giving off bursts of noxious fumes that made my eyes water. By the time my vision had cleared, Velika had taken flight. Shardas leaped into the air after her, no longer whispering, but shouting in the dragon tongue. I called out encouragement to him, wishing I could fly, too. Then a flapping of wings made my heart leap: if Feniul or Niva found me, I could ride in pursuit.

But it wasn't one of the collared dragons. It was Theoradus. He could barely keep himself aloft; sizzling blood from a dozen wounds spattered onto the ground, killing whatever plant life it touched. He folded his tattered wings and skidded to earth a few paces away from me.

"Oh, you poor thing!" I cried, stretching my hands out to him. I didn't care if he was still under the thrall of the slippers, seeing him so badly injured made me reckless. I realized that, with the coming of dawn, Earl Sarryck had begun his attack. A broken spear jutted from Theoradus's side and an arrow was lodged painfully in the soft flesh under his foreleg.

Theoradus's head sank to the dusty ground, and he

heaved a mighty sigh. He was so exhausted and so weak that only a little steam emerged from his mouth, no fire.

"Kill her!"

It would have been too much to ask that Amalia had not followed us, I saw as I whirled around. She was standing in the mouth of the tunnel, hands on hips, glaring at Theoradus.

"He's dying, you evil creature," I said to her. "He's dying because of you!"

"He *exists* to serve me," she snarled back. "And if he is too weak to serve me, then good riddance!"

I couldn't help myself, I lunged for her. I would get the slippers back and put an end to this madness or die trying. And if I had to kill Amalia in the process, well, I didn't think anyone would shed many tears over the loss.

I struck her in the face, knocking her to the ground. She yanked at my skirts, pulling me down after her, and we rolled on the ground, clawing and tearing at each other. A lucky punch from Amalia made my nose bleed, and I bit her shoulder in retaliation. While she was clutching at my face, I twisted around and grabbed one of her ankles, reaching for the slipper with my free hand.

"Kill her, kill her," she continued to shout.

Theoradus groaned and scrabbled at the ground, but could do nothing else. Then, arrowing out of the sky, Velika returned with Shardas close behind. Other dragons were flying in her wake, and I saw with a sinking heart that they were dragons still controlled by the slippers. Amalia kicked me in the face and I lost my grip on her leg.

"Niva, Feniul, Amacarin!" I yelled for the collared

dragons, desperate as I struggled with Amalia and tried to keep one eye on Velika and the others at the same time.

Hearing my cry, or perhaps merely arriving at the most opportune moment, Niva came flashing down from the sky with Amacarin and Feniul to either side and began to battle with the other dragons.

"Give up," I raged at Amalia. "You've lost. Velika and Shardas won't obey you, three other dragons are safe from the slippers, King Caxel still lives. You've lost."

"Not yet," she retorted. "Kill her, Velika, I command you!"

The scarred queen of the dragons soared down to land beside Theoradus. I let go of Amalia and scrambled backward on the slick rocks, uncertain if the slippers had regained their hold on Velika. The queen dragon reached forward and scooped me up with her left foreclaw. With her right she snatched Amalia. Velika rose high above the Boiling Sea and hovered there, holding us apart like a harried mother separating two squalling siblings.

I clutched at Velika's claw, fearful that I would slip out of her grasp and fall to my death. Silently I prayed to the Triunity that the power of the slippers would break, that Velika would come fully to her senses at last. I saw a flash of gold and my heart gave a little leap: Shardas had fought off the slippers' power. I added Shardas to my prayers, lumping him in with the gods and pleading aloud for him to save me.

Holding me upside down by a handful of my ruined skirts, Velika lifted me to eye level and studied me with eyes that looked sharper now than they had in the tunnel. Tears streaming from my eyes, I looked back at her, saying her name in a trembling voice.

Then she extended her foreclaw . . . and flipped me into the air.

Screaming in terror, I spun through nothingness. I might have survived a fall onto the rocks of the shore from this height, but I was falling into the Boiling Sea. My stomach and my heart rose in my throat, and as I rushed toward the steaming water I thought that at least I would be with my parents again. I closed my eyes and prayed that death would come quickly. But instead of feeling the searing pain of boiling water, I hit something hard and scaly with a smack, and felt myself borne upward.

Claws closed around me, gently holding me safe as Shardas plucked me from the air only seconds before I struck the surface, saving me from being boiled to death by the beautiful blue sea. I wrapped my arms around one golden claw and sobbed. A reassuring snort of breath stirred my hair, and I kissed the claw. I was drenched with cold sweat and my legs shook so badly I didn't know if I would ever be able to walk again. I had set out for the palace with Luka knowing that I might die, but I hadn't come near to imagining the true horror of it.

Shardas carried me back up the hill and deposited me beside Theoradus, who barely stirred. Then the golden king of the dragons rose into the air just as Velika, still holding Amalia in her other claw, dived into the Boiling

Sea. It was as if the whole sea turned into noxious steam, obscuring the sky thousands of feet up and as far as I could see to either side.

"Velika!" Shardas's roar made my head ring and several rocks tumbled down the hill and into the water.

I found the strength to stand. I stretched out my hands to Shardas, even though he was far above me. Sizzling drops of water from the Boiling Sea spattered me, but I didn't flinch.

Shardas spread his golden wings to their full width. His long neck snaked around and he looked to me. Our gazes locked for the length of a heartbeat. He turned back to the swirling water where Velika had disappeared. Then with a clap he folded his wings tight to his gleaming sides, and dove after his mate, sending up a great plume of water as he entered the blue depths of the Boiling Sea.

The dragons battling above froze in the air. Roars burst from their throats, and they slowly descended to hover near the fringes of the great cloud of steam. The uncollared dragons appeared bemused and weakened, but the thrall of the slippers was gone. All of them were silent, their tails whipping the air and bursts of fire coming from their mouths as though they couldn't control themselves.

I called out to Niva, who was nearest to me. "Are they . . . ?" I couldn't finish.

She circled down slowly and landed beside me. "So it would seem," she said, her head drooping. "The poisons in the waters of the Boiling Sea are lethal even to dragons."

"Oh, Shardas," I sobbed, sinking to the ground. I put out a shaking hand and laid it on Niva's near fore-claw. She gently nuzzled my head with her nose. Then I stretched out my other hand, and laid it on Theoradus's muzzle. It was cold.

Picking Up the Pieces

L ater I learned that while I had been in the caverns beneath the palace, the three collared dragons had been
fighting their friends above. Niva had tried to plead with
the others to go to the Mordrel estates and be collared,
too, but the slippers' hold had been too strong. The en-
suing battle had destroyed the east wing of the New
Palace. As Feniul and I flew over the rubble, still stunned
by the deaths of Shardas and Velika, we heard shouting.

Feniul swooped in for a closer look, and we saw a
hand reaching out of a pile of roof tiles. I dismounted,
and helped Feniul dig the unfortunate person free. It was
Crown Prince Milun, with Pippin, Amalia's little white
lapdog, stuffed into his shirt.

He had spent most of his imprisonment in the attics
where unused furniture and unwanted princes were
stored, lying in an old bed with only Pippin as company. When the roof collapsed, the heavy canopy and

tree-trunk-thick bedposts had formed a protective cage around him. His leg was broken, but he was otherwise unharmed.

Pippin circled Feniul, barking ferociously for a dog the size of a muff. But the dragon lowered his head and made a trilling noise, and she stopped barking and pranced right over to him. She gave his proffered muzzle a lick, then ran up his tail like it was a ramp and settled herself amid the horns crowning his head.

Back at the Mordrel estates, Luka and I assured Feniul that he could keep the dog. We doubted anyone would care, but he wanted to make a fair trade. So he gave Azarte to Prince Miles. Miles was delighted, and Azarte leaned against the prince's legs and lowed like a cow. I shook my head and warned Miles to keep all sweets well out of the dog's reach, but I don't think he was listening to me.

King Prilian was killed in the battle beneath the palace. The Feravelan soldiers, fighting for home and hearth, had rallied and defeated the Roulaini in the cavern beside the waterfall. The soldier I had found hiding in the kitchens had slain Prilian with his own hand, and was now captain of a regiment.

The new Roulaini king, Prilian's nephew Rolian, had been quick to send messages declaring his goodwill. The Roulaini army was recalled, and King Rolian was making noises about tithes of appeasement and demonstrations of brotherhood, whatever that meant.

Larkin had been found by the King's Guards as they

swept through the palace hunting for Roulaini. She claimed that the Roulaini had tried to torture her for information, but the kitchen maid who was asked to bring her some hot tea recognized her as Princess Amalia's uppity maid. Luka and I both testified against her, and she was sentenced to life in prison for treason. To give her something to do—idle hands crochet the devil's stockings, as my silly aunt would say—she was put to work hemming sheets and rolling bandages for the Royal Hospital. I thought the monotonous work a fitting punishment.

So now there was just the little matter of rebuilding the New Palace, the Winter Palace, and the King's Seat. Not to mention that the dragons, absent from the lives of humans for centuries, were now still very much among us. Niva was leading a vigil along the shores of the Boiling Sea, where more than two dozen dragons had gathered to sing a mourning song for King Shardas and Queen Velika, Theoradus the Brown, and the handful of others who had died in the battle. They would remain there, fasting and singing, for a full cycle of the moons. Whenever I had time, I went down and stood between Niva and Feniul, putting a hand on the foreclaw of each and listening to their song.

King Caxel declared that Theoradus's hoard should be a gift to the public. I didn't know what that meant, but Luka explained that the shoes would be put in a special building so that the public could come to admire them. I said that I thought Theoradus would like that, but also that I thought it should be available to the dragons, too. Luka squeezed my hand and said he would make sure there was a dragon-sized entrance. The display house would be built in Carlieff Town, and Luka promised to hire my brother, Hagen, as a caretaker. I sent a note for Hagen with the nobleman designated to design and build the display house.

Then the king had discussed repairing and displaying Shardas's hoard as well, but I had vehemently disagreed. Just thinking of how Amalia had ordered Shardas to destroy his beloved windows made me sick inside, and the idea of thousands of people, people who had never known Shardas when he was warm and humorous and *alive*, trespassing in his cave caused me even greater distress. Instead, Feniul promised to seal the entrance to Shardas's cave. Niva thought that we should remove the contents of the alchemist's room, and let other alchemists study his work, and I said that I thought both Shardas and the alchemist would have approved.

"Which brings us to you, Mistress Carlbrun," the king said at last, looking down the table at me.

It was the end of a very long meeting, after a week of very long meetings. I had been included in this council on the insistence of both princes and the Duke of Mordrel, who had all pointed out that I was more involved than anyone, and deserved to be there.

"To me?" I asked. "Your Majesty?"

"I think that a reward is in order, for our resourceful Mistress Carlbrun," the king said. "I have heard that the populace is referring to her as the Heroine of the Dragon War."

I looked down at my hands, feeling awkward. The Duke of Mordrel, sitting next to me, patted my arm. I straightened the cuffs of my gown. It was one of the duchess's, hastily altered, so that I would look presentable enough to sit at the king's council table. She had said that I could keep it, and I was already planning to add panels of embroidery to it, in honor of friends lost. Blue and gold, I thought, in a pattern like scales.

"It's really not necessary, your Majesty," I mumbled. "I was only trying to help. After all, I'm the one who brought the slippers here to begin with."

King Caxel made an airy gesture with one hand. "You had no way of knowing what they were. No, the populace has become enamored of you, and you must be rewarded."

I got the distinct impression that had the "populace" reviled me, the king would have reviled me. And had they ignored me, I would not be sitting here, between a duke and a prince, being addressed by his majesty.

"As the marriage to the Roulaini princess is no longer feasible," the king went on, ignoring several snorts of incredulity at the overstatement, "other arrangements for Prince Milun will have to be made. Perhaps a fitting alliance would be for him to marry the Heroine of the Dragon War, who saved him from a terrible fate."

"What?" I half-rose in my seat.

The king frowned at me. "Pardon?"

"You can't want Miles . . . Prince Milun to marry *me*," I squeaked, sinking back down. "I'm a commoner." I looked to Miles for support and saw that he was wearing an uncomfortable expression. He caught my eye and gave me a pained smile. It seemed he didn't like this idea, either.

"I am very much aware of your common roots," the king said with a hint of disdain. "And that is why you do not understand affairs of state." He turned to look at the scribe sitting in the corner of the room. "Send out a proclamation: on this day, We, King Caxel the Third of Feravel, do decree that our eldest son and heir, Crown Prince Milun, shall marry the Heroine of the Dragon War, etc." He made a circular gesture with his hand and then turned back to the table. "Now, is there other business before lunch?" He looked around, his face bland.

"Your Majesty," I said loudly. "I'm sorry, but I don't *want* to marry Miles."

Everyone froze, and the king glared at me. "Young woman," he said in a low voice, "I am your king, and as a commoner it is not for you to question my decrees."

I felt my indignation rising. This was the man who had been too blind to recognize that the Roulaini were plotting something terrible. This was the man for whom dragons had died, for whom humans had died, and I was finding that I didn't much care for him or his decrees.

"Well, according to you, your Majesty," I said as politely as I could manage, "I am the Heroine of the Dragon War. And as the Heroine of the Dragon War, I wish to refuse this offer of marriage." I ignored the fact that it hadn't so much been an offer as an order, and privately vowed that I would never use my "title" again.

The entire room, including the scribe, stared at me in disbelief. I plunged on, thinking that I might as well continue, seeing as I had already put myself in harm's way.

"I am very grateful to your Majesty for wishing to reward me for my humble service," I said, thinking back to the fancy dialogue of my aunt's romantic novels. "But if your Majesty wishes to make me a more appropriate gift, I would be greatly pleased to have a dress shop of my own."

The king's eyes bulged, and beside me, Luka began to laugh under his breath, and the Duke of Mordrel applauded softly.

"You would rather work in a dress shop than marry the crown prince? The future king? I am offering you the chance to be the queen of Feravel one day!"

"And I am respectfully refusing," I replied. "Not that the offer isn't tempting, but I really don't think I would be a very good queen. And I don't want to just *work* in the shop, I want to *own* the shop," I corrected him.

Luka was now laughing aloud. "Oh, Father! Creel's right. She doesn't want to marry Miles—although I think she would be a wonderful queen! Let's buy her a dress shop and everything she'll need to make a go of it: furnishings, living quarters . . ."

"Cloth and ribbons, shears and thread," I put in. I saw an expression of profound relief cross Miles's face, and I winked at him.

"You'll need to hire a staff," Luka reminded me. "We'll pay their wages for the first six months."

"Marta will be my partner, and I think Derda's planning to retire, so I might be able to get Alle to work for us," I said, feeling myself flush with excitement.

The king cleared his throat loudly, and my flush faded to pallor. "Very well," he said. "Strike that last decree, scribe. Make out a title for a shop—"

"I want it called Marisel's Fine Dressmaking, after my mother," I told the scribe.

"Yes, yes," the king waved his hand. "Find something big and stock it with . . . whatever Mistress Creel requires. Buy it off the old owner, if they're still alive. And have the title read, 'Bequeathed by his Majesty, King Caxel the Third of Feravel, on this day, to Creelisel Carlbrun, the Heroine of the Dragon War, this place of business, etc.'" He made a circle with his hand again. "Any other matters of import? No? We shall continue this council after lunch to discuss reconstruction of the chapels."

I got to my feet with the rest, somewhat dazed.

"Well, it seems that you will not need to attend the Merchants' Ball next year," the duke said lightly. He took my elbow and steered me from the room after the king had exited. "I shall have my carriage take you to Ulfrid's inn, so that you may inform Marta of this change in your fortunes. I might add congratulations, as well."

"Er, thank you." I gave him a weak smile. It was starting to hit home that I had defied my king. I must be completely mad.

"Don't worry," Luka hissed, taking my other elbow. "The old man's probably relieved. Imagine if you'd turned out to be as crazy as Amalia *and* a commoner? He'd die of embarrassment." He gave me a roguish smile, and I elbowed him in the ribs.

Luka rode with me to Ulfrid's inn. It was nearly full: so many people no longer had homes or jobs that they had nowhere else to go but to an inn to drink away their sorrows. Ulfrid served them, if not with a smile, then at least with a sympathetic nod, and also provided fresh bread and hearty stews to soak up some of the ale in their stomachs.

Sitting in pride of place before the fire on a bench padded with cushions and sheepskin, Tobin lay recuperating. He and Luka had faced over a dozen men in that corridor, with Tobin bearing the brunt of the attack. Finally, Luka's sword had been broken and his right arm gashed to the bone. Tobin had insisted that his prince flee, and stayed behind to finish off the last three men. Luka had gone to the kitchens, where the formidable head cook had bandaged his arm and sent an army of scullery maids with carving knives to help Tobin. They had found him sitting atop the stacked bodies of the last three men, bloodied but triumphant.

When we entered the inn's common room, we saw Marta sitting beside the mute hero, working her laborious way through a book of epic poetry in Moralienin. Ulfrid had confided to me that Marta's accent was atrocious, but Tobin didn't seem to mind. Both his arms were heavily bandaged, one leg was splinted, and there was a long gash across his tattooed scalp that Marta had stitched with her own hands, insisting that her stitches would be far neater than any surgeon's.

"I got a shop for us," I told her, plopping down on a stool by Tobin's side. I made the "hello" gesture to Tobin that Luka had taught me. He made it back, grinning.

"What?" Marta looked up from the poetry. "You did?"

"She only bullied my father into it, is all," Luka said breezily, calling to one of the serving girls for tea.

"You did not!" Marta closed the book with a snap, goggling at me. Tobin was laughing silently. She poked his shoulder. "That isn't funny!"

"Well," I drawled, "first he offered to marry me to Miles and make me the crown princess and future queen, but I said I shouldn't care for the job. So I asked the king to give us a shop instead."

"I think I'm going to be sick," Marta said, fanning herself with the book.

"Oh, don't be," I said, laughing. "We got the shop, and that's all that matters."

Tobin nudged Marta and said something with his hands that I couldn't follow. She blushed to the roots of her strawberry blonde hair, and then looked at me, biting her lip.

"What is it?"

"Well, er, we also have good news, although you might be disappointed," she said.

"Tobin, you didn't!" Luka looked delighted. "Four mugs of cider," he hollered to the serving girl, who was on her way toward us with a tea tray. She halted in confusion.

"Didn't what? What's happened?" I looked from Marta to Luka to Tobin, but they were all too busy grinning at each other.

Marta set her book in her lap and held out her right hand. There was a beautiful sapphire ring, wide and foreign-looking, on her middle finger. She was betrothed.

"Tobin?" I gawked at her, then at him. "Tobin!"

He nodded, and slipped one bandaged arm around my friend's shoulders. She leaned close, laying her head on his chest, looking like a very contented angel.

"Congratulations," I said past the lump in my throat. I wondered if Alle would like to be my partner. It wouldn't be the same, but at least I wouldn't be running a shop on my own.

"So, we'll be moving to the New Palace," Marta said, lifting her head. "I'm sorry, Creel. I'll come and help, though, I just won't be able to be your partner."

"Actually, you will," Luka said, looking a bit deflated. "I spoke to my father before the council this morning, Tobin. He's decided that you should be retired."

Tobin's eyes narrowed. His fingers flickered.

"No, no, it's not that." Luka shook his head. "Just from your bodyguard duties. Father feels—and I agree— that you've served our family more than faithfully for over ten years, risking your life to protect us, training me and Miles. My father wants you to take on an advisory role. Train the King's Guards, and our personal body-guards. We'll double your salary, and give you a house in the King's Seat so that you can leave the palace and relax at the end of the day."

Tobin's grin was back, broader than before. He beamed at Luka and gave Marta another squeeze.

"We'll get a house near the shop," Marta declared. "And can I still be your partner?"

I nodded eagerly.

"Good. And Tobin can take care of all the children!" She gave a satisfied nod. Then we both laughed at the alarmed look on her betrothed's face.

Ulfrid came over with five mugs of cider and joined us in toasting the happy couple. Then Luka gave her the rest of the news, and we toasted Tobin's new career and the opening of Marisel's Fine Dressmaking.

It was one of the better days I'd had since Shardas died.

Stolen Glass

It had been more than a year since the Dragon War. I winced every time I heard mention of it, but at least I was no longer hailed as the heroine of those terrible days. Now I was known more for my gown designs and my fine shop just a stone's throw from the Jyllite Square.

Despite my close proximity to the New Palace (which was even newer now that it had been almost completely rebuilt), I rarely saw Luka. His father kept him busy riding the borders to check the defenses, and meeting with delegations from Roulain, who continued to reassert their most humble apologies. Prince Miles was still skittish about the Roulaini, and a great many of his former duties had been passed to Luka.

So when the door to the shop opened and a tall young man came striding in, I didn't recognize him at first. Nor did I recognize the leggy hound by his side, except to wrinkle my nose.

"I'm sorry, good sir, but I'd prefer that your hound not enter," I said, the light coming from the large front windows casting the young man's face in shadow.

"Oh, but Azarte has been longing to see you," Luka said with a laugh. "I borrowed him from Miles specially."

"Luka!" I ran from behind the counter and threw my arms around him. "I haven't seen you in ages!"

He squeezed me back. "I've been in Roulain for the last month," he explained. He had grown at least a handspan and was very tan.

"Ugh, how was it?"

"Boring, but sunny," he said with a shrug.

I patted Azarte's narrow head with one hand, and tried to keep him from leaning against me with the other. I was wearing a new gown, pale green with darker green embroidery, and didn't fancy picking white and black dog hairs off it for the next five hours.

"It looks as though your shop is doing well," Luka said, gazing around. "Could you help me find a gift for a lady friend of mine?"

My heart plunged to my green satin slippers, and I had to stare down at Azarte for a minute, petting him hard. Naturally Luka had a "lady friend." She was probably nobly born: the daughter of a count or a duke. I imagined her having thick dark hair and clear skin, and was bitterly jealous. "Of c-course," I stammered after a time. "What would she like? A gown? A sash?" If she came in for a fitting, I decided to "accidentally" poke her with every pin.

"Hmm, well, she is wearing a lovely gown today," he said. "Although no sash."

So. He'd already seen her today, and it was not yet noon. I rubbed Azarte's ears furiously. "What color is her gown?"

"It's sort of green, with more green, and the design looks like stained glass windows," he said. "It's very beautiful, like her."

I stopped petting the dog and looked up at him, not sure what I was hearing. "Oh?" My heart thumped painfully.

"Yes, so perhaps she doesn't need a sash after all. No sense gilding the lily." He gave a melancholy sigh. "But I really would love to give her a very special gift. I was hoping if I did, she might give me a kiss in return, instead of the brotherly hugs I always get instead."

I raised my eyebrows, trying for casual interest even though I could feel my pulse beating in the blood rushing to my cheeks.

"I know!" Luka snapped his fingers. "Forget a sash. I'll give her this!" And with a flourish, he pulled a roll of parchment from his belt pouch.

More confused than ever, I unrolled the paper and read. It was a letter from a priest in the Southern Counties, addressed to King Caxel. In it the priest begged for a grant of money. They had recently built a large chapel, the finest that had ever been dedicated to the Triune Gods in that region, and it had only been completed the year before.

"But we do need another grant from the crown," the priest wrote. "For a most heinous act of vandalism has taken place. Our rose-glass window, which illuminates the Triple Altar in glorious colors pleasing to the gods, has been stolen. It was removed from its frame the night before last, and not a pane of it can be found."

"Shardas?" I looked up at Luka with my eyes brimming. "Shardas!"

"I have a pair of horses waiting outside," Luka said. "We can be at Feniul's cave by nightfall."

I threw my arms around him again, and this time I gave him the kiss he'd been waiting for.

"Creel!" Marta came out of the backroom. "What in the name of the Triunity. . . . Oh, hello Luka!"

"Shardas is alive," I shouted to her. I ran back around the counter and danced her about until we ran into a rack of ribbons and sent them tumbling to the ground.

"What? You're joking!"

"No, I'm not! A window's been stolen, a window's been stolen!" I sang. "Can you and Alle manage the shop until I get back?"

"Of course, but where are you going?"

"We're going dragon hunting!" And I ran out of my shop, with a large hound galloping ahead and my own prince following after.

ACKNOWLEDGMENTS

I would like to acknowledge that this book would never have been written if not for the following things: First, in 1989 my sister checked out from the library Robin McKinley's fine Damar books and then left them on the floor of our bedroom, where I tripped over them and then fell in love with them. Second, for many years my parents lovingly supported both my book-buying habit and my book-writing ambition, taking me out of school to meet people like Robin McKinley and Patricia C. Wrede, and forking over lots of hard-earned cash for books about dragons and magic and heroic rescues, before finally handing the (financial) responsibility over to my husband. And third, when the first line of this book leaped into my brain one night, my poor, dear husband agreed to walk the floor for hours upon hours with our colicky baby so that I could get some writing done.

I would also like to acknowledge (or confess, really)

that when Melanie, the editor of my dreams, called to tell me that Bloomsbury (the publisher of my dreams) was going to publish my book, I was still in my bathrobe.

It was noon.